This item is a donation to
the La Jolla Community
Collection.

THE
WICKED
AND THE
JUST

The Wicked and the Just

J. ANDERSON COATS

HARCOURT
HOUGHTON MIFFLIN HARCOURT
BOSTON NEW YORK

Harcourt is an imprint of
Houghton Mifflin Harcourt Publishing Company.

www.hmhbooks.com

Text set in Celestia Antiqua and Letterpress Text
Design by Christine Kettner

LIBRARY OF CONGRESS CATALOGING-IN-PUBLICATION DATA

Coats, Jillian Anderson.
The wicked and the just / by Jillian Anderson Coats.
p. cm.
Summary: In medieval Wales, follows Cecily whose family is lured
by cheap land and the duty of all Englishman to help keep down the
"vicious" Welshmen, and Gwenhwyfar, a Welsh girl who must wait
hand and foot on her new English mistress.
ISBN 978-0-547-68837-4
1. Wales—History—1063-1536—Juvenile fiction. [1. Wales—
History—1063-1536—Fiction. 2. Middle Ages—Fiction.
3. Prejudices—Fiction.] I. Title.
PZ7.C62927Wi 2012
[Fic]—dc23
2011027315

Manufactured in the United States of America
DOC 10 9 8 7 6 5 4
4500456840

To Michael and Owen

1293

ASSUMPTIONTIDE

TO

SAINT JOHN'S EVE

TONIGHT at supper, over capon and relish, my father ruined my life.

He smiled big, scrubbed his lips with the end of his cloak, and said, "We're moving house."

"Thank the Blessed Virgin!" I sat up straighter and smoothed my kirtle. "I'm weary to thimbles of Coventry. Will we be back at Edgeley Hall in time for the Maypole?"

"No, sweeting. We're not going back to Edgeley. We're moving to Caernarvon."

"*What* in God's name is *that?*"

"It's a town in Wales."

I'm in my chamber now. I will never speak to him again.

Unless he buys me a new pelisson for the journey.

I'll not go to Caer-whatsit, not while there's breath in me.

I'll not eat. Not till my father gives up this foolish notion. At supper, I enter my uncle's hall with my nose in the air and sit at my father's right and sniff as the plates pass.

Betimes I glance at my father to see if he notices, but he's too busy loading his gob with sowce so grease-slick shiny it catches rushlight, and pies with crusts that dissolve at the touch.

I eat in silence. But everything tastes as bitter as wormwood.

So I refuse to speak to him. Not one sweet word from his beloved daughter, his only living child, the light of his otherwise meaningless life.

My father merely smiles and remarks to the saints, "My, how delightfully quiet it's become."

I've no wish to resort to manipulating him, but it's rapidly becoming necessary to end this worrisome notion of moving with a slightly underhanded blow.

So I confront him in the public of the hall with my most piteous Salvo-eyes and wail, "How can you do this to me? I'll die an old maid! There won't be a suitable man for leagues out in the wilderness!"

"A pity you were not born a boy, sweeting," my father replies. "What a King's Bench lawyer you would have made."

And then he arranges for our household goods to be brought to Caer-whatsit by pack train.

An unwelcome feeling is coming over me. This might really be happening. And there might be naught to do for it.

Alice and Agnes pull me into the hearth corner, their eyes as big as trenchers. They want to know if it's true, if we're really leaving. I cannot speak, not even to Alice, who gave me her only ribbon to cheer me when Salvo went lame, nor to Agnes, who has held her tongue about how I kissed Wat the groom last May Eve.

Coventry was bad enough when we came here last Easter. Filthy and crowded, not a patch of green anywhere. Only for a while, my father promised, since already we were straining my uncle's hospitality. Only till we got Edgeley sorted.

Now this. Giving up his birthright to live among savages. Dragging me away from my two dearest friends and any chance at all of making a decent marriage. All with good cheer, no less! I'd think ruining a family would weigh heavier on a father's conscience.

My father may be going mad. Apparently I'm the only one who sees it.

Says my uncle William: "No service owed for your holding? Neither here nor overseas? Only twelvepence a year and that's all? Blast it, what fortune you have!"

Say my cousins: "Hey, Cesspool, how will you keep your precious undershifts clean now?" "Poor Cesspile, you'll have to give them up for want of lye!" "Cesspit, you'll tell us how the Welsh lads kiss, won't you?" "That's if you make it back alive, eh, Cesspile?"

Charming. You'd think that one being a squire and the other a journeyman goldsmith would make them too grown-up to mock my name. You'd be wrong.

My aunt Eleanor is the only one with something sensible to say: "Oh, Robert, how can you take a young woman into that den of vipers? Leave poor Cecily here with me."

I seize my father's sleeve and beg, "Please, Papa, couldn't I stay?"

But my father only laughs, big like church bells. "I would miss you far too much, sweeting. Besides, it's perfectly safe. I wouldn't put you in danger for all of Christendom."

One morning in April just after Easter, my father rents a cart and hires a man who smells of cabbage to drive it. Most of our belongings will follow us by pack train, but my father would bring the valuables with him. The pewter and a strongbox are hidden among some of our simplest goods, and those will keep us till the pack train arrives.

The cart fills up fast. Our things are stacked two and three bundles high. I direct two of the townsmen to load my coffer into the wagon. The coffer contains my most treasured possessions, so I know my father would want it with the valuables.

Salvo limps out of my uncle's townhouse. He stumbles over the doorframe and heaves his way to the cart, where he collapses against the wheel. I kneel and pet him, and he lifts his tail high enough for a single friendly whap.

Then I peer into the wagon crammed back to front.

Salvo whines quietly, nose on paws.

This won't do, so I climb into the cart and shift the bundles and crates, but the stacks I make grow so high that the goods will end up in the mud at the first deep rut.

Salvo closes his eyes. His sides are still fluttering.

My father is arguing with the carter. As usual, it's up to me to make things right.

I catch one of the townsmen by the sleeve and tell him that my coffer should be removed from the wagon to the pile of goods being brought later. The space it leaves is just big enough for Salvo, and I bring his sackcloth bed from my uncle's hearth with my own hands.

My relations turn out to say farewell. My uncle William clasps wrists with my father and tugs cheerfully on my veil. My aunt Eleanor kisses us again and again, sobbing into her handkerchief. She leaves wet smears on my cheeks.

Alice and Agnes cling to my elbows and weep. My two friends are all that has kept my exile in Coventry bearable.

I embrace them both and whisper, "I'm coming back. I'll not be in that dreadful place forever."

They weep harder. They don't believe me.

The wagon is loaded. All is ready. My father embraces my aunt and uncle once more while I hold on to Alice and Agnes as though Hell's great maw has opened beneath us.

Alice and Agnes and I lean together in a tight knot and pledge to be friends forever, no matter how far apart we are. Their shoulders are warm and wisps of their hair tickle my cheek and I'm choking out my promise because I'm going to wake up tomorrow and Alice's elbow won't be jammed in my ribs and Agnes won't be there to lend me a length of thread when mine goes missing in the dim.

As I climb into the wagon, Alice catches my sleeve. She presses a soft folded packet into my hands and whispers, "We want you to keep it. To remember us."

I weep as Coventry rolls out of view. I am like the saints who were sent into the desert to be killed by infidels.

I run out of tears and rub my stinging eyes. The wagon jounces along a rutted track, hitting rocks and chuckholes. I have a blurry view of the carter's faded hood and the oxen's rumps, and Salvo is heavy on my feet.

There's something in my hands. The packet Alice gave me. I unwrap it and my throat closes up tight.

It took us a year, all three of us perched like dolls shoulder to shoulder, bent over one long frame. My fingers throb just looking at the two dozen saints lined up before the throne of God.

Alice was keeping this altar cloth we made to present to Saint Mary's in Coventry at Whitsuntide.

Instead she gave it to me.

To remember them.

As if I need an altar cloth for that.

When dusk is falling, we stop at an inn. Supper is a meat pasty with stale crust and some small beer in a wooden vessel. I'm so hungry that I eat the pasty in three bites without thinking too hard on what might be within.

Then I find a hair in my teeth.

I must share a pallet with two alewives. They both snore like pigs. The fleas devour me toe to crown.

Once we're stuck in Caer-whatsit, I will go to Mass as

faithfully as an abbess and confess my sins every quarter-day. If Hell is anything like this journey, I want to be certain of my soul.

I'm restless all night, and I rise even ere dawn and watch the whey-pale daughter of the house blearily stir the fire to life. After she drags herself away, I wrap up tight in my cloak by the struggling fire and stare hard into the flames.

Right now it's lambing season at Edgeley, and I should be on the uplands watching the little darlings frisk and stagger. I should be admiring the clean cuts of the moldboard as the plowmen follow the oxen up and down the strips. I should be sowing my garden behind Edgeley's kitchen with rue and madder.

"How are you holding up, sweeting?" My father glides out of the darkness and nudges my foot cheerfully.

"Fine."

"That well, eh?"

His good humor makes Edgeley seem even farther away.

"Oh, Papa, why do we have to go to Wales?"

My father kneels at my elbow and squints into the fire. "I'm trying to decide what answer to give you. The one I'd give a child who needs to hear everything is well, or the one I'd give a grown girl who can cope with a bit of the world's ill."

"I'm not a child, Papa."

"Very well." He sighs like a bellows. "I lost the suit."

"Oh, Papa, no! They found against your claim to Edgeley? How could they, when you ran it so well for so long?"

He shrugs sadly. "Simple. Roger is my elder brother. The manor goes to him. I must wish him well of it."

"I wish he'd never come back." I fold my arms. "I wish the infidels had *eaten* him."

My father stiffens. "Watch your tongue, Cecily. Your uncle Roger is a Crusader who followed his Grace the king to liberate the Holy Land."

"And when he comes back, he liberates *your* land," I mutter.

"Sweeting, come here." My father holds out his arms and I'm so tired and heartsore that I shift into his embrace as if I'm six again and scared of the bull. "I'm not happy about it, but such is the way of the world. In Caernarvon, I can get a burgage for twelvepence a year without any military service due, not foreign or domestic. It's all I can get if I'll not have the humiliation of being a steward on a manor I was once lord of."

"What about me? Thimbles, Papa, Edgeley was to be mine! Now I don't even have a dowry!"

My father hugs me tighter. "You let me worry about that, sweeting. In the meantime, you'll be lady of the house once we have our burgage."

Lady of the house. Keys at my belt. Servants doing as I bid them. Like my mother once, at Edgeley.

"Besides, Roger has no heirs, and he still gets those spells from so many years beneath the Crusader sun." My father looks pensive. "If we live quietly in Wales for a few years, who knows? I might find myself in possession of Edgeley after all, as will you and your husband when I'm gone."

That year in Coventry was bad enough, chewing my fingers to pulp and waiting for assize judges and King's Bench lawyers. That year within walls was merciless without Plow Monday or Rogation, without Alred's Well and Harcey's Corner and my mother's grave in the churchyard, where the yew trees grow in thick.

I'm ever so weary of endless green fields and priory floors and travel bread. I want to go home. To Edgeley.

But every turn of the cart's wheels takes us a little farther away, so I ask the carter if he knows anything about the Welsh.

"Oh, aye, demoiselle." His breath smells like onions. "A tricky lot, those. Say one thing and do another. Can't trust 'em farther than you can throw 'em."

Charming. We're going to be murdered in our beds.

"Are they . . . Christian?" I whisper.

The carter smacks his lips. "After a fashion, I suppose."

Even better. We're going to be murdered in our beds by infidels.

My father must not be aware of this. He can wield a falchion and knows a goshawk from a sparrowhawk, but he can be rather dim betimes.

"Oh, demoiselle, beg pardon. It was a poor joke." The

carter smiles like a dog that's used the hall floor as a privy. "Aye, the Welsh are Christian and hold Our Lord and His Holy Mother as sacred as we do."

I pull my hood over my head. At Edgeley I heard Mass every day surrounded by Edgeley people who tilled the fields and drove the beasts and never once looked me in the eye.

"And don't you worry, demoiselle," the carter rushes on. "The Welsh are harmless. It's been ten years since his Grace the king subdued the land of Wales, and there are over a dozen good Englishmen in Caernarvon's garrison. Walls like Jerusalem. Caernarvon's the last place there'd be trouble, mark me."

Today I'm driving the cart.

Well, I'm holding the reins and keeping the oxen while my father and the carter rock and grunt and heft a wheel back onto the road.

The oxen's mouths pull at the strips of leather, as if all they want is my hand to guide them.

As if I'm holding the reins of the whole world.

I could grow accustomed to driving.

When we arrive in a town called Chester, my father hires a guide who has the temper of a sunburned boar. He smells like one, too. My father says we need him to pass safely, though, for he knows the Welsh tongue and every path within a day's ride.

"The Welsh tongue?" I frown. "You mean . . . they don't speak as we do?"

My father shrugs. "They're different from us in many ways, sweeting. Why do you think the king wants us there? How else will they learn to behave?"

At dusk, we stop at a rickety thatchpile house. A woman comes to the door and speaks to the guide in a tangle of sound that makes no sense, but our guide answers in a like manner. Then he tells my father that she's offering hospitality, and my father bids the guide to thank her.

This must be the Welsh tongue. When the guide speaks again I listen carefully, but it's as if someone stretched out his tongue with red-hot pincers and left it to dry in the sun. The sounds he makes are not like proper words at all, and I'm glad when he speaks in good English once more.

I suspected my father mad ere this, but I know it certes now. If the Welsh cannot even speak properly, we have more work before us than I wish to do.

It's late afternoon, right about the time we usually knock on someone's doorframe and request the hospitality of what passes for a hearth in this misbegotten land, when my father reins in his palfrey next to the cart and points.

"There it is, sweeting."

"*That's* Caernarvon?" I put a hand to my mouth. "Saints, Papa, it's *beautiful!*"

No one said anything about a castle. And not just any castle. Possibly the loveliest, most elegant castle in all of Christendom. A wall of gray stone lit orange by the sunset, thin window-slits, high towers. And bands of purple stone threading through the gray like the finest embroidery. Where the castle leaves off, there spans a wall studded with towers. It looks like a subtlety of stone.

"But I thought . . . I thought the Welsh . . ."

My father chuckles. "The Welsh didn't build this, sweeting. His Grace the king did."

His Grace the king has excellent taste.

Even the beasts seem to hurry. We stream down an incline toward a river mouth where boats bob against a series of docks, then we curve around the docks to the south. Little wonder. I can see no gate, only towers that bristle from the wall like cloves in an apple.

As we pass the docks, one of the brawny lads unloading a barge looks at me. Right in the eye, without dropping his gaze or ducking his chin. As if he's my brother. Or my sweetheart.

Tenants at Edgeley would never dare such a look. They all know better.

But I am a long way from Edgeley and there is naught to do for any of it.

We arrive before a massive gate, and the men guarding it approach my father to parley. My father hands over some silver and they nod us through. Above us, the city walls are as wide as several men lying head to toe. The walls are dark and damp and cold, but thick.

It would take a lot to get through walls this thick.

What opens up within the walls does not look like Coventry. There are no townhouses overhanging the roads, blocking out the sun. There are no muddy gutters and middens.

There are open spaces greening with furze and narrow plots with new-turned furrows waiting for May planting. Unfinished townhouses rise golden like solid honey, and older houses, gleaming white with limewash, sweep up from green plots.

I can have a garden here. Just like at Edgeley.

My father looks smug. "More to your liking, sweeting?"

"It's not Edgeley. But I suppose it will do. For now."

The street we follow veers slightly to the left and ends abruptly with the city wall. We pass one cross-street, then another, ere the guide calls gee and directs us down the endmost street.

The castle is massive now. I can just see a curve of tower and a tangle of scaffolding when we lurch to a stop.

"What do you think, sweeting?" My father gestures to a house that rises tall and graceful out of a tidy yard. The bottom part is stone, the top timbered with bright limewashed panels.

"Is that our house?" Not a mud-and-thatch midden-hole, and certes a hand up from my uncle William's crowded lodgings in Coventry.

But by no means is this Edgeley Hall.

My father smiles. "Welcome home."

A thickset woman of middle years answers my father's knock. She is Mistress Tipley. She and the servant have been caring for the place through the winter, and she thanks the saints that we've come through safely.

Mistress Tipley looks suspiciously like a chatelaine, when I'm to be the lady of this house.

At least she is speaking English.

"Sweeting, I must go see the constable," my father says. "Let him know we've arrived and find out what he requires of me. Mistress Tipley will show you the house."

My father swings back astride his horse with a faint groan, then bids the guide bring the cart into the rearyard and unload. I'm left in the foyer with Mistress Tipley regarding me as though I'm a child threatening the wall hangings with my damp little hands.

Being the lady of this house was promised me. I put my chin in the air and tell her, "I can show myself the house. You may go."

Her face reddens, but she bobs her head and disappears.

Abovestairs is a chamber halved by heavy curtains. I claim the half at the rear of the house as my own; my father can have the other. There's a pallet on the floor, but I sincerely hope my father doesn't think I'm sleeping on the floor now that we're here. We can stay at an inn with real beds until the pack train arrives.

I throw open my window shutters and gasp. The view is stunning. The sun is all but down and the land across the shimmering water is a rich, glowing purple. Boats bob and creak below, tethered to docks that run along the city walls. In our rearyard is a scattering of outbuildings and animal pens and a kitchen garden greening like a meadow.

If I'm not murdered, this might not turn out so badly after all.

I trudge belowstairs in search of a place to rest my cart-rattled bones, and I come upon the hall. Salvo is already asleep before the hearth, where a girl about my size is raking the coals. She's dressed in unbecoming gray wool that has been patched and repatched with tight, careful seams.

The servant, like as not. And I am the lady of the house. Like my mother once, at Edgeley.

I wave a hand at the girl and say, "Fetch me some wine."

Rather than leaping up and skittering toward the kitchen, the girl regards me so fiercely that my belly seizes up. Her eyes are dark as currants and unblinking as a bird's.

I stiffen from jaw to fists. "You will bring the wine. Then you will beg my pardon."

The servants at Edgeley would never have dared to so much as raise their eyes to me.

And this girl is fighting a smirk.

"I am the lady of this house," I say in small, bitten-off words, "and you are dismissed from it. As of right now. Be gone!"

I wait for her to cower and plead, but she merely looks at me as steadily as a saint. At length she returns to raking.

"Did you not hear me?" I wrench the grate rake from her hand and haul her to her feet. "You will leave at once!"

The girl's expression hardens. For a long moment she does naught, neither word nor deed, and I'm about to prod her with the rake when she turns on her heel and marches toward the rear of the house.

I'm looking for a place to hang the rake when the girl returns with Mistress Tipley, and the crone is bristling like a sopping cat. "Gwenhwyfar is going nowhere. Now give her the grate rake and let her get on with her work."

"She's ill-mannered," I reply, "and unfit for this house."

"What's unfit for this house?" my father asks as he plods into the hall and tugs at his gloves.

"Her." I level a finger at the girl as she studies her bare feet.

My father runs a hand through his hair. "Cecily, please. We're all weary. Let it lie."

I sharpen my voice. "I'll not have her in this house."

My father sighs. "If it'll make you feel better, sweeting, mayhap—"

"My lord, begging your pardon," Mistress Tipley cuts in, "but if you dismiss Gwenhwyfar, you may as well dismiss me, too."

I turn on my father like a whipcrack. "She's lying! She cannot leave!"

Mistress Tipley draws herself up straight. "I've breathed town air much longer than a year and a day, so I can come and go as I see fit. I'm here for wages, and with the borough's leave. If this arrangement doesn't suit you, my lord, I'll gather my things and be gone by first light on the morrow."

My father blinks. "Christ, no. Mistress Tipley, please. Let's not be rash. Of course Gwen—Gwinny—of course this servant shall stay. And so shall you. And *no more*"—my father gives me a warning look—"will be said of it."

The girl, Gwinny, slices a triumphant look at me as Mistress Tipley hands her the tool. Then she kneels once again and begins to rake around Salvo in long, taunting strokes.

I sulk on the bottom step of the stairs. I will see that crone Tipley on the street by midsummer. Her and her precious Gwinny. No one makes a fool of Cecily d'Edgeley and gets away clear.

A KNIGHT and his daughter, she said. No mistress.

More fool I, to have thanked God for small blessings too early.

No mistress, and new English might be bearable. No sniping. No accusations of familiarity with the master.

No insistence that I live in this town. In this house.

But what I get is worse again, and from a girl no older than I who stands there hands on hips, eyes narrow, brazen as a cold-water drench. As if this is her house already. Her grate to be raked. Hers from splinter to beam.

Wait for the master to slap her senseless. But he does not.

Expected a lot of things from new English. Did not expect to be ruled by a brat.

Long winter days, and I should have known better than to grow accustomed to the blessing of stillness. To grow to love the way quiet could fill space. To close my eyes one too many times and think mayhap new English would never arrive, mayhap this place could stay waiting forever.

Now it's spring, English are here, and I could kill the brat a hundred different ways.

Could strangle her with one of her foolish ribbons. Dump hemlock in her breakfast porridge. Push her down the stairs. Would be no different than killing a rat.

She is English.

The lot of them should burn.

MY FATHER refuses to get us into an inn. When I presented a clear and thoughtful argument, his eyes bulged as if I had spit at the king. Then he said blather-blather-"silver" and blather-blather-"ruinous" and ended the discussion. It appears that cushioning his beloved daughter's poor bruised body is not worth a few measly pennies, so I must sleep on the floor. On the pallet. With all the fleas.

I want my bed.

My father says the pack train like as not won't arrive for another fortnight. If it's not waylaid.

Even in Coventry I slept in a bed.

I must have been more tired than I thought, for I awaken to Prime ringing. Mayhap they are Christian here.

There's a bucket of washing water in the corner. I splash some on my face, brush and plait my hair, then slide on my gown. It takes hardly any time to ready yourself when there's no one to hide your shift or tease you about your shiny forehead.

My tread echoes in the chamber. In this morning light, the space spreads out like sown fields. No elbows to bump. No feet to trip over. It's just me.

Agnes talked too much and Alice couldn't keep a secret to save her soul from Purgatory, but it's all I can do to swallow down my tears. I take out our altar cloth and sit for a long time on the floor, tracing every stitch with my fingers.

But the lady of the house cannot sit and mope. I rise, hide the altar cloth beneath my pallet, and head belowstairs. In the hall, there's bread on the trestle table and I fall on it like a hungry raven. Mistress Tipley bustles in, adjusting her wimple. She picks up the market basket near the door.

The lady of the house does the marketing.

I must sort out a way to get rid of Mistress Tipley.

"I'm coming with you," I inform her.

She blinks rapidly. "Demoiselle, you must be tired after your—"

"I'm coming with you." I look her in the eye till she huffs.

"Very well," Mistress Tipley replies, "but we must leave now."

I lead her into the street, where women lug buckets of water and men sweep refuse into the gutter.

And I remember where I am.

I will be murdered as sure as God hates sin. Some big hairy Welshman will beat me to death with my own market basket. I shouldn't even *be* here; I should be at Edgeley Hall throwing sticks for Salvo's grandpuppies and stitching my bridal linen.

But the passing townsfolk do not lurk or creep or even menace. Most greet Mistress Tipley. In English.

The last place I expected to hear the English tongue is this back-end of Christendom's midden.

We have been walking forever. Mistress Tipley is either lost or daft, or possibly both. I match her pace and say, "Surely we must be at the market common by now."

"It's not a market day," the old cow tells me. "We're just going on the rounds."

"But how can you market on a day that isn't market day?"

Mistress Tipley sighs. "It's a privilege, demoiselle. Hurry, I'm busy today."

Charming. Next she'll be telling me the mayor is a heathen Turk and wine flows through the gutters and this place isn't in fact full of cutthroats and barbarians.

We stop at the bakery. The baker is just lowering his stall-front into a counter and propping up the awning when Mistress Tipley trundles up. The smell of bread is divine.

She pulls out a linen-wrapped parcel and slides it across the counter. The baker counts five wads of bread dough and places the parcel beneath the counter, then he withdraws four cross-stamped rounds from a shelf behind him.

"Half a penny, mistress." In English. Like any of my neighbors at Edgeley.

Mistress Tipley arranges the bread in her basket and pays the baker.

"Why only four?" I ask. "You gave him five loaves. Why do we not get five in return?"

"Castellaria," Mistress Tipley replies as she herds me into the street. "Everyone must contribute to support the castle garrison."

I cannot think of men I want better fed than those of the castle garrison.

Mistress Tipley bustles up the street like a hen. She does not seem to worry about being murdered.

At the coster's counter, Mistress Tipley buys a pan of onions. The coster weighs the pan and says, "That's a penny, mistress."

No one is speaking Welsh. I haven't heard a word of tongue-pull since our ill-humored guide took his leave.

I ask the spicer where he's from.

"King's Lynn, demoiselle." He hands a small packet of pepper to Mistress Tipley.

"You're an Englishman, then."

The spicer chuckles. "Of course I am! Where else would I come from?"

"Er." I gesture around. "Wales?"

The spicer roars laughter as if I've made the most uproarious jest ever in the annals of jesting. "Wales! Oh, saints, listen to the little maid! Did you fall off the turnip cart this morning, or are you laughing in your sleeve?"

I clench my fists. It's a decent guess, as we're in the thick of Wales. But for some reason it's high amusement to mock poor Cecily who asked an honest question and expected an honest answer.

Mistress Tipley swallows her rude laughter and pulls me up the street. I'm itching to ask what's so funny, but I will not give her the satisfaction of mocking my ignorance, too.

We're heading toward the house when I see *him* again. The lad from the docks who seems to think it proper to look upon me squarely. And as he drives past on a rubble cart, one sturdy bare foot resting easily on the foreboard, sure enough, he does it again. He looks right at me, and this time he *smiles*.

Mannerless vermin like him would be cartwhipped at Edgeley.

Not soon enough, we get back to the townhouse. I follow Mistress Tipley down the greenway to a rearyard that's frightfully mucky. But it's my duty to know it well, so I pace it off while holding my hem out of the mud.

The kitchen takes up a good portion of the yard and houses a massive cookfire and several trestle tables. Alongside the mud-splattered kitchen wall is a small roost for hens, and a pig keep. A pigling trots to the pen's rail and grunts hopefully as I near. I haven't any scraps for him, but I scratch his back with a stick of kindling. Next to the lovely garden are a shed and a covered space where two barrels sit empty. The yard ends abruptly at the city wall, which rises like a shield stuck in earth.

Standing in the yard between house and wall is like being folded into your father's embrace after losing at chess or delivering a particularly harrowing confession.

I never thought I'd like walls so much, not after looking over Edgeley's rolling yardlands.

But Caernarvon is not Edgeley. It can never hope to be.

So I'm glad for the walls that stand between me and all that is without.

We go to Mass. I wear my second-best kirtle and my cloak trimmed in fur, despite the sun roasting me like a Michael-mas goose.

Though my father has not yet taken the oath, the bur-gesses welcome him into their midst with back-slaps and bellowed greetings and extended wrists. Their wives cluck over me, and I duck my chin and flutter my lashes in case they have comely sons who might pay me favor.

They are English, to the smallest babe.

I'm beginning to wonder if there are any Welsh at all in Caernarvon.

When I lead Mistress Tipley out to do the marketing after Saturday Mass, she does not turn onto Palace Street toward the baker's shop. Instead she plows up the big main street toward the city gate. I suffer walking at her elbow and ask, "Are you lost? Palace is behind us."

"Today is market day," Mistress Tipley says, "and the mar-ket proper is held without the walls on the common, so we must go there."

Market day, at least, makes sense. Unlike so many other things here.

When we reach the city gate, a massive trestle bars the way through the dark arch. A straggling queue stretches along the walls and curves out of sight. There's no space to get past the trestle save a single gap near the wall, and that space is blocked by a big serjeant bearing a long knife.

Two men sit at the trestle. One guards a wooden box with thick hinges and a sturdy lock. They, too, have knife-hilts clearly pushing back their cloaks.

Mistress Tipley nudges me from behind. "Come. We're not required to pay murage."

She approaches the serjeant and taps his elbow. He steps aside, nodding politely. Ere I can speak, she seizes my sleeve and drags me forward, wrinkling my plum-colored gown.

"This is the daughter of the Edgeley house," Mistress Tipley tells the serjeant. "You will be seeing her as well."

Edgeley House. I must admit it has a music to it.

The serjeant inclines his head to me, then pushes aside the first few men in line so that the old cow and I might pass. The men mutter in tongue-pull.

I stand very still. Surely they'll not murder me while an armed serjeant stands within a knife-slash.

The Welshmen don't even look at me. To a man they push their hoods back and study their bare feet while Mistress Tipley brushes past them, towing me by the sleeve.

Outside the gate, the Welsh appear like worms in cheese. The bridge and fields are crammed with them. Tongue-pull and singsong English ring all around like birdcalls. You can't turn around without roughening your elbow on homespun.

Mistress Tipley plows through the Welsh so briskly that it's all I can do to follow. The poor wretches plod like oxen, even the children, as if this is a quarter-day and not a market day when all the shopkeepers have their awnings out and ribbons on their poles and criers are hawking everything from meat pies to smoked fish.

There's a worn path leading past the castle, and a long queue of Welsh people stretches beyond the gatehouse and the wharves. They're bearing boxes and crates, packs and satchels, animals on tethers and wheelbarrows piled with graying vegetables.

They must be from the countryside.

Mistress Tipley does not join the queue. She strides purposefully to the front amid a flurry of elbows and shoves. I hurry to catch up.

The queue is held up by a trestle that bars the mill bridge, much like the one beneath the castle gate. Three men sit at the trestle. One has a strongbox. Another has an array of eggs, spun fibers, fish, apples, and cheeses in baskets both on the trestle and at his feet. Several armed serjeants stand in the only gap.

"Come," Mistress Tipley says over her shoulder. "There's no toll for us." To the serjeant she says, "Edgeley of Shire Hall Street."

The serjeant nods and stands aside. As we move past the trestle and onto the market common, the first Welshman in line drops something in the strongbox. It clinks like metal.

One of the men at the trestle marks the Welshman's shoulder with chalk and the serjeant steps aside to let him pass.

How sensible. A toll to keep the riffraff out.

So the Welsh are only permitted near the walls once a se'ennight and they must pay for the privilege.

Mayhap I will not be murdered after all.

On the market common, the Welsh kneel before their wares spread out on homespun. Mostly they offer milk and meat, but some have cured hides and rolled fleeces and wool in skeins. The wool is rough and grainy, hardly fit for monks. Our wool at Edgeley was ten times better.

It's a charitable thing indeed for the burgesses of Caernarvon to allow these folk and their pitiable goods near the walls in the first place. The Welsh ought to thank the burgesses on bent knee for the opportunity to trade with the English in the shadow of their walled town.

Mistress Tipley buys a sack of oats and a big wedge of cheese, then she says we must go to the wharves to get the best fish. She leads me past all the lambs and cattle to the edge of the common, to a board straining beneath baskets of fish.

The fishmonger scrambles to his feet and pushes back his hood. "A health to you, mistress." He speaks properly, but barely so, for his words are made singsong by tongue-pull.

"Five of your best sparling," says Mistress Tipley.

He fumbles through a big covered basket and pulls

out fish by the tail. Three are shiny and gray-green, but the others are stiff like planking. And they smell.

Mistress Tipley had better not think I will be carrying those fish.

She shakes her head. "Your best."

"They're the best I've got," he grumbles. Then he straightens and adds, "If it pleases you, mistress."

"Half price, then," Mistress Tipley says. "Those two aren't fit for anything save a stew."

I'm sure as anything not eating them. I'll give them to Salvo. He likes foul dead things.

"Naught wrong with them," the fishmonger insists. "Just listless from being at the bottom of the basket."

"Then a levelooker shall decide," Mistress Tipley says firmly. "The judges at Piepowder Court won't mind settling the matter."

I giggle. Piepowder. Mayhap the judge is a baker and you're amerced in sacks of flour.

The fishmonger growls something in tongue-pull, then sighs. "Very well. What'll you give for them?"

Mistress Tipley squints. "Twopence."

"I'd rather have the sack of oats that your daughter there is holding."

I jerk back as though he hit me. That he could even *think* such a thing, much less speak it!

"Twopence," repeats Mistress Tipley.

The fishmonger looks bellysick. "Please, mistress. Lastage is the worst tax of the lot, so there are no costers out here."

Let him rot. That'll teach him some manners.

"Twopence or nothing."

The fishmonger closes his eyes for a long moment. His jaw is working. Then he deliberately pushes back his ratty cloak and drops a hand to a knife-hilt.

I choke. I freeze. I cannot even stumble out of his reach.

"Don't." Mistress Tipley's voice is steady, her posture rigid. "That's trouble you don't want."

I garble out a prayer in an undertone. I will stand before my Maker ere my Ave is done.

"What you want is to finish this trade," she goes on in a voice even I can tell is too calm. "Then there'll be no trouble."

The fishmonger's wrath falters and his shoulders slump. At length he drags his cloak over the knife-hilt. "I . . . I just haven't the coin . . ."

Now that the knife is out of sight, I manage to tumble behind Mistress Tipley like a days-old puppy.

". . . it'll be county court because of the blade . . ."

Mistress Tipley regards him steadily. "What blade? I've come for fish. Twopence for sparling."

The fishmonger gapes like a pardoned man on the gallows. At length he pleads, "Half the oats, then. Half for all five sparling, plus a handful of herring. *Your* handful."

Mistress Tipley puts a thoughtful finger to her chin, and it's obvious now that she's not fit to do the marketing.

There's naught to consider with such a bargain. He's offering easily fivepence worth of fish for a piddling halfpenny's worth of oats. And after the fright he put on me, the wretched brute deserves to come up short.

"Very well," she says. "Half."

The fishmonger piles the fish into a cloth she holds out, penitent now, babbling like a lackwit. "A blessing on your kindness, mistress, for I've two little ones to feed, and with all the tolls it's enough to drive a man to—"

"Shhh!" snaps Mistress Tipley, and she jerks her chin at me.

The fishmonger bobs his head, smiles, cringes like a whipped hound. "You are kind indeed, demoiselle, and God Almighty and all the saints will reward you for it."

An Ave ago, this wretch was ready to gut me like a fish. Now he's heaping blessings on me. And pulling his cloak firmly over the knife-hilt, hoping I'll forget.

I don't, though. When we pass the toll table on our way out, I tug on a serjeant's sleeve and whisper in his ear.

"He had what?" The serjeant draws back, startled. "Where?"

I gesture toward the wharves, trying to look frightened. It isn't hard.

"Good work, lass." The serjeant nods to his fellow and they peel away from the toll line, pawing through Welsh people and drawing their weapons as they go.

Soon there's shouting and commotion and the slushy

sound of fish dumped on the ground. More shouting, then a cry of terror and the thrash of struggle.

I smile as I follow Mistress Tipley back toward Caernarvon, despite the black look she's giving me. Somehow I'm not as frightened anymore.

THE brat never looses me ere sunset. Most days it matters little.

On market day, it means we starve.

The last few shopkeepers will be drawing down their awnings and folding up their counters by the time I reach the market common.

Only one thing to do.

Promised Gruffydd I would not. But we must eat, and this is what they've left us.

Down the road, beneath the dark grave of a gate, toward the mill, bracing myself. Deep breaths. Steady on.

Knuckles against the weathered rearyard door. The Cadnant laps quietly below.

A face, doughy and wroth, peers through a cracked door. "Whaddaya want?"

"Oats."

The doughball's eyes flick up and down. Then he gives a greasy smile. "Threepence."

Open my hand. There he is. Staring out, hair like the waves, becrowned. Bastard has the gall to smirk, even cast in silver.

He is why.

It is he who reduced us so.

Turn the penny over. The cross is better. Must think of the saints, though. Not the churchmen.

"How much for a penny?"

"A curse," the doughball spits. "Filthy whore. I've been amerced enough today."

Turn. Walk away. Won't limp here. Not beneath walls of bone and stone.

"Unless . . ."

Keep walking. Already know what he'll want for a miserable half-sack. Back along the path, head down, feet raising dust.

Squeeze the penny tight. Mayhap hurt him whose likeness is stamped here, can men of silver hurt.

Toward Porth Mawr. With luck it's not too late and he'll have something left. Sun isn't completely down yet. Mayhap, since the Porth Mawr mill is farther from the walls. But English watch him more closely for that very reason.

"Three measures," whispers the miller through the crack in his rearyard door. "And you did not get it from me."

"Crown measures?"

"Christ, yes. What else?"

Stuff the sack through the crack. A rustling, and the sack returns dangling from a grizzled hand. It looks empty still. Weak and limp. The levelookers must have been here today.

Peer in. Oats at the bottom, a finger's depth.

Crown measures.

It's all I can do to keep from stuffing them in my mouth. Handful after handful, oats clinging to my lips. Feel full. Just for a moment.

Give the penny one last squeeze, my thumb over his face. Press hard. Hurt, silver king. Die.

"Now get gone," the miller hisses, "ere I'm amerced again."

Hug the sack. Hug it close.

The lot of them should burn.

The path unfolds, some last hints of sun at my right. Skirt fields, fine greening swaths of oats and barley. Mustn't tread there. Watchers are about. Traitors all. Like their miserable fathers.

Should be Gruffydd's. And men like him. Every handswidth. Instead it belongs to burgesses. Given by a king who had it to give because he took it. Sown with blood. Every handswidth.

Woods are nearing. Stumps and holes in waves where the timber gangs have been. English always need wood. Firewood. Castle scaffolding. Townhouses.

Gallows.

Timber gangers never want for coin. Smug bastards with their steady wages and their woodboon and their wretched quarter-day feasts on the borough's penny. Hand-picked by the English, every man, to keep the rest of us jealous and compliant.

At the top of the rise is a dull bulk of shadows. Hidden. They'd have to care to find us.

Shoulder through the curtain. The fire is down to embers, and next to it Mam lies on her pallet. She looks dead. Just a pile of threadbare blankets. The one I got from the porter for showing my tits. The one Gruffydd got for spading up and sowing the first mayor's curtilage garden. And the one that smelled like Da for almost a year till the dirt crept up from the floor and the mold crept down from the walls to take him away from us one last time.

Go to her. Kneel. Her eyes are clenched closed. Her face is lines all cracked like thirsty ground. Her bone fingers pick at the blankets. She is never warm.

Rise. Legs throb all the way up, throb and ache and feel wobbly inside, bones of water. Turn from her, quiet. Mustn't wake her. Feed the fire enough ill-gotten sticks to keep it sputtering. Mash a small handful of oats into gruel. She'll be hungry when she wakes.

Lift the gruel spoon, watch the liquid oats dribble. Almost more than I can bear, empty as I am. When I'm at the brat's, the chatelaine does what she can—a wedge of bread at midday, a covert mug of ale—but there's naught to do for Crown measures and market penny.

Drink some watered mead. Tricks my belly into feeling full.

"Babies."

Crawl to Mam's side. "I'm here. Please be still."

"They're coming." Mam's eyes are flat like coins. They have not looked in years. "They'll take everything. The herds. The pewter. They'll kill my babies. They'll kill my poor little lambs."

Mam's eyelids flutter and her limbs begin to thrash. Slide a bit of wood between her teeth and press her shoulders against the pallet till the shaking dies away.

"Your babies are alive." Pitch my voice calming. "Sleep now. They're alive."

Mam's face is bloodless. Tug the stick from her sagging jaws. Cover her with blankets. Spoon some gruel into her mouth.

Your babies are alive. Every time, I lie. We are alive in body, my brother and I. English should have put us to the sword, though. Spared us this.

Muck out the byre, toss the leavings on the midden, then haul bucket after bucket of water. It's long past dark when everything is set. A bucket of water at Mam's right hand. Her knife carefully sharpened and cleaned. Chips for kindling the fire and wood enough to keep it burning all day. Her privy rags and bucket, dumped and squeezed and scrubbed. A pottle of mead, nigh empty.

Now, with God Almighty's help, Mam might live another day.

Drink mug after mug of water. In the blackest part of night, I will rise so I can be at the brat's house by dawn to haul water and cook pottage and listen to the lackwit prattle on about how unfair it is that she must sit so still while the buttermilk bleaches her freckles.

I'VE DRAGGED one of the hall benches into the frontmost chamber, the one with the big windows that open onto Shire Hall Street. Most likely it's meant to be a shop of some kind, or a workroom. It's the only place I can spin or sew in peace. If the pack train ever arrives, I'll set up my embroidery frame here. It'd be perfect but for the flies and the smell of the road out front.

My father clumps in crowing like a cock. "Oh, my girl, get dressed! They're waiting on us even now."

"A moment, Papa." I'm squinting at a particularly tricky curl of a peacock's tail. "Let me finish this stitch."

My linen is jerked from my hands. My father tosses it onto the bench and pulls me up by both wrists, grinning like a fool.

"Hey! Papa—"

"Hay is for horses, sweeting. Now go put on your surcote. Quickly now."

I weave my needle into the corner of my linen and bundle the lot into my workbasket. "What's the hurry?"

"The Coucys have invited us to dinner. Now go!"

Right. Yes. There was someone by the name of Coucy at Mass. Bark like a mastiff and hands like a smith. I put on my yellow surcote with the vine stitchery around the collar and off we go.

Up the road. Toward the High Street.

We stop before a door twice my height that's set in a building all in gray stone, four stories' worth.

The Coucys live on High Street in a house of gray stone.

I suddenly realize my hair is a mess.

A girl in a homespun apron lets us in. We're led into a paneled hall and given hippocras. My father beams down at me and pets my plaits, putting them in further disarray.

"Edgeley." A sun-browned man fills the entryway.

My father crosses the room with big strides and clasps the man's wrist, then inclines his head. "My lord, you are kind to invite us. We are honored to take meat at the table of Sir John de Coucy."

Sir John nods. "You're most welcome to Caernarvon."

"Thanks to the goodwill of *honesti* like yourself."

"Well, don't think it comes cheap," Sir John replies to the wall behind my father's head. "You'll take the oath as soon as we can convene. By quarter-day at the latest."

My father blinks. "B-but that's midsummer."

"So it is. Sooner the better, eh?"

A woman and a girl come through the doorway after Sir John. The girl is about my size and has hair that flutters about her waist. It's the color of sunlit flax.

My hair is plaited. It's the color of wet sand.

I hate this girl already.

She is called Emmaline. When I'm presented, she smiles at me, and I mark that her teeth are more crooked than mine. This pleases me.

At table, I'm seated next to Emmaline, so we must share a cup of wine. I manage to refrain from spitting in it since my father is watching me like an unpaid gaoler.

We're served stuffed pigling and gingerbread. Gingerbread! I eat two whole pieces and I'm reaching for a third when my father kicks me under the table. I reluctantly pull my hand into my lap.

While the apron girl is clearing away the pewter and horn, Emmaline asks her mother, "May I show Cecily my embroidery?"

"Of course you may," says the harridan, so I'm obliged to follow Emmaline abovestairs.

The walls of Emmaline's chamber are tinted a delicate shade of orange. There's a cushioned windowseat and a brazier that smells faintly of sandalwood. A small table stands near the bed, and on it are a brass bowl and ewer, some vials, a scattering of combs, and a bronze looking glass.

At my house, I sleep on the floor.

Emmaline goes to an embroidery frame beneath the window and unpins a length of linen. "I'm working this veil for my brother's wife. Do you think she'll like it?"

She's holding out the linen, hopeful as a dog with a stick,

so I take it carefully in both hands and pretend to care. The stem stitches look loose, like gallows-rope, so I sneak a quick peek at the back. The knots are a mess, all tangled and lumpy.

I grin outright. I can do better work with my feet in the dark.

"I spent all winter on it," Emmaline says proudly. "My brother and his wife live in Shrewsbury, but they're coming to visit this summer."

"Ugh, why?"

Emmaline looks puzzled. "Why not?"

I gesture around. "Who would set foot in this town if they could avoid it?"

"You mean Caernarvon?" Emmaline cocks her head. "But it's a lovely place! You've come in spring, true enough, and it's a bit gray now, but come summer you'll fall in love with it."

"What about . . ." I grimace. "The people. Who live out there. Without the walls."

"The Welsh?" Emmaline smiles as if we're sharing a secret. "Don't be troubled by them. Most newcomers find them odd at first, but once you know them, they're charming. They have the most beautiful children, and you should hear them sing."

Somehow I doubt that Emmaline has ever been within spitting distance of a Welsh person, much less been saddled with an ill-mannered one as a servant.

The apron girl appears at the top of the stairs bearing a tray loaded with honey wafers.

Honey wafers *and* gingerbread. Sir John ought to change his name to Croesus de Coucy.

Emmaline sits on the bed and holds out the plate of wafers. I take a big handful and cram them in my mouth without anyone to say me nay, while Emmaline's happy chatter about the Eden that is Caernarvon flows over me like rain over feathers.

I have a bellyache. Emmaline's company must have upset my digestion. I retire to the floor of my plain, cold, untinted bedchamber with a cool cloth over my eyes and a mug of weak small beer infused with chamomile.

I'm better by supper, and I grumble belowstairs to eat sparling and cabbage with antler spoons.

Up the street, Emmaline is eating honey wafers and wasting gold thread on that excuse for a veil.

"So," says my father, "a nice surprise at dinner today."

I sniff and stab at my sparling.

"You're always complaining how much you miss Alice and Agnes. I thought you'd welcome the company of another young female."

"That girl isn't Agnes or Alice."

My father lowers his meat-knife. "You will be pleasant to Emmaline de Coucy. Her family built this borough. Sir John was one of the first Englishmen here."

I wrinkle my nose at my trencher.

"Cecily." My father's voice has an edge I shrink from.

"Very well. I will be pleasant."

"She would make you a very good friend," my father says as he tears off another piece of bread. "Invited to an *honesti* home within a fortnight of arriving—I barely believe such fortune. The saints are looking out for us, sweeting, to bring us into the graces of the town's elite. To say naught of my taking the oath by midsummer, when I thought Martinmas at the earliest. Almost six months early! It's most fortunate, and we must make of it what we can."

My father can make what he wants of this place. It'll be all I can do to run this house and keep my gowns in good repair and not get murdered until we can go home to Edgeley Hall.

God is merciful to sinners! The pack train just arrived! And at its head is Nicholas, my elder cousin.

"Cesspit!" he crows, hopping down from his palfrey and throwing his arms about me. He smells like horse and sweat and sweaty horse, but I hug him hard. It's Nicholas, the lop-eared oaf who puts horse apples in my shoes and hides my hairpins, but my throat is choked up as if I've swallowed too big a bite of pie.

"I could really use a mug of your strongest," Nicholas says, clasping my father's wrist, "but first let's set this lot to their labor." He gestures to a group of ragged men hovering like locusts at the corner of the house among the crowd of laden mules. "I hired them without the walls. Will they understand a word I say?"

My father shrugs. "Usually there's one or two who will."

"Very well." Nicholas bawls at them, as if they're hard of hearing. "Unload the mules. Put things where my lord of Edgeley"—Nicholas claps my father's shoulder—"bids you. A penny per man when you've finished."

One of the laborers steps forward and speaks in tongue-pull to the others. I freeze right there in the yard with Nicholas's arm still about my waist.

It's *him*. The one who *looks* at me.

Of course he'd be a Welshman. I should have marked him by his stabley manners and his scruffy gray tunic that's laced all crooked, revealing far too much in the way of dirty collarbone.

I ought to bid Nicholas knock his front teeth in, just on principle.

But Nicholas is already halfway inside, telling my father of the journey and the river crossings and an inn in Chester where the girls did some shocking things. I turn and follow ere *he* has a chance to look at me.

My father sits at the trestle table with Nicholas and laughs and brags and hears the news, so it's my task to tell the laborers what goes where. In my own house and with two armed men present, the laborers wouldn't dare try to murder me. But I'm on my guard nonetheless.

I don't look at the men. I look at what each is bearing,

then point with sweeping gestures and use small words so mayhap they'll understand. Hall. Kitchen. Abovestairs. Workroom. They nod and duck out and do as they're told. Like dogs.

Dogs do not murder.

The laborers heave and haul and tote from midmorning well into the afternoon. They sweat like oxen and they're twice as filthy, but by sunset our little house actually looks like a house. There are cooking pots and fireplace tongs and linens and saints be praised, my bed is finally here and strung together.

As soon as one of the men brings up my coffer, I carefully lay our altar cloth within, next to a bunch of dried flowers from Edgeley's garden and my mother's handkerchief, the one she pressed to my bleeding palm when I tried to imitate her slicing bread on a trestle I could barely see over.

When the mules are unloaded, the laborers look and smell like an army of pigs. One poor wretch has jammed his thumb so badly it's turning purple. They line up in the gutter while *he* hovers at the front door, waiting to be paid. Like as not he's looking at me even now, but I'm stringing my embroidery frame in the workroom and ignoring him for the beast he is.

And I can ignore pretty well.

Apparently my father can, too, for it's quite a while ere he groans up from the trestle and clumps outside while pouring coins into his hand. He sifts through them, then drops a halfpenny far above each sweaty palm. By the time my father gets to the one who *looks*, there's a lot of grumbling down the filthy line.

"Beg pardon." His English is singsonged by the tongue-pull. "A penny was promised us for this work."

"You were promised nothing of the sort," my father replies. "Half a penny is more than you deserve, so get gone lest you'd have the Watch on your backsides."

I come to the window in time to see a shadow of rage move across the boy's stubbly jaw. Half a penny might be more than they deserve, but I'd be wroth too were I denied what was promised me.

But he only grunts something in tongue-pull to his mangy fellows and they troop down Shire Hall Street in a cloud of sweaty dust.

At supper, we celebrate with a haunch of mutton with sage. The trestle is set properly with linens and pewterware. I sleep like a babe in arms in my own bed.

God is indeed merciful to sinners.

Nicholas is here two whole days ere he works up the courage to lay out the terrible news. My thieving uncle Roger has posted banns. He will marry a girl half his age at midsummer. Which means there could be an heir to Edgeley Hall by next Easter.

I could be stuck here forever. And there'd be naught to do for it.

I wonder just how much penance I would have to do for praying her barren.

My father is taking his burgess oath ere the month is out. I have nothing to wear.

There's the green kirtle that was small on me last year, which hovers around my calves as though I'm a ratty little waif. I may as well brand UNMARRIAGEABLE on my brow. The yellow surcote has a gravy stain in the lap that no amount of fuller's earth can remove, and the alkanet kirtle is barely fit for rags.

My father cannot think I'll stand before the whole town wearing one of these excuses for a garment.

As soon as I've finished supervising Mistress Tipley doing the marketing, I go down the road to the common stable just within the walls. My cousin is there, brushing his palfrey.

"Nicholas." I lean prettily on the stall. "You love me, do you not?"

"I do, Cesspit. You're my favorite cousin."

I'm also his only cousin, but that's a tired jest. "How much do you love me?"

Nicholas combs the horse's flank with long, chuffing strokes. "Not enough to do whatever it is you want of me."

"I only need someone big and strong to escort me around this filthy place."

"And?"

"And . . ." I make my voice small and sweet. "And lend me the price of a new gown."

Nicholas pops up over the horse's rump. "Hellfire, Cesspool, do I look like a man with the price of a gown?"

"All right," I grumble. "Be mean and pinch your pennies. But come with me. Please? You're going to miss me sorely."

He groans and tosses the comb onto a ledge, mumbling something unflattering about women. I let his remark fall, though. Doubtless he secretly likes ferrying me around. I must look fair upon his arm, and if Fortune favors him, people will mistake me for his sweetheart.

We head up High Street and turn on Castle, where I spot a swinging sign bearing a faded ship. At the counter is a falcon-faced graybeard measuring cloth nose to fingertips. He looks up as we approach.

"G'morn, my lord. Have you come for wool?"

"Something suitable for a gown," I jump in, ere Nicholas can ruin things. "For a special occasion."

The merchant glances at Nicholas, who nods. Then the merchant turns to me and holds out the wool he's been measuring. "There's this, just back from the fuller. A good tight weave."

It's just minnet. I frown. "What else have you?"

"This ochre is fair." The merchant brings out a scrap.

I pet it and it's like sand. "Surely you've something better."

The merchant glances again at Nicholas. My cousin

shrugs. Then the merchant holds up a finger and disappears into the shop. In a moment he's back with the most beautiful bolt of finespun I've ever seen. It's the color of fresh blood and as soft to the touch as a lapdog. I pet it and pet it. I cannot take my hands off it.

"How much?" I ask.

"Fifteen shillings a yard."

I blink. Even Nicholas looks a little stunned. Horses can cost less. "W-well, I'll take it. My father will come with me on the morrow to settle up."

"Beg pardon, demoiselle, but without some kind of surety, I cannot hold the wool for you. I could sell it to half a dozen buyers by the morrow. It's right off the boat from Flanders."

I must have this wool.

"Nicholas, what do you have of value?"

"Sorry, Cesspile, all I've got is gold plate," my wretch cousin snipes in a most flippant way.

I must have this wool.

The merchant holds the bolt close to his heart like an only son. Nicholas folds his arms and leans on the window frame as if this is boring somehow.

I swallow hard. "How about an altar cloth? All stitched in gold thread? It has two dozen saints. Took a whole year to make."

The merchant shrugs. "I'd have to see it."

"Nicholas, my dearest cousin, the kindest and most self-less Christian ever to—"

"Yes, yes, I'll go fetch it," Nicholas grumbles. "Where is it?"

"Folded in the coffer in my chamber. Nicholas, you are simply the most—"

But he's striding up the street like his cloak is afire. One little favor and he's worked himself into a lather.

In less than two Credos, Nicholas is back with a familiar packet that he slaps hard into my belly. I ignore him and unfurl the altar cloth like a grand banner. The merchant makes an approving little noise and puts out a hand.

I hesitate.

The linen is soft as a mare's flank. The saints are peaceful all in a line. Alice and Agnes would never speak to me again if they knew.

I push it into his hands all at once. "Take care with it. It's dear to me."

The merchant folds the altar cloth into a tidy square. "This'll be enough to hold the wool. You'll get it back when I've been paid in full. Your father will return on the morrow to pay?"

"Oh, indeed, my lord," I reply. "Mayhap even today. The sooner, the better."

But as the merchant begins to unfurl the wool for measuring, a tall cock of a man slides up to the market counter and smiles all teeth at Nicholas.

"You are a foreigner," the cock-man says to my cousin.

Nicholas frowns. "What do you mean?"

"And trading on a Wednesday. Amerced a penny." The cock-man holds out his palm.

Nicholas squares up. "I made no trade."

The merchant draws back, clutching his bolt of finespun. "I knew not, Pluver. I swear I didn't."

"I made the trade." I step before Nicholas and glare a brace of daggers at this wretch Pluver. "My father is Robert d'Edgeley, and I will see you cartwhipped for your baseless threat against my kinsman, you filthy swine."

"Robert d'Edgeley." Pluver squints thoughtfully. "Newly of Shire Hall Street. Not yet admitted to the privileges and still a foreigner. That makes you a foreigner, too." He holds out his hand. "A penny."

"I've no idea what you mean," I reply through my teeth, "but I'll not give you a single blasted thing merely at your word."

The merchant has withdrawn and stored the bolt of finespun out of sight.

"You are a foreigner trading on a day that is not Saturday, the recognized market day in Caernarvon," Pluver explains, as if I'm a halfwit. "You are amerced a penny for this trespass. In my hand, or it'll be Court Baron before the bailiff."

I sneer. "I'm not a foreigner. I market every day with Mistress Tipley and she said we owe no market tolls. She said only the Welsh must pay tolls."

Pluver seizes my wrist and it stings like sin. Nicholas starts toward Pluver, but the brute says, "One hand on me and I'll haul you in for assault, lad, and then you're waiting on his Grace the king's itinerant justice. Six months at best."

The filthy swine drags me through alleys and greenways. My hem is a mess and my wrist afire. If anyone ought to be hauled before Court Baron, it's Pluver. We go up and over and up to a tall timber building in the shadow of the castle. It's the Justice Court and no more than ten doors from my own.

Nicholas is my shadow till we arrive, then he mutters something about bringing my father and disappears like an angry ghost.

Justice Court is lit by braziers and two big windows with ornate shutters. There are lecterns and rustling clerks and the moldy smell of damp parchment. I'm sat on a bench and told to keep still. The bailiff barks at me whenever I so much as shift.

My backside is sore. I could do with a cup of wine.

My father arrives, Nicholas on his heels. I leap up and move to throw my arms about my father, but he curtly bids me sit and pulls Pluver and the bailiff into the corner. They mutter like conspirators.

I sit. My father will demand they apologize for the rough way they treated me. For putting hands on me right in the street like they might some red-handed felon.

It's several Aves ere my father returns with the bailiff

and Pluver. I rise, brush dirt from my gown, and prepare to receive my apology with grace and dignity.

". . . appreciate your discretion and understanding in this matter," my father is saying to the bailiff. "You have my word it'll not happen again."

I smooth my hair and glare at Pluver.

"As soon as your daughter has begged my pardon," Pluver says to my father, "she can be quit of this place. Doubtless you of all men have no desire to see the inside of Justice Court right now."

Nicholas will explain. He'll tell my father how I was goaded into defending him and ill-served as a result.

But Nicholas won't even look at me. His back is turned. Like everyone else's.

"Papa, I—"

My father squeezes my elbow and fixes me with such a look that I grit my teeth and mutter to my toes, "Begging your pardon, my lord."

The words taste of sulfur.

Pluver has agreed to forgive the amercement for trading on an unlawful day since no trade was actually made, but I am being amerced a half-penny for calling an official of the borough a filthy swine. It's been entered into the *rotuli* and everything, and I will be required to present myself at Court Baron to answer for it.

Now in the sight of God and Crown, I'm a slanderer. I will die an old maid surrounded by twenty cats.

My father steers me out of Justice Court by the elbow and propels me up Shire Hall Street. "What were you thinking? Haven't you the sense God gave a goat?"

"Papa, I—"

"Do you realize the weight of this matter? How will this look to the *honesti* who vouch for my good name before mayor and community?"

"It's not my fault!"

"And whose fault is it?" My father is turning purple. It's most unflattering. "Christ, Cecily, that levelooker was ready to bring *Nicholas* in! Nicholas, who taxed the goodwill of his lord to safely bring our belongings all the way out here!"

I pull my arm free. He's hurting me. "How was I to know? How could you let them treat me like one of the Welsh? Amercing me for *trading*."

"That half-penny is coming out of your clothing allowance, Cecily, and going right to alms for the poor. And you'll stay in the house a solid se'ennight."

"That's fine!" I shout back. "Because I don't want to even look upon you for *twice* that long!"

I'm in my chamber ere I recall that the wretched merchant still has my altar cloth. *Our* altar cloth. And God only knows how I'll get it back now.

I cannot bear to stay housebound for a whole se'ennight, so at cockcrow I busy myself with things that will put my father in a kind and favorable mood. I air all his linen and replace the birdlime flea-traps in his chamber. I make a whole pottle of the sage wine he favors, then I brush all the snarls out of Salvo's tail.

When my father comes in for supper, the trestle is perfectly laid. The pewterware shines. The pottage is still steaming. There's even a bunch of violets tied with twine arranged on the broadcloth.

For a while, the only sounds are chewing and the snick of meat-knives. I wait till my father has emptied his mug and poured himself another. Then I clear my throat.

"I regret that Nicholas almost got amerced. I'll ask his pardon when he's back from the Boar's Head."

My father snorts quietly. "What in God's name were you even trying to do, you silly creature?"

"My garments are a mess. I thought to get some decent wool to make a gown for your burgess oath-taking." I give him Salvo-eyes. "I would hate to reflect poorly on you."

"What a sacrifice for you," my wretched father drawls.

I stab at my supper. If he would mock me, I'll not speak to him for a fortnight this time.

"Sweeting." My father lowers his meat-knife. "Until I take the oath, we're foreigners. It may seem difficult to believe, good English that we are, but until I have the privileges we're legally no better than the Welsh."

"What of Mistress Tipley? Why can she market freely?"

My father takes a heaping bite. "She cannot, unless she

buys for this house. This house has privileges that we don't. Not yet, anyway."

I spear a turnip cube with my meat-knife. Foolish town rules. Foolish townspeople.

"So you must mind yourself better, at least till I'm admitted to the privileges. You're damn lucky the bailiff believed your tale of misadventure."

"I knew not, Papa. I truly didn't."

"I know you didn't, sweeting. Just as I know you truly did not expect me to pay fifteen shillings a yard for finespun."

I groan. "Very well. Let me put on a sackcloth smock and roll around in the midden."

My father laughs aloud.

"It's not funny! They'll all be watching. Do you not want me to look like a burgess's daughter?"

My father closes his mouth abruptly. Hitting him square in the pride rarely fails. I want to remind him that my favorite color is green, but I dare not risk his changing his mind. At length he licks his lips and mutters, "Mayhap . . . mayhap you might wear her vellet gown."

I gasp. "You're jesting."

"I'm serious as the grave."

My mother kept the gown wrapped in lavender-sprinkled linen and took it out every quarter-day to brush it and flick it with holy water. It's as close to indigo as the likes of us dare get, brought all the way from some southern place near the Pope's front courtyard. It must have cost a small fortune.

I've not seen it since she died.

"Th-thank you, Papa."

My father grunts and turns back to his meat.

She'd let me touch it only after I scrubbed my hands twice in the ewer and dried them on clean linen. The gown looked vast lying on the bed, yards and yards of sleek cloth, and it was softer even than newborn lambs or kittens.

I'd beg my mother to put it on and show me how it looked, but she'd just shake her head and smile and wrap it back up, laying it reverently in the coffer, as if it belonged to a saint.

Cannot get without the walls quickly enough. Step lively till the gray stone beast is all but gone among the trees.

Through the doorway curtain, shoulder first. It's stifling in the windowless steading. There's a fire. Gruffydd is feeding it sticks.

My little brother has fresh bruises across his forearms and his feet are black as soot.

Little. Gruffydd hasn't been littler than me in years. But he's still my little brother, even if I must look up at him.

Didn't expect him till Sunday. He said he'd been hired to cart stone for a se'ennight, and the lads would be staying at the quarry to save the walk. The quarry is heavy work, but at least the wages are certain. Not like standing idle without the walls waiting to be hired by burgesses to do donkey-work for a pittance.

Move to hug him, but he holds me off with a simple embrace about the shoulders. Gruffydd says I should not touch him, for he's always covered in road dust and town filth, but even when he's just out of the river he puts me off.

"Hey, Gwen." He presses a hand to his lower back and grimaces. "Please tell me there's supper."

"No quarry, I take it." Pull out the bread the chatelaine gave me, the stale round I've been saving since midday.

Mouth waters, but I tear off a piece for Mam and hand him the rest. "You look like Hell's own castoff."

Gruffydd grins at me lopsided as he wolfs down the bread. "You too."

"What happened with the quarry?"

"Burgesses."

Tear the bread into pieces for Mam. "Bastards all."

He shrugs. "I take what they give me. They're the ones with the coin."

"They hired that lapdog Tudur Sais again, didn't they? And you said naught and let them."

"What would you have me do?" Gruffydd asks wearily. "Raise Cain? End up like Maelgwn ab Owain? His youngest finally died. She didn't weigh much more than a hearthcat at the end."

Kneel, check Mam. Her breathing is steady. Stay knelt, even when there's naught more to check.

At length, Gruffydd says, "I saw Dafydd on the wharves. He asked after you."

"We are not speaking of Dafydd now." Shoot to my feet, glaring. "We're speaking of how you must not let the likes of that slavish hound Tudur Sais take all the best work, especially when that work was already promised to you!"

Gruffydd smiles sadly. "I know not what you did, but Dafydd is absolutely besotted with you."

If Gruffydd knew what I did with Dafydd, he'd beat him senseless instead of playing errand boy.

Turn away. "Doesn't matter what I did. I'll not marry him. That's the end of it."

Gruffydd flings a hand. "Because of me? I'm not a child, Gwenhwyfar! I can look after myself."

Today's quarry incident would suggest otherwise.

"Saints, how many times must I say it? To you, to Margaret, to Dafydd himself? Must I carve it into my forehead? The answer is no!"

Gruffydd shakes his head. "And Marared is so kind to you. She says naught when you arrive late at the townhouse. Slips you food. Stands up to the master, if what I hear is true."

"Margaret. That's what she calls herself within the walls." Snort, roll my eyes. "If Margaret Tipley chooses to be kind to me, it should be because I work hard and do as she bids me. Not because she used to plait Mam's hair, and certes not because she'd see me wed to the only son of her dearest friend."

"It's because she'd see the burgesses humbled and made to follow the law," Gruffydd says. "And she'll always be Marared to me."

"She cannot be, not in there. Not as a burgess running-dog. And she's in no hurry to leave."

"I'll not throw stones at anyone for how they made their way when the English came," Gruffydd replies quietly, "nor how they must live now."

Only so many times I'll suffer this discussion.

Hold up my coin cross-side out. Gruffydd takes the hint

and pries up the hearthstone. There's a moldy scrap of wool beneath. He unwraps it carefully on his palm. Together we count. Five. There are five silver pennies all together.

"It's not enough," he murmurs. "They'll take something."

"May God strike them down." Can barely speak for choking.

"They can distrain what they like should we not pay," Gruffydd says. "Damn taxmen will be here any day now."

Rub my eyes. Head hurts. Smoke rises like a shroud, silts me down.

My little brother's hands are cut up and sown with splinters. They hang limp at his sides like some lord's kill.

He should be wearing rings. Sitting at the dais of Pencoed and riding the land his by right. He is not, though, and he'll not be. Not now. Not ever.

Nicholas is leaving for Wallingford. I drag my feet while walking him to the door. "You'll come back soon, will you not?"

"If I can, lass, but my lord has little business here."

I study my felt shoes and swallow hard. The house is so much fuller with him in it, belches, bootsteps, and all.

Nicholas smiles suddenly, lighting up like a Candlemas altar. "I nearly forgot to tell you the joyous news, Cesspool. Alice de Baswell is wedding Adam Baker at Lammas. *Your* Alice! The mousy little thing got herself a husband, can you believe?"

She'll have flowers in her hair and her mother will make her the loveliest gown and away she'll go with her comely new husband and I'll miss the whole thing. The ceremony at the church door and the bride ale and the bedding revels. Alice, who sings like an angel and taught me to cheat at tables.

And here's me, adrift in the wilderness without half a yardland in dowry and waiting for the Crusader sun to finish off my uncle so I can go home.

Nicholas is still grinning like a halfwit, as if he's paid me some sort of favor, so I make myself smile. "Godspeed." I squeeze his forearm. "Ride safe."

He yanks my plait with one hand and unties my

apron with the other. Then he winks and he's out the door, down Shire Hall Street. Ere long he's just one of the crowd, and I lean against the doorframe watching all the strangers go by.

An affeerer for borough court comes to the house to remind my father that I'm due in Court Baron for my offense against the levelooker Pluver.

My father stabs me with a quick glare and tells the affeerer that we'll be there.

It's cruel for my father to throw that incident back at me. It's dustier than Adam.

When the affeerer is gone, I slam down my spindle and huff. My father pulls out a whetstone and his meat-knife, so I huff again, louder.

Finally he gets the hint. My father is truly not the brightest-eyed dog in the pack. He sighs and asks, "What is it, sweeting?"

"If I'm to be dragged into court and humiliated, I'd have some justice for my own loss."

"And what would that be?" He shings the blade down the stone and doesn't even look at me.

"The merchant kept the altar cloth I gave him for surety," I reply indignantly. "That's thievery."

My father snorts. "Sweeting, I'm more worried about our future right now than about a strip of linen you embroidered. We'll discuss it after Court Baron. I want no trouble with the law here. Especially not ere I've taken the oath."

"But Papa, they'll—"

"Look at it this way, sweeting," my father cuts in. "A burgess of Caernarvon has a better chance than a foreigner of getting your whatsit back. Does he not?"

It's very annoying when he has a point. I've no liking for his thinking he might be right too often. But I say naught, kiss his prickly cheek, and pick up my spindle, because I want my altar cloth back more than I want to be right.

Court Baron is held in the churchyard. My father holds my elbow firmly as if I'll flee. He's in a foul humor. It's as if *he's* the one who was provoked into slandering a borough official, who was roughly treated and spoken to unkindly by small-minded brutes.

There's a big crowd around the portal of Saint Mary's down at the end of Church Street. At the top of the steps is a trestle, and sitting at it are two men. One I recognize as the bailiff from Justice Court. The other is as sun-browned as the guide who brought us here, and looks like a mouthful of vinegar.

I stand beneath a yew tree for a gasp of shade.

They start calling plaints.

Oath-breaking, amerced a penny. A dog tore up someone's curtilage garden, amerced twopence. The master, not the dog. Someone's pig wandering the streets. I can feel my hair growing.

A beardy burgess all in graceful saffron is called up for breaking a contract, but he isn't two moments before the trestle ere the bailiff intones, "Trespass forgiven, no amercement."

"By God, there will be!" A Welshman leaps from the crowd and lashes a finger at the beardy burgess. "This man sold me sheep with the murrain and passed them off as healthy! I demand justice!"

My father's hand tightens on my elbow.

I stand on tiptoe and crane my neck. Mayhap there will be a scandalous brawl right here in God's yard.

No luck. Serjeants fall on the Welshman, seize his arms, and force him still.

The bailiff points at him. "Amerced twopence for slander."

The Welshman is turning an interesting shade of red. "You'll regret it, by your beards. You'll regret your every last act sooner than you realize."

"Serjeants, put him out." The bailiff flicks his fingers. "Without the walls. Where he belongs."

The serjeants drag the Welshman out in a flurry of elbows and scraping of heels that seems awfully harsh for a man merely seeking justice.

And my turn is coming.

When I'm finally called, my father pushes me forward

with a firm hand between my shoulder blades. I have to walk through the big mob of scofflaws like I'm one of them.

I stand before the bailiff and the sourpuss. I clasp my hands and push my lip out the smallest bit like I'm innocent as a babe. Poor Cecily, motherless little lamb, victim of a woeful misunderstanding.

My father is yammering about the respect he has for borough government and how he would rather die than break one of its laws out of malice and his firm commitment to attaining the privileges to defend laws such as this one and his close friendship with *honesti* like Sir John de Coucy.

Poor little Cecily. Let her keep her halfpenny. She has learned her lesson.

The bailiff sits up straighter. "What did you say men called you?"

"Edgeley, my lord. Robert d'Edgeley."

Even the sourpuss is alert now, and he and the bailiff tilt their heads together and mutter.

"Of Shire Hall Street? Down from Justice Court? White timbered house?"

"Yes, my lord." My father seems confused. But that's nothing new.

The bailiff mutters something to the clerk, then announces, "The borough forgives Cecily d'Edgeley her amercement. In light of your taking the privileges, Edgeley, and staying in that house. Is that clear?"

My father nods, but he still seems bewildered. "Thank you, my lord."

The bailiff smiles at me. "Go on, now, lass."

I twitch my hem and take my father's elbow merrily. Poor motherless Cecily has hoodwinked the fools at borough court!

There's a distinct murmur in tongue-pull as the clerk scritches something on the *rotuli*, but the serjeants clear their throats and fidget with their knife-hilts and the churchyard falls quiet so the borough can finish handing out justice.

1293

SAINT JOHN'S DAY

TO

MICHAELMAS EVE

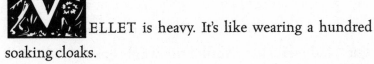ELLET is heavy. It's like wearing a hundred soaking cloaks.

But my mother put this gown on once. She rustled it over her head and tightened the lacing.

This gown seemed as vast as Heaven once. But when I slide it on, it extends a mere fingerlength beyond my wrists and pools just slightly on the floor. Some places are bulgy. Others hang in folds. But mostly it fits.

Then I try to walk, and I catch my toe in the hem and fall into the wall.

I wager a whole shilling my mother never fell into any walls.

My father is waiting in the hall. When I appear in the doorway, he gapes at me like a landed eel. "Glory, when did you grow such? Were you not playing dolls last month?"

I laugh and tug my hem. "Papa, don't be daft!"

"By God, but you are her image." He mutters it, hoarse, as if she left us yesterday and his knees are raw from vigil.

I hold my breath and will him to say more. Anything. To tell me her favorite flowers. Whether she liked sweets. What she might have thought of this place, of what he goes to do today.

"Well, we'd best be off," my father finally says, and yet again all my willing comes to naught.

Even though the castle is a stone's throw from our door, my father has hired horses so that we might arrive as befits our new station. We ride up Castle Street toward the King's Gate, and we're just crossing the weed-choked castle ditch when my mouth falls open.

The castle wall that faces the town is not made of the same purple-banded stone as the town walls or the rest of the castle. It's made of sturdy wooden palisades limewashed and stained to ape the stone. The wall still rises so sheer and high it hurts my neck to look at the top, but I held Caernarvon to be a great massive pillar of stone, solid as an anvil and mighty as a saint's resolve.

The castle is not as it seems.

The sentries at the King's Gate nod us through. Inside, the purple-banded parts form a meandering, drunken shell that's still webbed with scaffolding and awash in mud.

Edgeley and its greening yardlands are a world away, like something from a nursery story.

My father dismounts before a wooden hall that's ochered a deep red, and I do likewise. It's not made of purple-banded stone, but at least it makes no pretense of being something it's not.

A man with a falcon-sharp face and a heavy gold chain about his shoulders beckons my father to the front of the hall. My father squeezes my elbow and departs, so I slump on a bench and cinch my arms over my belly. No one sits next to me. As other burgesses take seats, I catch sight of Emmaline de Coucy and her parents across the aisle.

Emmaline is wearing a gown of the red Flanders finespun that nearly got Nicholas amerced and landed me unjustly in Court Baron. She lifts a cheerful hand when she sees me.

I face forward.

Even petting my mother's vellet does not cheer me. Seeing that finespun on Emmaline's back puts me in mind of my stolen altar cloth, which puts me in mind of Alice and Agnes and how far away they are. How far away Edgeley is.

My father places his hand on a wood-bound book held out by the gold-shouldered man and swears to maintain the privileges of Caernarvon and conduct the town's business thoroughly and a lot of other things I pay little heed to because I'm too busy wishing the castle were more like it should be and wondering who's noticing me since I'm wearing my mother's gown and hating Emmaline for her sleek, effortless plaits while mine look hagstirred from the buffeting wind off the strait.

The gathered burgesses abruptly raise a cheer. My father clasps wrists with the gold-shouldered man, then steps into a crowd of burgesses who all clap him on the back or clasp his wrist or both.

Good. It's done.

I rise and shake out my gown. There's a clammy skin of

sweat over my whole body. My hair is heavy and damp on my neck.

Something seizes my arm. My father, and he's grinning like a well-fed monk.

"Oh, sweeting, it's set and sealed! I couldn't be happier!"

I could. If a runner brought word that my uncle Roger was dead and we could go home to Edgeley. If I had that dratted gown of finespun on Emmaline's back, which is rightfully mine. If I had a mouthful of wine.

"It was lovely, Papa," I lie. "Where are the horses?"

My father beams down on me. "It's not over, sweeting. Whenever they swear in a new man, they must check that the town's liberties haven't been encroached upon, so we must walk the boundary stones."

I look down at my clean blue hem. My vellet hem. My mother's hem.

I am sweatier than a pig in Purgatory.

For all that the privileges of Caernarvon are costing me, they'd best pay off to the hilt.

It's hotter than perdition. I have been walking forever. If I were a saint, I'd be a martyr by now. Saint Cecily, scorched to death on a forced march.

I trudge behind my father, step after miserable step. My slippers are ruined beyond salvage, so I labor to keep my hem off the ground. There is less mud out here, but the vellet across my arm feels like a cartload of masonry bricks.

We seem to be walking a circuit around the town walls. We keep passing these bits of quarry-stone poking out of the ground like teeth in an old man's head.

By all that's holy, why must this town be so large?

Someone falls into step at my side. A wineskin appears before me, hovering like some strange trick of a heat-addled mind.

If it is a trick of my mind, it's one that pleases me. He's got hair like a blackbird's wing and a careless smile and the most charming dimple.

My hands are shaking, but I take the wineskin and raise it to my lips. No wine comes out. He laughs and uncorks the bung, then offers it again.

If God Almighty had any mercy at all, He'd let me melt through the desolate wasteland below my feet ere making me face this comely stranger before whom I've just made a fool of myself.

"Thirsty work, this," he says, "and you seem thirstier than most. Would I had something for you to ride."

The wine is bitter and warm, but I drink it so I'll not have to look at him, or speak. Then I hand the wineskin quickly back.

My father has noticed my new companion and drops back to take my elbow, which he holds much too tightly. "Edward Mercer. A health to you."

"Oh, come now," my wine-saint replies. "You must call me Ned if we're to be neighbors."

He says it to my father, but he looks right at me.

My father snorts so quietly that I'm certain he's merely clearing dust from his throat.

My wine-saint is still smiling at me. My father would flay me alive should I call a man I'm not wed to by his Christian name, but my father would also not want me to be ill-mannered.

So I smile at the mercer. At Ned.

"And welcome to the privileges, Edgeley. How does it feel to be a friend of the king?"

My father worms his way between Ned and me. My elbow is fiery where the vellet scratches.

"It'll feel better when those privileges begin to take effect. I put down quite a sum on murage just getting my household through the gate."

"Well, you're free of those tolls now. The king does not wish to burden his friends here with such bothersome details. We'll let the Welsh maintain the walls and roads, right?"

"So there is actually some advantage to being here?" I ask, partly because I'm interested but mostly because Ned will have an excuse to speak to me directly. "It's not just where all the castoffs and vagabonds end up?"

Ned winks at me and my father's hand on my elbow tightens enough to burn. "Why, demoiselle, you couldn't drag me back to York, God's honest truth! I can charge their lot what I like and they must pay, for they're not permitted to trade outside the Caernarvon market. Not even an egg can pass from one neighbor to another without the both of them being dragged into borough court and amerced."

Saints, but Ned has a shivery smile. I cannot look upon him without feeling all hot and sloshy.

"The sheriff of Caernarvon cannot even peek beneath the canvas on any of my loads, and all it costs me is keeping this place safe, which I'd do anyway." Ned half draws a short sword at his belt and adds, "There isn't the Welshman born who'd dare touch me."

My father shifts enough to block Ned and loudly asks how the borough enforces trading restrictions. Ned speaks of chalk and levelookers and county court in a voice smooth and mellow like a summer evening. Even so, listening to them is tedious. Would that they would stop talking about tolls and start talking about something important. Like whether I can have another drink from Ned's wineskin, and when this barbarous death-march will be over.

My father is now a burgess of Caernarvon. Friend of the king. The mayor leads the other burgesses through our house in a long, meandering line while bearing a rather heinous-looking mace over his shoulder.

Ned is among them, all leather boots and a finespun woolen mantle. He winks at me and I get a bellyful of shiveries.

My father shows the burgesses his sword and falchion. He shows them the sacks of barley and millet, the salted meat, the bins of peas and turnips.

The mayor approves. My father's stores are sufficient and his weapons sharp. The burgesses give a rousing cheer and my father grins as if he just made peerage or sainthood. They clap him on the back and paw his shoulders and crowd around until I cannot tell him from any of the others.

THE brat sets me to cleaning her blue gown. Mud clings like stolen goods to a thief's hand.

Off they went, the pair of them. The master and the brat. Back they came clad all about in town privilege.

Knew it would happen. It's why they came here. It's why any of them come here.

But watching them ride upstreet made what happened at Pencoed yesterday and nevermore all in one gasp. Horseback English, a decree from their king, and my first taste of foreign rule went down bitter and clear.

One more burgess. One more friend of the king. One more stone in those purple-banded walls.

The mud has worked into the very weave of the wool. It'll take lye and scrubbing to bring it clean.

As a burgess of Caernarvon, my father has been endowed by the king with some cropland. It's without the walls and comes with Welsh people to till it. It's been sown since March with oats, so all that's left to do is weed and chase away crows. That job is done by a sullen little boy whose only words in English are *bastard, whoreson,* and *rot in Hell.*

I go with my father to look at the land. He stands hands on hips and gazes over the greening yardlands as if they're Eden. "Of all the privileges that come with this place, sweeting, land without tenure is the cream."

"I like Edgeley better," I say.

"I owed service for Edgeley," my father replies. "I had to be ready to go armed where my lord bade me at any time, for any reason. This land I hold of the king for twelvepence a year. That's all. It's that simple."

I still like Edgeley better, but my father is grinning so big as he walks among the rows of plants and ruffles their leaves as he might Salvo's ears that I say naught.

Mistress Tipley is hollering at me to help with the brewing. My shutters are closed so I can pretend not to hear. I tiptoe down the stairs, past the hall—where my father would notice me and bid me go help the old crone—and out into the glorious sunshine.

Down the street I stride, dodging puddles and horse apples. It's a fine day for justice, and I cannot wait to taste it.

Now that my father has the privileges, I will have what is due me.

There's the shop, just as I remember it. I've been waiting for this moment for se'ennights. I'll march up, rap at the counter, and demand what's mine. The merchant will be vengeful but pale, but all that's good and right is on my side and he'll reluctantly pull my altar cloth from behind the counter and pause just a moment with sublime regret ere putting it in my deserving hands.

I will tell him how fortunate he is that I am such a good Christian that I will not haul him before Court Baron for theft, and he will gibber in gratitude for his good name. It will be most embarrassing for him, with all of Caernarvon watching.

I cannot wait.

The awning is down, but the sign is different. It's not the merchants' ship. It's a spool of thread and a needle. A tailor's shop.

I freeze in the gutter, my hem in the mud. I check and recheck. Yes, it's the right stall, between the empty building and the house with faded crates full of dead herbs.

An amiable redhead comes to the shop window-counter and asks if he can help me with something.

"Wh-where is the merchant?" I ask. "This used to be a merchant's shop. Where is he?"

The redhead shrugs. "Gone. One too many unlawful trades. The borough revoked his license. His loss is my gain, though."

I turn on my heel. Muddy road is flashing beneath my feet. My fists are stiff at my sides. I round the corner of Shire Hall and knee an illegally kept pig out of my path, then slam our gate hard enough to echo.

I find my father in the hall and shout, "How could you?"

My father looks up from a bowl of chestnuts, bewildered. "Do what, now?"

"He's gone, he took it with him, and now I'll never get it back, never, and it's your fault, Papa. You're the one who let him go, and I'll never forgive you for it!"

"Sweeting, I—"

"It's all I had left of them! Now I don't even have that much! It's gone forever, just like they are!"

My father puts aside the bowl. "What are you on about?"

"My altar cloth," I sob, and collapse in a weeping heap at his feet. It's best that I'll never see Alice and Agnes again, for they'll never forgive me this.

There's a muffled groan, then a heavy shape sinks at my side and there's a warm weight over my shoulders. My father has put his arm around me and I fall against him, hugging him and sobbing.

"Forgive me, sweeting," he says, holding me tight. He

smells like leather and dust. I sob harder and hide beneath his arm. "You can make another one, though. A better one."

Just because a thing is new doesn't make it better.

But I say naught and let him hug me, all pokes of leather and scratchy wool and strong embrace like city walls about my shoulders.

After Mass, Emmaline de Coucy invites me on an outing.

She knows a little place where the river pools, where there's shallow water for wading and a good grassy place for rest and food. She played there often as a child, pretending to be queen of the water sprites with her shift hiked up to her knees.

Emmaline leans in close when she tells me this, glancing at her parents sidelong even though my father has snared them in a conversation they seem to be reluctantly tolerating.

There's nothing I want more than to sniff and tell her not for all the damask in Damascus would I pass one more moment in her wretched golden company than I'm forced to.

But the air in the townhouse is like curdled cream and everything smells of sweat, and I'm ever so weary of the square of street that's visible from the workroom window.

So I agree. Emmaline squeals and claps her hands and bids me meet her by the gates as soon as I'm ready.

Back home, Mistress Tipley is clarifying lanolin. There's a massive fire in the rearyard and she's leaning over a potbellied kettle. Her face is as red as the Adversary's backside and she's sweating fit to drown.

I come into the rearyard to get my shoes from the stoop, and the old cow aims the stirring paddle at me.

"Here, stir this. I must get more firewood, and the lanolin will burn if it's not tended."

My father has gone to Watch and Ward. He'll not be back till sundown. I breeze past her toward the greenway as if she's speaking Welsh.

Mistress Tipley hisses like a cat. "You don't think to leave, do you? There are fleeces to roll and wool to comb. They must be ready for the Saint Margaret's market."

I'm already up the greenway and almost in the street when I hear her holler for Gwinny to come take the paddle, and by then it's too late. She'll never find me in the crowd.

Emmaline waits at the gate. A knot of people I don't recognize stand with her. The man has Emmaline's flax-colored hair. The women are veiled, but one has a sharp face like a wolfhound, and she curls her lip at me and smirks.

"Oh, Cecily, I hope you don't mind," Emmaline says. "My brother and his wife and our cousin would come with us. And our maids, of course. It's too nice out to keep the servants inside all day."

The maids are elegant girls in plain wimples who stand like statues at a proper distance, hands folded, chins tucked. They hold baskets that smell faintly of bread.

"Do you not have a maid?" Emmaline asks, peering over both my shoulders. "We can wait for her."

"Her?" snickers the wolfhound. "A *novi* with a maid? Hardly."

"Now, cousin, don't be unkind," Emmaline says cheerfully to the wolfhound. "Cecily cannot help it if she's new to the Principality. Not everyone has the good fortune to grow up here."

I breathe deep and harness all my hating. I'm to be pleasant to Emmaline de Coucy, and that means not taking her wretched cousin down a peg.

"As a matter of fact, I do have a maid," I reply, just short of haughtily. "She's poorly today. I bade her stay abed."

Emmaline is all concern. "Summer chills are the worst. We'll pray for her health. Shall we go, then?"

I nod. Best get it over with. I trudge like a penitent a pace behind them, just in front of the maids.

Without the walls, big spans of green open up. Naught but plots of summer-bright crops stretching out for leagues, all endowed to burgesses. Emmaline directs us across the mill bridge and tells us to follow the river.

Emmaline's brother is called William, and he is tall and long-limbed with a friendly, crooked smile. He inclines his head politely and asks, "How do you find Caernarvon?"

"We found it same as anyone, I reckon," I reply, a little bewildered. "The road from Chester that runs along the water."

The wolfhound snorts. "Lackwit. Any fool knows how you *find* it. He means how do you *like* it?"

My whole face is hot and scorchy. I would give anything short of my immortal soul to reply to this viper as she deserves, but I'm to be pleasant to Emmaline de Coucy.

I turn away from Emmaline's wretched cousin. To William I choke, "Fine. I like it fine."

William smiles lazily and paws my shoulder like a mother cat. "Don't mind Elizabeth. She's living proof that girls should never learn to read."

William's wife is called Aline. She narrows her eyes at me and then makes a show of taking William's elbow. Then she glances at Cousin Evilbeth and they trade cruel smiles.

"We're almost there." Emmaline points at a dark smudge ahead. "Look, where those willows are thick."

I hurry ahead of the others. Aline says something to Evilbeth as I brush past, and they both giggle.

Let the hens cackle. I would put my feet in the water.

It's shady beneath the willows, dapply-cool. The river moves slowly here and murmurs over round rocks. Even the air feels lighter, and there's a breeze.

All at once I'm back at Edgeley, splashing in the creek that turned the mill-wheel and held tiny silver fish that girls could catch in their handkerchiefs if they had patience enough.

It's just like home.

Then I see them.

Across the stream, half a dozen ragged men in home-spun are gathered close like sheep in a storm, their heads bent together.

I freeze.

They're deep in conversation. I cannot hear any words over the stream's murmur, but their lips are moving.

"Hey!" William leaps past me like a roebuck, his short sword drawn and brandished. "I'll see the lot of you in the stocks for a se'ennight!"

One of the men shouts something in tongue-pull and they scatter in six directions. William is knee-deep in the stream when they're all out of sight.

"Bastards," he mutters as he wades out. He slams his sword into its scabbard and squishes up the bank.

I crane my neck, but naught remains of the men save swaying branches and trampled mud.

I hurry to catch up with William. "I agree with you. Welshmen should all be put in the stocks."

He shrugs, but his face is still dark. "Men who follow the law ought to be left to their business. Those who break it must pay."

"Standing on a riverbank is unlawful?" My father certes does not want to see the inside of Justice Court again.

"It is for Welshmen," William replies grimly, "should they gather in groups. Twice over, should they be armed. As that lot was."

All at once the world seems very large, away from

the castle and town walls and armed sentries who incline their heads.

Emmaline does not seem shaken. She even hums as she spreads a blanket where the grass is dry and bids the maids set out pasties and apple tarts and slices of cold meat and cheese. Piles and piles of everything, straight from the kitchens of Croesus de Coucy.

I drop to my knees and pick up two pasties and a tart. Evilbeth puffs out her cheeks like a pig. I take a third pasty and stick my tongue out at her ere I can stop myself.

Aline is still standing, her arms cinched tight as a girdle. "It's not safe here. Let's go back."

"They're gone, love," William tells her. "Half a league from here by now. Welshmen want no part of the law, believe me."

"They were here," Aline insists. "They might come back."

William eats a pasty in two bites. "Not today."

"You don't know that. Who can know what they're capable of?"

If Gwinny is any indication, the Welsh are quite capable of airing linen and laying fires and scooping dog leavings onto the midden.

"Come now, Aline," Emmaline says. "Surely you've seen Welshmen ere this. You've been staying in Shrewsbury for months."

William sighs. "Really, love, Em's right. You may as well fear the cattle."

"You're cruel to mock me." Aline wrings her hands in her sleeves. "Both of you. I would go home. Not just Shrewsbury, either. Home to England."

I grab two wedges of cheese and another tart. I've not even put my feet in the water and this whiny little mouse would drag us back to the sweltering town merely because she fears her own shadow.

William takes her hand kindly. "I should never have allowed you to come. The fault is mine. But Belvero and Whetenhale would never spare me to bear you home to Warwick, or even to our lodgings in Shrewsbury. The part of the fifteenth we collected back at Easter was barely adequate, so the October sum must make up for it."

"I'm weary to death of hearing of this fool tax!" Aline shakes off William's hand and folds her arms like an ill-mannered child.

I'm weary to death of hearing her fool voice, but I'll not be rude about it.

William selects the biggest apple tart, gently untangles Aline's arms, and tucks the pastry into her hand. Her surly pout cracks, then she cuts her eyes to him and takes a bite. He grins and plants a smacking kiss on her cheek.

If we were still at Edgeley, there would be ten kind, comely souls like William lined up outside the door, every man of them begging for the chance to become the heir to a well-run manor like Edgeley.

But we're not at Edgeley.

I shove the last of a tart into my mouth and tromp down to the river. I kick off my shoes and pull up my hem just the smallest bit. The ground is cold and moist, the water deliciously freezing. Like balm against my sweaty feet.

I take out my handkerchief and peer into the creek for fish, just as I used to do on the bank of Edgeley Run.

When I risk a glance behind me, William and Aline are feeding one another tidbits and Evilbeth has taken out her spindle. Emmaline stands apart, gazing toward the angry purple mountains that rise sheer and stark to the south, one hand gently stroking the broad leaf of some bushy plant.

I've seen that look ere this. My father has it as he strolls town and castlery, whistling just as cheerfully as he did walking Edgeley's yardlands.

It's midafternoon when we pack up to leave. At least, they do. I'm still in the stream shallows with a wet hem. The trees dapple shade on my hands and bone-cold water ripples around my ankles and I never want to go back to the dank rotting town, never.

"Come, Cecily!" Emmaline calls as she hands the hamper to her maid. Her feet are rubbed pink, without even a line of mud beneath her toenails to betray her.

Evilbeth rolls her eyes and mutters to Aline, who grins.

God save me from being a shrewish harridan when I'm grown.

I look around one last time, drinking in the graceful

limbs and the gentle murmur of water over stones. I never thought to memorize Edgeley Run like this. I never knew it would be needful.

I'm glad to know this place is here.

The others are already disappearing among the trees and I hurry to catch up. William strides at the fore, Emmaline is a few paces behind him, and then come Evilbeth and Aline, with the maids trudging at the rear. I whisk past the maids, then push past the two shrews. I've just shouldered past Emmaline when the bushes shudder.

Men rise out of the brush like ghosts, at least a dozen, on both sides of the deer track.

Behind me, a girl screams.

William drops a hand to his sword.

But ere he can draw it, the men pelt him with rubbish. Rotting turnips, handfuls of mud, horse apples, all flying in a stinking wave from every side, splattering, smearing, whacking, and thumping. The men jeer and shout in tongue-pull as they throw.

William holds both arms over his face to ward off the barrage. He's cursing like a drunken carter.

A handful of muck splatters my gown just above the knee. Slimy green and brown, God knows what.

"You miserable misbegotten *brutes!*" My voice is shrill and brittle. "I will see you all *hang* for this!"

But the men have already vanished, leaving naught but waving branches and a vile midden stink.

William straightens, lowers his arms. His tunic is motley with chunks and smears of refuse. Something pulpy caught him upside the head and clings in gobbets in his hair. He looks like a mad leper thrice-spurned by God.

Emmaline rushes to his side and makes to seize his shoulder, then pulls away. She looks a little greensick. "William! Are you sound?"

He skins off his hood and wrings murky liquid from it. "It'll avail them not a bit. Not one bit."

I turn to William and bare my teeth like an animal. "Hang them. Hang them all."

He uses his hood to wipe rotting muck from his arms and chest. "I regret your gown, demoiselle. That was not meant for you."

I sputter. I stammer. I stomp and kick the brush. I've sworn enough curses to earn a hundred Aves at my next confession. And I have to bite my tongue to keep from earning a hundred more.

"They're getting bolder," William says with a grim laugh. "Last time it was just words, and words these days are enough to get a Welshman amerced."

A splatter of muck on sky-blue linen. Stains mocking fuller's earth already, and my father as miserly as a miller in debt. I shake my skirts and a shower of filth tumbles down. "A curse on every Welshman ever born. God be praised they're not permitted within the walls. Caernarvon is almost tolerable without any Welshmen in it."

"We will go house to house to collect this tax, *hafod* to *hafod* if need be." William draws his sword and nods us down the path. "No man wants to pay his taxes, but the Welsh must put their share forward, same as the rest of the realm."

We walk in silence for some time. William's bootsteps squish. Evilbeth and Aline creep like cats and leap at the smallest sound. Even Emmaline walks on her brother's very heels. William grips his sword till his knuckles whiten.

"I warned you," Aline snivels. "It's not safe anywhere in this dreadful place."

"It's not common for them to harry a *taxator*," William says over his shoulder, "but it's not unheard of. It's getting worse, though."

"You're a *taxator*?" I ask. "When did his Grace the king call another tax?"

William snorts. "This is the tax of the fifteenth that was called two years ago, demoiselle. Wales is not easy to tax. But his Grace the king will not give up. He beggared himself bringing the Welsh to heel. High time they repaid it."

"My father won't be happy to hear from you," I tell William. "He was on his knees with his paternoster for blasphemy for a whole se'ennight the last time he was assessed."

"Your father has naught to worry about," William replies. "Burgesses in the Principality are never subject to taxation."

"They're not? Not ever?"

"Heavens, no!" William laughs. "Nor are they required to pay a penny in tolls, not even market tolls."

I've passed that trestle on the mill bridge dozens of times, dozens of Saturday markets, and skimmed past the Welsh lined up for leagues with their grubby coins and wads of butter and baskets of eggs.

They must want to trade at the market pretty badly to stand in line for so long and part with their goods to pay tolls.

William insists on seeing me to my door. Aline is one massive scowl and Evilbeth is drawn tighter than a bowstring. Emmaline squeezes my arm and thanks me for coming.

"We shall have to meet again," Emmaline says cheerfully, as if William is not covered in filth and the rest of us skittish as colts. "When your maid has recovered, you'll come to my house and we'll spin."

Yes. My maid. My nonexistent maid.

I try to seem pleased at the prospect as I hurry toward my door. When I look over my shoulder, I catch Evilbeth's cruel, knowing smile.

POOR girl is almost dry. She lows as I milk her, but there's naught to be done for the heat that parches the soil.

There's even less to be done for Crown measures and market penny, and God help you should you seek redress. Fanwra from down the vale may never recover from that month on the gatehouse floor.

Almost a bucket of milk. Mayhap it will be enough. Silver in their palms and mayhap they'll leave us our cow. Part is better than naught. Even taxmen must know that.

Bucket in my hand sways like a hanged man as I set off toward that eyesore on the strait. Handle digs into my palm, gritty.

Take the long way. Fewer Watchers. And with any fortune, Dafydd will be waiting on the other path, the one the timber gangers use.

Saturday, and the roads are full of dusty feet and baskets on backs. Fall into step with them. Say naught. None of us do. Plod toward the castle. Toward the swarm of souls without the walls on the market common.

Horseback English ride, pressing horseflesh through the queue. Step away from hooves and heels. They watch, not us but our goods. They watch our hands to make sure naught passes between us. If we trade away from the walls, they're denied their share of our sweat.

If we trade away from the walls, they amerce us and take more.

English at the trestle looks me up and down. "Lastage, and market penny."

"Half measure milk instead?" My words in their tongue are purposefully stumbling, purposefully broken. It's never good to let them know what you know.

"Silver," says trestle English. "Or be gone."

Could bribe him. Others do. A heaping Crown measure, and the need for silver is suddenly weaker. But betimes the "gift" disappears and still they demand silver.

Slam the coins down before him. The whole trestle shudders. Horseback English turn, poised like wolfhounds. Trestle English narrows his eyes as he slides the coins into his palm.

Brace for the blow, standing to like a foot soldier. Some take special pleasure if you beg or cower.

But trestle English merely reaches across to chalk me, to keep the levelookers off. Mustn't flinch. Not a hairsbreadth. The milk will spill, and part is better than naught.

He chalks me across my tit, cups it, squeezes, smiles. Stand to. Not a hairsbreadth. Stare through him.

Eyes are stinging. Must be the dust.

Sway past the trestle, into the market beneath the walls. Find the other dairy girls, chalked over the tits same as me, the cheeses and butter and endless buckets of milk already ripening in the sun.

Flies in my milk. Scoop them out, cover my pail with what's left of my cloak.

And he comes through the crowd, damn him, golden and glowing like a war-band chief. My penance for a lapse in judgment I'd have back at any price.

Pull my hood over my eyes and slump, but it's for naught. Dafydd is already heading toward the dairy row.

"They charged me double toll again," he says cheerfully. "You can be sure it'll go in my next petition to the king. I'll tell him, 'Your Grace, not only is it unlawful, but I'll be obliged to court my beloved in my smallclothes.'"

He means to make me smile, so I try for courtesy's sake. But the walls cut a harsh shadow across the market, even at midday.

Dafydd kneels, pretends to examine the milk. "If they're resorting to such petty tricks, the nerve I hit is raw. My petition will eventually be granted. They cannot keep me out forever."

It isn't. It won't. They can.

"Caernarvon won't change unless we make it change," he whispers. "There's naught in the king's law that says a Welshman cannot take a burgage. All this ill is just the burgesses guarding their privileges. Changing anything takes strength, and I know no one stronger than you. I need you."

Choke on a sound, an animal sound. All the strength in

the world did naught for Da. "Changing anything takes sacrifice, and that's a luxury I cannot afford."

"When we're successful, you'll be able to afford all the luxuries to hand, and some you just dream up."

"That's not what I meant."

"I know." Dafydd lifts my chin with two fingers. "I love you. I want you as my wife."

Flinch. Remember despite myself. His gentle hand sliding up the small of my back, his warm breath against my neck.

Look down. My knees dig into sun-baked dust. A chalk gash over my tit.

Shake my head, curt, like a fist to the jaw.

"Why not?"

Two pennies poorer and naught to show, horseback English watch my hands, and above us all rise those purple-banded walls that can be seen for leagues.

He must notice how my eyes slice over the market, for he sobers and says, "It just wants one crack, Gwenhwyfar. Just one crack and then time will do its work."

It does want a crack. One dealt with knives and fists and red, raw anger. One dealt with the gallows in plain view. English understand naught else.

Pull my hood over my eyes, stare into the milk. Dafydd takes the hint and rocks to his feet. "Right, then, I'm off. But you'll see me again. I don't give up easy, you know." His voice softens. "Not for the things that matter."

Linen shuffles, and he's gone. Risk a glance after him.

Hate him for that square of shoulders, that proud, lovely stride.

This is why, Dafydd. Because you're a fool.

They come at night. Man-shaped shadows, sleek like wolves and faceless in the dark. By morning, something English will be in ashes or hamstrung or torn to pieces or just plain gone. They've come for Peredur's son, and Gruffydd ap Peredur goes to the door to give them his regrets.

"This is not the way." Gruffydd glances over his shoulder at Mam and me. "Too much risk and naught to gain."

"Your father thought otherwise." The voice without the door is harsh, disparaging.

"Aye," Gruffydd replies, equally cold. "Look what it got him."

Somewhere in the rafters is Da's spear. Slid there to wait by some comrade lost to memory while Da still hung from the walls. But Gruffydd does not look up. He meets the gaze of the hooded shadow and does not flinch or beg pardon when he tells the men to go with God, that for everyone's sake they were never here.

Gruffydd's tread is heavy as he makes his way fireside and collapses on his pallet.

Lie back on my own pallet as the fire sputters its last orange breath. Mam next to me sleeps as if she's dead already. Stare hard into the thatch, trying to make out some stray wink of steel. Just so I know it's still there.

BEASTLY-HOT AIR drafts through my shutters. I'm in bed wide awake. My bare skin is damp, my bedclothes are damp, and Gwinny's going to have to air the linen again today because I'm sick to bleeding death of this sticky-foul cling of damp cloth.

I rise and open the shutters. The sky is a most lovely shade of deep blue. It was never this blue at Edgeley.

The house is silent. There are no thumpings in the rearyard, so no one has risen to prime the kitchen fire. It must be very early.

I should just go back to bed. But then I'll have to lie in mucky-damp linen.

I struggle into a shift and put on my bedrobe. I pad belowstairs into a hall that's much cooler than my chamber. By the rear door, there are two buckets full of water. Just as there should be.

Gwinny may be difficult, but at least she's a decent-enough servant.

The rearyard is deliciously cool. Salvo sleeps against the kitchen wall, sprawled like a dogskin rug. I check his water pan, then lift my leaky watering bucket off its peg, dip it into the bigger bucket, and swing it dripping toward my garden.

That's when I see the child.

The little urchin is wearing naught but a sleeveless shift and she's standing smack amid my neat rows of herbs. Her fat fists are crammed with bright blue borage.

"Yook," the herb-trampler tells me, "fow-ers."

My garden is pulverized. Stalks crushed, smashed, pulped, uprooted. Chunky little footprints criss and cross through the disaster, and in case there is some doubt as to who the culprit might be, this little thing is filthy knees and elbows and—saints preserve me—mouth.

The urchin smiles. She holds out the crushed borage, dirt dangling from the roots.

"You must be one of those tenscore Glover creatures from next door," I mutter. "Your rotten brothers throw mud at my laundry."

She smiles and opens her hand. Mangled borage falls at her filthy feet.

"You need to go home. Go away. Shoo. Back where you belong." So I can see what can be salvaged of this mess.

I point to the greenway that leads to the street out front, but the child makes no move to obey. Instead she stomps her stubby feet in what's left of my tansy.

God save me ere I have any babies. They are grabby, clingy little beasts who steal your figure and always want a ribbon or a wooden sword. And who sometimes make you die bearing them.

"Come with me, then." I rise and unstick my shift from my backside, then head down the greenway. The child doesn't follow. She's uprooting fennel and flinging it and chortling.

I consider dragging her by the wrist, but then she'd squawk and bring not only the house but all of Shire Hall Street to gape and snicker at me in my sweaty underthings when I haven't even washed my face or put a comb to my hair.

Cringing, I hoist the urchin up, one hand beneath each armpit, and hold her at arm's length. She doesn't protest. In fact, she giggles as if we're playing some game. I stagger through the greenway into the Glovers' dooryard, lower her gritty little feet onto the hearthstone, dust off my hands, and head up the path.

There's a pattering and she's right behind me, treading on my heels, grabbing at my bedrobe.

"No. You stay here." I shoo her back to the hearthstone as if she's a halfwit baby Salvo. "Stay. You stay."

She sucks in a big sobby breath and lets it out as a throaty whine that steadily grows in volume.

The sky is still a deep night-blue and all the buildings are black. Caernarvon is utterly still, like we're the only souls within.

She is really quite small. Too small to know better than to throw mud at laundry.

"Very well." I hold out a hand and she leaps at it. I am the most selfless Christian in all of Christendom. "Let's go back to my house. What are you called?"

The child doesn't answer. She's obviously not the sharpest little knife in the Glovers' brace.

As soon as we're back in my rearyard, she's tumbling away like a fat wobbly puppy. By turns she's carefree or intent on tiny things like dew on the greenery or the dregs in the pigling's trough. She giggles like a drunkard and spins like a whipping top.

I cannot imagine chasing a baby all day if this is what they're like, but whenever she runs up and hugs me, a sticky embrace made fierce and swift like an attack, I always hug her back.

The sky is still a deep sapphire when the row next door starts. There's a lot of thumping and the clatter of feet and someone shrieking like a lost soul. The Glovers must have risen and found themselves a child short, though how that's noticeable I know not.

I tighten my bedrobe. "Come, let's go find your mama."

"Mama," echoes the baby, and she takes my hand and toddles with me up the greenway, through the gutter, to her door.

No one answers my knock for several long moments, then a tousle-head boy peers out. He gives a great whoop and throws the door wide.

"It's Nessy! Mama! Nessy's here!"

Mistress Glover is at the door in moments; she scoops up the baby and squeezes her tight. Even with her great swarm of children, Mistress Glover kisses this small one and pets her hair and coos and embraces her again and again.

Then Mistress Glover turns her petting on me and hugs me across the shoulders as much as she can with children hanging off both arms and crowding at her skirts. She thanks me up to the heavens for bringing back her lost lamb, who she thought for sure was down the well or in the mill-pond or beneath the hooves of some beast.

I peel myself free and smooth my hair. "She was in our rearyard. I live next door."

"Oh, dear." Mistress Glover hoists baby Nessy on her hip. "I hope she didn't do you any ill."

My borage. My tansy, my fennel, eyebright, rue, lady's mantle, coltsfoot. All gone. A whole year's worth of herbs, stomped into pulp by small feet.

But Mistress Glover is regarding me doe-eyed as if I'm a saint and running a hand again and again over Nessy's thread-thin hair as the child snuggles against her mother's shoulder, so I grit a smile and say, "No trouble, Mistress Glover. Really."

My father presents me with a piece of fine linen. He struts around like a peacock, proud of his largesse.

"Now you can make a new altar cloth," he says cheerfully.

"A better one." And he stands there with his chest puffed out waiting for hugs and squeals.

I don't want a new altar cloth. I want my old one.

I hug him and thank him. I cannot muster squeals, but he doesn't seem to notice.

When he leaves, I pin the linen on my frame. It's soft and smooth, a clean panel just waiting for saints and holy figures, vine borders and spirals.

I stare at the linen and my throat chokes up. So I unpin the cloth, fold it carefully, and retrieve my spindle. It's possible to spin and cry. I've done it many times.

It's been raining for a solid se'ennight. This place has no seasons. Even summer is winter here.

Ned Mercer calls just as dinner is ending. His black hair is damp and tousled from the mist, and he asks my father if he might take me on a walk since the weather has finally turned from deluge to heavy gray.

Gracious, but he is lovely on the eyes.

And I am wearing a kirtle with two different stains on it.

My father squares up like a mastiff. "I think not, Mercer. Cecily is very young, and—"

"Can I go, Papa?" I know my father is thick, but not so thick that he doesn't notice a comely suitor doing his work for him. "Please? Getting out of the house would do me much good."

My father pauses. The war between paternal smothering and scrabbling for position in this backwater is plain in his every line.

Finally he says, "If you'd have it so. And only because you'd have it so. Mistress Tipley goes with you."

Ned inclines his head politely. My father calls Mistress Tipley, and in a moment she appears in the hall in a jingle of keys that rightfully belong at my belt.

I force down a scowl. A man should never see you scowl till after you're married. My mother used to say that whenever I was surly, but I rarely saw her so much as frown.

I kiss my father's prickly cheek, then Mistress Tipley, Ned, and I squish into the dull gray chill.

My hands are shaking. I grip my cloak and try to hide the worst stain, a dark gravy patch from breakfast.

Ned moves easily at my side, graceful as a wolfhound. He's speaking of the weather. I'm glad for it, since my throat is stoppered firmly and I couldn't speak to save my neck.

Mistress Tipley huffs and pants to keep up. Already she has fallen a stride behind. I take big steps to match Ned's pace even though I'm almost trotting.

Ned walks me past his townhouse, a brilliantly ochered structure across from the church. Through the window, I see a workroom much like my own, only this one is tinted a strong and living green. There's a big trestle table, and seated there is a well-groomed apprentice busily sorting skeins of silky-looking yarn.

The whole room smells like ginger and wool.

I could very much get used to it.

I'm fussing with some transplanted seedlings in my garden when Mistress Glover appears at the fence.

"Have you seen Nessy?" she asks.

"Sorry, no." And thank goodness for that.

But then I notice that her eyes are wild and her face is as pale as her wimple.

"I haven't seen her since breakfast," Mistress Glover whispers. "And she likes your house, so I thought . . ."

I rise and dust off my hands. "She's not here. Are you sure she's not just hiding from you? Playing a trick?"

Mistress Glover shakes her head. "Nessy is too small for tricks. Besides, I've searched the house from top to bottom. The lads have been up and down the street. No one has so much as seen her."

"She has to be somewhere nearby," I say soothingly, but my stomach is full of odd little pangs. "Let me ask my father if I can help you look."

Not only does my father give permission, he joins the search himself. "She could not have gotten without the walls on her own."

My father underestimates Nessy's ability to get places she isn't supposed to be.

But by sundown, we've knocked on every door and searched every empty lot and outbuilding. Mistress Glover is all but raving and Master Glover quietly sits on the threshold drinking claret. There's nary a sign of a lost baby anywhere in Caernarvon. It's as though she's vanished from God's green earth.

Nessy Glover is still missing. Hue and cry has been raised, but a formal search of the town by the constable himself and both bailiffs has turned up nothing.

Today they're dredging the castle ditch and both mill-ponds.

The town is so tense, I nearly forego supervising Mistress Tipley's marketing. Men mutter in doorways and women don't tarry long at the well. Even children move about quietly. No frantic patter of feet and no shouting in street or yard. I breathe easier when we're safely home.

I search our rearyard for the fifth time, Salvo limping at my heels. Mayhap an impish golden head will pop out from behind the rain barrel, chortling nonsense baby words and oblivious to the panic she's caused.

No luck.

Around midday, Ned turns up on my doorstep. I've been changing the linen and my hair is in a state. I start frantically smoothing stray tendrils behind my ears, but he says, "I beg your pardon, demoiselle, but today I've come for your father. We must question the Welshry." He's slapping a sturdy blackthorn cudgel against his palm.

"But why?" I'm still fighting my hair into some kind of order and covertly biting my lips to redden them. "My father says Nessy couldn't have gotten without the walls."

"Unless one of those—people—abducted her," Ned replies with a tight, forced smile. "So we must, er, question them."

God only knows why anyone would want to steal a baby, troublesome creatures that they are. But I don't tell Ned this. Instead I bid him Godspeed and try to enjoy the back of him when I see him and my father off.

Caernarvon is still as a graveyard. Usually the streets are bustling and the gate is crowded, but the serjeants have closed the murage trestle and only burgesses may pass.

I know not what else to do, so I take a loaf of sweet bread to Mistress Glover's house. One of her sons silently shows me to the hall. The whole room is packed with women and the trestle is loaded with stews, cakes, and even a haunch of mutton studded with cloves. Mistress Glover sits ashen and dry-eyed at the hearth, her flock of sun-browned children arrayed like quiet dolls at her feet.

I stay as long as I can bear, then escape home.

My father isn't back from questioning the Welshry till long past curfew. I'm dozing before the banked hearth, but I leap up to hear the news when I hear him banging down the corridor.

Just one look at him and my heart sinks. They've not found her. Not even a trace.

My father is muddy to the knees and his forearms are badly scraped. He tosses a blackthorn cudgel into a corner and curtly bids me go to bed.

Dim, but growing louder every moment, is a clacking of clappers and the echoey thudding of drums. I make it to High Street in time to see a scruffy Welshman being rattle-and-drummed toward the castle by a crowd of raging townspeople. The bailiffs ride grim-faced and the Welshman must stagger behind them since he's tethered by the wrists to their horses, but he's hollering his innocence with every stumbling step.

At supper, my father is in high spirits and answers my question ere I can even ask it.

"Black Reese of Trecastell," my father tells me. "A vile brute of a highwayman who haunts the king's road to Chester, but he'll hang for the abduction and like as not murder of Nessy Glover."

"Like as not?" I ask hopefully. "They haven't found her body yet?"

My father shakes his head and pours himself a mug of undiluted wine. "Black Reese swears he's never laid eyes on the girl, but the bailiffs have him in the darkest hole in Caernarvon. He'll confess soon enough."

"Do you suppose he really did it?"

My father shrugs. "No reason he wouldn't."

I chew my bread thoughtfully. "If he did abduct her,

what does he gain by denying it? Would he not instead demand a ransom?"

My father bangs his mug down. "Jesu, Cecily, the burgesses are doing the whole castlery a favor by sending this cur to meet his Maker."

"But isn't it unlawful to—"

"Enough! The man is guilty of *something!*"

I nod slowly because I know better than to challenge that tone, but if Black Reese is to be hanged for something, it should at least be a crime he's actually committed.

THE priest's boy comes to the door. He asks if I know of anyone in the vale who is missing a baby.

Long past sundown. On my feet all day. Wrung out like a rag. But the word stills my hand on the kettle.

"Baby?"

The servant nods. "Girl-baby. Two milk-teeth on top. She doesn't say a word, so they don't know her name. Yellow curly hair. Like a little angel, they say."

"They?"

"A herdsman out in Llanrug found her. Cadwallon ap Goronwy. His wife is called Gwladys. No one they know recognizes the little lass. They've no idea what to do. They're too old to raise another." The boy shakes his head. "Poor little thing. Her mam and da must be frantic."

Girl-baby. Curly yellow hair. Like a little angel.

It cannot be. It's too far. And without the walls.

It has to be. Her mam and da *are* frantic.

Release a long breath. "The baby belongs within the walls. She's an *honesti* baby."

The boy crosses himself, babbles a string of oaths. "Christ help us. What'll I tell the herdsman?"

"Tell him . . ." Grit my teeth. No way out but through.

"Tell him to bring the baby to the Saturday market and hand her over to the gatemen."

The boy gapes. "I'll not! You're mad!"

"English will praise the Almighty to find the baby alive." Press a hand to my eyes. "Besides, would it be better for English to find the baby at Cadwallon's steading? They'll go croft to croft soon enough."

The boy shudders, reluctantly nods, takes his leave.

By dying firelight, look down at Mam curled like a stringy corpse beneath her blankets. *Honesti* mother had better thank God on her knees for the safe return of her child. It's a lot more than some mothers get.

MY FATHER has been given an office of charge. He says it's almost unheard of that a burgess so new to the privileges is entrusted with responsibility in the borough government, and he does his mad capering dance the length and breadth of my workroom before all the neighbors of Shire Hall Street.

I would we had better shutters.

He is now Officer of the Town Mills. He is charged to regularly visit the two mills, the one on the Cadnant and the one at Porth Mawr. He's to survey the grindstones and ensure that the millers take no more than their due and that the quality of the flour is acceptable. The Officer of the Town Mills is also required to regularly ride through both the castlery and the Welshry to ensure that no man has a handmill, and if any man is grinding his own grain, to bring him before borough court for amercement.

My father is very proud of his office of charge. We have a haunch of mutton and sage wine to celebrate. His office will give him something to do and keep him out of trouble. And hopefully out of my workroom, too.

Mistress Tipley and I are heading home with the day's bread when we hear an earsplitting shriek near the gate. I fling the bread at Mistress Tipley and fly toward the clamor.

Just within the gate is Mistress Glover—hugging Nessy!

Townspeople crowd around, cheering, blessing the baby, patting both Glovers as they hug and squeeze their errant child. I can barely see Nessy through the welter of arms and bodies, but her cheeks are pink and she's squealing merrily just as I remember.

I grin big as market day. God is merciful to sinners.

Nearby, three serjeants form a well-armed ring around an elderly couple, who cringe and glance about uncertainly. One of the serjeants clears his throat and says, "Master Glover?"

Mistress Glover looks up over Nessy's blond head. Her eyes are streaming and cold like a wolf's. "They'll hang with Black Reese."

I frown. If Nessy is safe, surely the burgesses will let Black Reese go.

The old woman says something in Welsh angled like a question. Her voice is a panicky stutter. The old man chimes in with a protest, calm but desperate. But the serjeants pay them no mind and jerk them toward the gatehouse.

Nessy appeared in my rearyard and tore up my garden. No one marched me off to be hanged when I brought her home.

I press close to Mistress Glover. "Mayhap we should ask them how they came to have Nessy."

"They *took* my Nessy," Mistress Glover growls. "When you're a mother, you'll understand."

"Look at her," I insist. "Nessy has been gone a fortnight

and there's not a scratch on her. It wouldn't be right to hang them with no cause. What if they *helped* Nessy?"

Mistress Glover looks down at her pink, healthy child for a long moment, then nods reluctantly. The elderly couple are manhandled before her and both begin a frantic chatter in Welsh.

"Speak properly!" Mistress Glover shrieks, and both of them cringe and fall silent and gesture with gnarled hands.

"I don't think they can," I say into the quiet that's descended.

"Then they hang!"

Mistress Tipley pushes to my elbow and bobs her head to Mistress Glover. "They're saying they found the baby eating turnips in their garden. They live all the way out in Llanrug and none of their neighbors recognized her. They had no idea she belonged within the walls or they would have brought her sooner. They beg you to show mercy."

I stare openmouthed at Mistress Tipley. She can understand Welsh!

"Nessy looks well fed," Mistress Tipley adds, "and look how clean her face and feet are."

Mistress Glover scrubs at her wet cheeks. "Oh, you lot deal with them!" And she turns on her heel and bustles up High Street with Nessy peeking over her shoulder.

I turn a pleading gaze on Master Glover while Mistress Tipley glowers at him, hands on hips, and at length he bids the serjeants to release the couple. The two poor souls lean on each other, faint with relief, then fly through the city gate as if the Adversary is seeking them.

If it had been my baby returned hale and plump, all but back from the dead, I would have at least thanked the people who fed and tended her.

Even if they were Welsh.

IT'S all over the Welshry. Gwladys and Cadwallon of Llanrug were as good as dead, accosted at the city gate with the baby they'd been wringing their hands over. The baby they'd been tending with the last of their milk and borrowed oatbread.

The *honesti* baby that castle English have been threshing the Welshry to find.

Gwladys and Cadwallon of Llanrug were as good as dead, sent to their fate by naught less than my foolish belief that English would celebrate the baby's safe return more than they'd demand vengeance for her disappearance.

But Gwladys and Cadwallon were spared because of an English girl who spoke for them brassy as you please right before castle English who would have strung them up then and there.

Mayhap they helped Nessy, she said. It wouldn't be right to hang them without cause.

And castle English stayed their hands.

They're saying it was the brat. *My* brat. Brattily Bratly of Shire Hall Street.

Gwladys and Cadwallon live. Their home intact. Limbs aright. Not even a bruise. For no other reason than the kindness of the brat.

Wait for her to crow and preen. But all she does is wrap a honey cake and bid me take it to the *honesti* baby next door.

The brat wraps the cake so carefully that it's hard to recognize her work.

FOR THE SECOND TIME in a year's worth of saints, my father has ruined my life.

"I've had the most joyous tidings!" he crows at supper over his plate of trout.

"Uncle Roger has died and we can go home to Edgeley?"

My father serves me a dark look. "No. Mind your tongue."

I bow my head and try to look sorry.

He brightens as he reaches for the nef. "The good news is that the lady de Coucy will be helping you learn to get along among the ladies of Caernarvon. On the morrow, you're to present yourself at her door at the ringing of Sext. Be sure your chores are done in the morning."

"Papa, no! I don't want to!"

My father pinches two fingers of salt from the bow of the small wooden ship and dumps it in his visorye. "Your opinion on the matter is acknowledged. The ringing of Sext. Don't tarry."

"I know all about how to run a household!"

"It's got naught to do with running a household, sweeting," my father says. "I might have taken the privileges, but there is more to being a burgess than I realized. I'll not have you at a disadvantage. Since you get on so well with Emmaline de Coucy, her mother has agreed to take you under her wing. So you will be attentive." His voice sharpens. "And well-mannered."

I nod miserably and push my trencher away. I'm not hungry anymore. "It'll serve no purpose. When we go home to Edgeley, I'll need none of these foolish town customs."

My father blinks rapidly and chokes. He must have taken too large a bite.

As Sext rings, off I dutifully go. A servant answers the door and directs me to the solar, where Emmaline is ruining linen with her disastrous needlework and the lady de Coucy is spinning. When she sees me, the lady sets aside her work with a faint jingle of keys. She's blinking rapidly, as if a dairy-maid has entered the solar, or mayhap her cow.

"Saints," the lady mutters, eyeing me up and down. At length she puts together a smile and gestures me in.

My father did not raise a cow. I lift my chin. I straighten my shoulders. I walk like a queen through the solar to stand before her, and I regard her steadily.

"Emmaline," the lady says, "what did this girl do wrong?"

Emmaline bites her lip, toys with a trailing stitch. She meets my eye and shrugs the tiniest helpless shrug ere saying, "The walk . . . and the look."

"Dare I hope you've even been to a town ere this one?" the lady asks wearily.

I unclamp my teeth from my bottom lip. "Coventry, my

lady. We spent a year there. We were waiting to go back to Edgeley Hall, but—"

"Right, yes. That grubby little manor in the midlands." She wrinkles her nose as if she's caught a whiff of manure. "Your father is a burgess of Caernarvon now. For good or ill, you're one of us, and by all that's holy you will not bring shame on this town."

I nod because I'm to be attentive and well-mannered, but may God Almighty strike me down ere I become anything like the ladies of Caernarvon.

The lady de Coucy puts me through my paces as though I'm a mastiff whelp. Walk. Speak. Roll over. Not like that! Bad girl! Nones is ringing when she finally lets me leave. It's all I can do to incline my head ere fleeing from her solar like a loosed felon.

I stomp up High Street, kicking rocks and hating everything because I'll be at her mercy every wretched Monday and there's naught to be done for it thanks to my father's conniving.

I look up and see *him*. The miserable Welsh vagrant who *looks*. He's driving a timber-laden cart toward the city gate. The horse strains against its collar and the load lists dangerously beneath the tethers.

I'm sweeping past, nose in the air, when a cart wheel hits a puddle and a curtain of filth sluices up and drenches my gown and it's too much and I whirl on him like a soaked cat.

"Saints above, look what you've done!"

He barely spares me a glance, harried as he is and tangled to the elbow in reins. "Demoiselle?"

"As if it isn't bad enough that— How *dare* you?"

He manages to still the horse, but the load slides drunkenly with each jerk of the cart. "Beg pardon, demoiselle. Bad roads."

He certes doesn't look sorry. And there's naught I can do for it. There's naught I can do for a lot of things.

I glare at him with all my hating, trying to kill him where he stands, but it isn't working. He's waiting like some half-witted hound, not seeming to notice how much I'm hating him.

Waiting. And shifting uncomfortably and glancing at the castle every few moments as if it's a boot poised to kick. "Er, by your leave, demoiselle?"

He's a head taller than I and strong enough to break my neck with one throttle, but he cannot leave till I say he can.

An English person has spoken to him and now he must await his dismissal. Like any dog.

And there's naught he can do for it.

"Demoiselle?" He tries that smile, but something in my face must stay him because he squares up and fixes his eyes over my shoulder as if I'm my father. "By your leave?"

I put a finger to my chin and hold it there, pretending to consider. Then I stare back at him, right in the eye, till he looks at his bare feet and not at me. Not anymore.

"Mayhap," I drawl, "if you ask nicely."

"*Please,* then, demoiselle." There's an edge to his voice, no hint of plea. "I'll certes be thrashed as it is."

Good. May it cut to the marrow.

"Very well, off with you," I say, and it's not out of my mouth ere he's whipping the horse into a smart trot. He does not look back.

I breathe in deep and smile for the first time since Sext.

I'm holding the reins of the whole world.

Going to Mass is now a critical part of my day, since I can walk past Ned's townhouse twice without it seeming untoward. From without, Ned's house smells of bread and woodsmoke. Betimes the shutters are open and I can peek inside.

What slivers of workroom I can see are clear and tidy; floors shining, walls wiped, the trestle clear and waiting. Nothing like Edgeley when my mother came to live there. Despite the passage of years, she'd tease my father about the bench she'd had to peel her backside from and the pewterware with dregs caked at the bottom those many years ago, and he'd gallantly sweep a hand over Edgeley's hall, now clean and humming and cheerful, all the better for its lady.

When I peek in the windows of Ned's townhouse, I must admit I'm a little disappointed. There wouldn't be much for me to do. I would gain a house like Edgeley was. There would be no need to make this house into Edgeley.

R HYS Ddu of Trecastell has still not been released from the gatehouse. It's hard to know whether to curse or cheer. Fewer men deserve hanging more.

But the gallows on the market common cannot tell felon from hero. They both hang the same and end up just as dead, especially when the hand on the rope does not change.

Know not when I first notice. Watched burgess land no longer opens up with endless nodding furrows of oats and barley. The crops are shriveled now, poor things, sodden and pulpy and twisted, as if the Adversary himself whispered in their little ears. Field after field. The ravens circle overhead, searching in vain for a stray kernel or grain. Betimes a priest walks among the furrows, flicking holy water and begging the Virgin to have mercy and intercede with the Almighty to lift the damp.

They'll still have to bring the harvest in. Some of it must be salvageable.

Gruffydd waits for me at the wood-edge long after twilight, thumbs hooked over his rope-belt, kicking dust.

Fall into step beside him. "They'll be hiring for harvest work any day now. You'll be at the front of the queue, right?"

He nods. His cheekbones stand out like fence rails.

English fret and mutter. The master spends days at a time at his stolen land, comes back pale and drawn like a corpse. The barges pole in from Môn with fewer sacks every day, and they pass the common wharves that stand idle to tie up at the Havering wharf, the Whetenhale wharf, the Grandison wharf. Grain that lands on private wharves, burgess wharves, might as well not even be.

And still Gruffydd meets me when day is dying slowly over the stone-and-mortar eyesore. Every day. Bite my tongue and bite my tongue until finally I demand, "You stood aside, didn't you? For one of those blasted toady—"

"They're not hiring for harvest work."

Stop. Close my mouth. Stammer, "Wh-what?"

"No harvest work." He gestures helplessly at the pulpy fields, the crumbly, damp furrows. "I'll try the wharves. The burgesses import most of their grain from Môn anyway."

Gape at him. "The wharves? Jesus wept, we haven't the silver for a bribe that big! Especially not when there's no harvest!"

Gruffydd hitches a shoulder. "Have you a better idea?"

Burn them. Burn every last damn one of them.

Let out a long breath, then dredge up a smirk. "At least we'll get to watch the bastards starve."

Gruffydd squints at the horizon. "If anyone starves in the Principality, it won't be them."

"We don't need their wretched barley. There's the cow. Milk and butter and cheese."

"For now." He smiles sadly. "Until the taxmen come. Then back she'll go to Pencoed. Or mayhap Plas Newydd. All the old estates are filling up with distrained beasts."

The old estates. *Your* estate, Gruffydd. And men like you.

"We'll buy her out of lien ere winter." Say it forcefully, as if force will make it so.

"Dafydd had a horse distrained against tenpence at the Easter collection," Gruffydd replies. "When he went to redeem it, Whetenhale told him fifteen."

Roll my eyes. "But that's Dafydd. He may as well brand himself and spare them the trouble."

"Go ask Fanwra down the vale how much they demand for her cow. Or Maelgwn ap Tudur, or Llywelyn ab Owain, or—"

Fling a gesture, and Gruffydd falls silent.

"Very well," he says at length, "if we cannot afford a workboon for the wharves, I'll . . . I'll find something. I just . . . I cannot bear to take work from any man with little ones to feed."

Da went out. Da never came back. Little ones learn to feed themselves. Little ones learn to *fight*.

"We need the silver, too." Speak quietly, because he means it. "We have Mam."

Gruffydd nods. "I'll find something."

Little ones look after the littler ones.

Take my brother's arm. It's warm and rough and dusty, his elbow bound with a ragged, blood-smeared cloth. He places his hand over mine for a long moment ere he pulls away.

MY FATHER has learned about the outing Emmaline de Coucy invited me on after Mass. He leaps around my workroom like a mad fool, crowing with joy. Right before the big windows for all the neighbors to see.

My father can be such a trial betimes.

"And you'll invite her here, of course," he says. "You mustn't slight her by not returning the courtesy. You'll invite her, along with her cousin and sister-by-marriage and—"

"What? No!" My whorl clatters to the floor. "Please don't make me!"

My father frowns. He's going to insist because they're the Coucys. I cast about for something with half a chance of staying his hand.

"The linen is stained, the walls are plain white, the floor wants a scrubbing with sand, and there isn't a candle in the place." Square in the pride. "What would I even serve them? I would shame you, Papa, offering turnip broth and blackberry wine to daughters of the *honesti*."

My father folds his arms. "Honey, for wafers. And a mazer of good wine. But the walls stay white and we'll keep using pine knots and you can help Mistress Tipley scrub the floor and wash the linen."

Splendid. They'll take one look around this miserable

hole and mutter how presumptuous the *novi* are, placing themselves beside those who built the borough. Emmaline's coming would be bad enough. Aline and Evilbeth will split their girdles laughing, and their maids will snicker in chorus like chantry.

Oh, thimbles—the maids!

They'll know I lied about having a maid the moment they arrive, regardless of whatever perjury I come up with. And they'll laugh till they cry ere ensuring that every soul in this town knows of my airs.

Gwinny shuffles into the workroom with the broom. Her gray smock is stained with God knows what and tattery at the hem. She smells like goat.

No. There's no way.

My other choice is to stand humiliated before the sly and blackhearted daughters of the *honesti*.

All Gwinny has to do is hoodwink them for a single afternoon, but she must look the part.

I hurry abovestairs and rummage through my coffer till I find a moss-green kirtle given me last New Years by Alice's mother. The wretched gown bunches strangely beneath the arms and the color makes me look like a sick frog, but the cut is stylish and there are no patches and it doesn't smell of goat.

Even now, Saint Peter is recording this act of charity to my credit in his book.

I skip into the workroom waving the kirtle like a battle standard. "Gwinny!"

She sweeps around Salvo, long and even, and chuffs dirt out of the corner.

"Gwinny. Gwin-ny!"

She pulls the mound of debris into a pile, then looks me right in the eye as if we're the same.

Just as that mannerless wretch of a laborer did, the one who unloaded the pack train and *looked* at me right in my own yard. The one I cowed in the street. The one who'll not soon look at me again, should he have wit enough to study his lessons.

I wind my fists into my apron and make myself smile. "You're a fortunate girl, Gwinny. I'm giving you this gown."

Her brows dip. Her lashes flutter. And then she smirks. She actually smirks, the ill-bred hound!

At length she lowers her chin and the look is gone, replaced by the drum-tight mouth and blank birdlike eyes.

"You'll get your penny same as always." I hold out the folds of pond-colored wool. "This isn't payment. It's a gift."

Gwinny eyes first the garment, then me. She reaches hesitantly for the gown. I thrust the lot into her arms and beam.

"Good girl. Now put it on and let's see how it looks."

Once on Gwinny's back, the gown falls in graceful folds to the floor and the cuffs hang just over her wrists. And by all the saints if the color doesn't make her eyes glow like fish-ponds just after the weirsman's brush.

"There!" I clap my hands and grin. "Splendid. Oh, saints, mayhap this'll work. You hardly look Welsh at all!"

Gwinny stiffens as if she got a cold-water drench. She skins the gown off, leaves it in a pile on the floor, and puts on her gray smock once more. Then she goes back to sweeping.

I scoop up the kirtle and fling it at Gwinny. "Put that on! How dare you insult me so basely? Spurning a gift, a gift that's worth what you earn in a year."

Gwinny makes no move to catch the gown. It hits her shoulder and slides to the floor. She toes the folds of wool and closes her eyes for a long moment.

Then she retrieves it, strips off her filthy smock, and slides into the new garment slowly, as though it's a shroud.

"Good." I fold my arms. "For shame, Gwinny. Treating me this way when I seek to help you."

She collects her old goaty smock, folds it, and places it near the rear storage chamber.

"That new gown will be on your back tomorrow," I tell her, "and the next day, and the day after that."

She nods without looking at me and retrieves the broom.

I mutter a rapid prayer to any saint listening. Please let the *honesti* girls be fooled. Otherwise I will have to move house again or take up residence in the cellar.

Mayhap they won't come. Mayhap they won't want to be

seen with a *novi*. Mayhap Emmaline's father will forbid her. Mayhap William will forbid Aline.

If God Almighty has any mercy, none of them will come.

They all come. They bring their embroidery. Now we're sitting here in stifling silence while I try to think of things to say to daughters of the *honesti,* two of whom keep smirking and snorting and snickering whenever they glance my way.

Even their maids brought needlework. Margery and Maudie and May. The three maids sit in a row like little poppets on a bench dragged in from the hall. They sew shifts for their mistresses while my "maid" stands in the shadows like an effigy, smelling vaguely of straw.

Please don't let Gwinny ruin this. All she has to do is be still.

We've already spoken of the beastly weather. The way heat clings to floorplanks and leaves skin damp and sticky. We've spoken of William, Emmaline's father, my father, and Evilbeth's betrothed.

Now it's quiet. Sickly quiet. The kind of quiet that makes you stare at your needle and try to ignore the hair prickling at the back of your neck.

I clear my throat. I cannot stand it. "So . . . what are you all doing for Michaelmas Eve?"

Emmaline frowns. "Well, what else is there but—?"

"Nothing," Evilbeth cuts in. "That is, naught but silent

prayer and contemplation. And fasting. We fast and pray to honor the saint. Alone."

"But, Bet, you've forgotten the bonfire!" Emmaline wriggles and grins like a child on her year-day. "Oh, you'll love it, Cecily, there's naught else like it all year! There'll be cider and music and dancing, and if you're brave, you can put chestnuts in the fire and divine who your future husband will be!"

"As if that's likely," Aline mutters, squinting at a stitch.

Evilbeth glares at Emmaline, but Emmaline doesn't notice because she's toying with her half-finished veil and gazing dreamily into the hearthfire as if it's Michaelmas already.

I dredge up a smile. "That sounds lovely. At Edgeley, we'd crack nuts in the church. We could do that here."

"We could," Evilbeth drawls, "if we were *novi* and didn't know any better."

"I fancy a honey wafer." I leap to my feet and throw my linen blindly onto the bench. There's a tiny metal sound like my needle coming loose, but I pay no heed. "We have them all the time, so I'm sure there's a big pile in the kitchen. Gwinny!"

She shambles out of the shadows, tripping over her hem. She looks worse than usual, stains on her new gown and big dark rings around her eyes.

"Fetch the honey wafers from the kitchen," I say in slow, careful words. "Bring lots, because we always have enough to spare. And bring the wine. We're thirsty."

Evilbeth is smiling. My hackles go up like angry crows.

"*That's* your marvelous maid?"

"Yes." I cannot find my needle, so I pretend to stitch with small violent stabs.

"And of course she's one of *them.*"

I'm burning to demand what business it is of hers, but I'm to be pleasant to Emmaline de Coucy and my father will flay me where I stand if I'm rude to any of the *honesti.*

Especially a Coucy.

"I should have known." Evilbeth snorts. "*Novi.*"

"How can you trust one in your house?" Aline shudders. "Are you not worried she'll steal? Or break things?"

"The king would have the Welsh live cheek by jowl with us," Emmaline puts in, drawing her needle clear. "Within the walls and full privileges as burgesses. My father says there are already Welsh burgesses in Harlech."

Evilbeth sniffs. "It'll never happen in Conwy."

"A Welshman was supposed to live in your house, Cecily," Emmaline says. "Dav-ith something. Petitioned the king and everything. That's why your father was admitted so hastily."

Gwinny appears at the door, a plate of honey wafers balanced on her arm. In her other hand is a pewter mazer.

I can smell the honey wafers clear across the workroom. My father is still bemoaning the cost and swearing I'll not see another drop of honey till my wedding, but it's worth every penny because *I* am Croesus today.

As Gwinny approaches, I gesture to the coffer I lugged in from the hall and arranged before the benches, as if it's always there for the piles of honey wafers we always have.

Gwinny bends to set down the mazer and the platter of wafers tips. They're sliding, the whole pile, toward the gritty floor that never did get scrubbed with sand.

"No!" I lunge for the platter but instead catch Gwinny's wrist. She startles and corrects too much and the wafers fly like leper bread, scattering at the *honesti* girls' feet.

Evilbeth brays donkey-laughter and Aline cackles like a hen. Even Emmaline is tittering behind her hands.

I stare hard at the floor. At the wafers scattered there like fat straws.

All the honey in the house. Every drop.

"Gwinny, you clumsy ox!" My voice is high and choked. "I should have you cartwhipped! Look what you did!"

"No matter," Emmaline says cheerfully. "There are more wafers in the kitchen, right? She can just fetch another plateful. Here, Margery can pour the wine."

Gwinny studies her dirty bare feet, begging to be kicked and slapped into martyrdom for making a fool of me before these viperous *honesti* who built this vile town but haven't the manners God gave a goat.

Evilbeth snorts. "*Novi* and their airs. This little baby ought to unpack her dolls and go back to the nursery."

"Gwinny," I finally manage, "pick up the wafers. Margery can pour the wine."

As Gwinny kneels and collects the wafers, Evilbeth prods her shoulder with one slippered toe and shakes her head.

"Worthless," Evilbeth mutters, then narrows her eyes at me. "I'd dismiss a servant of mine on the spot for something so disastrous."

If I were really the lady of this house, I'd dismiss Gwinny in ten different ways and kick her rump on the way out. But as long as Mistress Tipley stands for her, and my father stands for Mistress Tipley, I'm stuck with them all.

I shake out my fists. I swallow till I'm fairly sure my voice will come out level. "Gwinny, I'll fetch the wafers from the kitchen. Give me the tray. You are excused for the day. Off with you."

She goes, and I make it to the rearyard ere angry tears get the better of me. I lean against the house and sob and hate Evilbeth as hard as any good Christian dares.

Then I take the platter into the kitchen, pick off the debris clinging to the wafers and stack them artfully back on the platter. They look a little mushy, but these girls deserve no better.

I splash water on my face, take a breath, then carry the tray back to my workroom.

My father had better appreciate all I'm doing for him.

Black Reese of Trecastell has turned up badly beaten near Llanfair, one of the very places he used to haunt to rob innocent travelers on the king's highway.

One of his arms hangs limply from the shoulder and his right leg is broken in two places. His tongue has been cut out and his face is swollen and purple. He draws breath in short raspy bursts when he's not coughing up blood.

Of course my father must relate this over supper. I push my trencher to arm's length.

County court conducts an inquiry. The bailiffs say they released Black Reese the very day Nessy Glover returned home, but the Welshry cries foul and demands that the porter of the city gates be called as an oathgiver to confirm the bailiffs' account of Black Reese walking out of the gatehouse in the same condition he went in.

The sheriff reminds them that Englishmen are not required to give evidence against other Englishmen when accused by Welshmen.

The bailiffs scoff that such a beating could come from any cudgel and that tongues could be cut out by any blade. Highwaymen make enemies of all, say the bailiffs, and such an accusation defames the borough when there's not a shred of proof.

That's when a Welshman seizes the plaint roll from the clerk and rips it to pieces, and the whole of the Welshry begins raising a row.

The sheriff shuts down the inquiry on the spot, and when he reopens it the next day, every man of the castle garrison stands behind him in a glowering, white-tabarded wall.

Black Reese dies halfway through the inquiry, but with

his tongue cut out he wasn't able to make oaths anyway. After deliberating for half an Ave, the sheriff rules misadventure and fines the Welshry for presentment, since Black Reese was one of theirs.

For the next se'ennight, my father does not ride the Welshry in search of handmills. He says he's feeling poorly, and he recuperates while honing his blade and carving a grip into the blackthorn cudgel that surely should have gone onto the midden after Nessy Glover's safe return.

Ned calls. He'd take me on a walk around the city walls. I turn my best Salvo-eyes on my father and he grunts his permission. While we wait for Mistress Tipley to wrap her bulk in her voluminous cloak, Ned thaws my father's icy scowl with an amusing tale of three Welshmen who attempted to arrange a buy-naught in the Conwy market. People were too frightened to refuse paying the market-penny, though, and someone turned them over to the bailiff, so the three poor wretches ended up rattle-and-drummed into the strait up to their necks and left there for two whole days.

My father is smiling by the time we depart.

Ned sets his usual stiff pace, which I can now easily match. Mistress Tipley is left well behind us, puffing and heaving in a most unflattering way. We turn up High Street and head toward the twin-towered gap in the wall that rises twice and thrice my height.

"The Water Gate," Ned says, smiling in that knee-melting

way. He strips off one glove and whistles with two fingers. A head bobs above us, then a rope ladder tumbles down. "You've not seen Caernarvon till you've seen it from the walls."

The hemp fibers are wet. And slimy. And the ladder sways like a three-wheeled cart and I'll fall and break my neck.

"Oh. You're frightened." Ned's face falls. "That's well enough. I just wanted . . . Never mind, it's naught."

"It isn't naught!" I crane my neck to catch his hangdog gaze. "Please tell me. Please?"

Ned glances at me sidelong through a windwhipped lock of hair. "It's just that I come to the Water Gate whenever I need some peace. And I wanted to share it with you because you're the only girl who . . . But I'd never see you frightened. Not for anything."

Something dear to him, and he's sharing it with me. And only me.

I seize the first rung. The ladder smells like pulp and brine. I take a deep breath and look up, and up and up.

A heavy hand falls over mine.

"I think not." Mistress Tipley pulls me away from the ladder and faces Ned, hands on massive hips. "You first. I'll follow the child up."

Ned shrugs. "As you would, mistress." And he shinnies up the rungs of rope like a squirrel.

I ignore Mistress Tipley and seize the ladder boldly, even through the stink of wet hemp will be on my hands till Christmas. Hand over hand I climb, clinging tight and not looking down. The ladder does sway like a three-wheeled cart, but I do not fall.

Ned helps me onto the wall. There's a walkway that runs behind the notches an armslength wide. The wind off the strait whips my hood back. He holds my hands longer than he needs to, rubbing my palms with his thumbs.

Caernarvon is below me now, rooftops and roads and patches of green all bound by the thin gray wall. Beyond are fields bristling with winter wheat, and farther away are dark purple jags where the mountains meet the sky.

The town does not look solid from up here. It seems naught but a jumble of toothpick thatch and parchment wall that I could grind beneath my heel while it begs for clemency. Or I could put my arms around it and protect it, like a child with a block castle when the dog walks by.

Mistress Tipley is still climbing the ladder. Her face is white as lye and her eyes roll around. She clings to the rungs midway up, as if the whole town is sinking.

"I can see why you like it up here," I say, and silently celebrate that my words don't come out choked or stuttery and I don't sound like God's greatest fool. "You have such a view of everything."

"You'd be surprised how many people have no liking for the walls," Ned replies, leaning on the stone in a way that lets our elbows touch. "I'm pleased you're not one of them. I didn't think you would be. You're too clever and brave."

My father thinks I'm restless and headstrong. The lady

de Coucy thinks I'm crude and dull. But Edward Mercer, burgess and *honesti* of Caernarvon, thinks I'm clever and brave.

"There's where I want to go, though." Ned gestures across the strait. "Anglesey. That's where the money is. That's where the *grain* is."

I parse his meaning. I want to seem clever. "We don't grow enough food here, so if you have extra grain over there, you could sell it at the Caernarvon market. You're a burgess, so there's no toll."

Ned grins at me, and hot shudderies clamor in my middle. *Thimbles,* but he is fair to look upon.

"Got it in one, demoiselle." He smiles slyly. "You know, a lot of men have no liking for clever girls. Me? I've no liking for girls who have vapor for brains."

Behind me, Mistress Tipley is struggling near the top of the rope ladder and Ned turns to help her onto the wall walk.

Now that she's here, Ned keeps a proper distance, but I can still feel the warm circle of touch on my elbow where he leaned against me. He is still speaking of Anglesey grain, but he often glances past Mistress Tipley and winks.

I am clever enough to know what this means, and betimes I am even brave enough to wink back.

MUCKING the byre when I hear hooves on turf and a clatter in the yard. Hooves are never good. Hooves mean they've come.

Seize Mam's pallet and heave. It slides backward and my knees pop and stab pain. She stirs, groans, flails. Drag Mam on her pallet into the byre, just behind the woven wall.

Make it almost to the hearth ere the doorway curtain is torn away. Three men, and they must stoop. Stand my ground behind the firepit, chin up.

"Householder." One has a roll of parchment that he holds up to doorlight and squints at.

"Gruffydd ap Peredur." Never give them more than they need, and besides, know better than to tell them that Gruffydd is my brother and not my husband.

English peers at his list. "In arrears. The total owed is a shilling and threepence. The amount collected in June, threepence. Your man owes his king a shilling, sweeting."

They're leering, all of them, and they're treading in their heavy boots right where Mam's pallet was.

Lick my lips. "Fivepence we have."

"Movable goods assessed in the summer of the king's twentieth year: one cow, a dozen sheep, a pig, a set of bed linens, a cauldron, and a pewter spoon." English scans, lip curling. "Take the cow."

One produces a rope, strides to the byre, loops it about the cow's horns. When he leads her out, she nearly steps on Mam.

"And where's the fivepence, sweeting?"

I almost tell him how high he can hang himself. Just for that surge of righteous bravado that goes to your head like claret and puts the moment squarely in your hand.

Then I remember June. What that moment will cost.

So I kneel. Pry up the hearthstone. They're hovering. Crowding in. Hot and sweaty and damp.

Se'ennights of scrubbing and burned forearms. Fingers like bones from cold water, scaly and red as the Adversary's.

Hand over the packet of coin. Se'ennights, and it's gone in an eyeblink. Tucked into a fine wool tunic and bound for the English king's coffers. From him it came and to him it goes.

"Tell your man he'll have a chance to get his cow again when what's due the king has been paid," English tells me. Then they swing up on their horses and disappear, the cow trundling peaceably behind.

Tomorrow she'll be in some Watched field. She and all the other cattle taken against their king's tax. Past her I'll walk to the brat's, barely looking, for even intent is enough to land you on the gatehouse floor.

All that coin still owed, and back they'll come at Easter.

God only knows what they'll see fit to take next.

1293

MICHAELMAS
TO⊙
CHRISTMAS EVE

EVEN ere I open my eyes, I know what day it is. Despite the dim light, I can make out the plinking of a lute and the high, shrill notes of a whistle beyond my window, and the whole house smells like roasting goose. It's Michaelmas!

I leap out of bed and wash, then I slide through the curtain into my father's chamber and check the bunting hanging from his window.

This far up, I can see over the rooftops of Caernarvon, row after row, all the way to the city wall and into the green beyond. The first hints of gold morning are broaching Saint Mary's, and the thatch roofs light up like firebrands.

Heavens, but for all its barbarism, this place is not without beauty.

Down below, in the yard out front, Mistress Tipley and Gwinny have laid out our largesse already. There are trestles with rows of steaming custards and piles of small birds in pasty crust for the fairgoers to help themselves. It will all be gone by Tierce, but we'll be the talk of Shire Hall Street for the sheer volume of food we've provided.

I go belowstairs and into the yard. At the trestle, Gwinny arranges fried lamprey in neat rows. Her cheekbones leap out of her face and her hand lingers over the meat, almost a caress.

No tenant at Edgeley ever looked so raw.

I comb my hair behind my ears. "Have something, Gwinny. Whatever you want. It's Michaelmas."

Gwinny hovers a hand over the pasties stuffed with spiced meat, easily the costliest and richest dish on the trestle. Then she cuts her eyes to me.

I nod cheerfully.

Without ceremony, Gwinny eats the pasty in two bites and licks her fingers. It's gone so fast I almost bid her take a second one. When I turn toward the house, her hand flashes between the table and her apron, but I say naught and head inside.

My father is rosy with ale and it isn't even Tierce. He bids me perch on his knee and pours pennies into my hand.

"Take Gwinny and go have fun, sweeting," he slurs, "but stay out of trouble."

I plow outside and grab Gwinny by the sleeve ere he sobers up enough to realize just how much coin he gave me.

In the street, I loose Gwinny's sleeve and we regard one another. Her bad humor will completely ruin my Michaelmas, but if she goes back to the house, my father will notice. He'll be upset that I'm roaming the city alone. And he'll come find me, drunk as Noah, and make a scene that will leave me twice humiliated before the *honesti* girls and him before Court Baron for disturbing the king's peace.

I sigh and gesture toward the road, and Gwinny looks as pleased to go as I must look to bear her company.

In High Street, we enter the fair proper, a solid wall of liveliness that chokes the wide street with stalls, carts, beasts, and children. There are baskets and woolen elbows and horse's rumps and glory but it's the Michaelmas fair!

And I have a handful of silver burning a hole in my palm.

I am in a better humor already.

I buy a big wedge of pandemain and slurp down mulled wine, giving Gwinny whatever I cannot finish. The treat seems to put her in a better mood, which cheers me all the more. I pet the silks and fondle the brocades and watch a trained monkey mimic a knight, a bishop, and a fine lady. I buy a new needle and a tiny packet of cloves and I'm eyeing a fine copper cloak pin for my father when I catch sight of a wretch I'd hoped never to see again.

On the corner, oozing among hawkers and dirty-footed shepherds, is Levelooker Pluver. The one who seized Nicholas and made me infamous before Court Baron with false charges.

Pluver wears a fine orange surcote and a tall floppy hat wrought in yellow. It looks like turds of butter. He's torment-ing a ragpicker, rooting through the poor wretch's rags and dumping them into the mud.

"That filthy swine," I mutter as Pluver seizes the ragpick-er's mangy hood and grinds it underfoot with one elegant boot. "Someone ought to teach him to study his lessons."

At my elbow, Gwinny snorts softly. "Will not happen."

I turn to her, chin high. "It should."

"What do you care?" Her voice is bitter like wine too soon from the cask.

"Justice," I say firmly.

Gwinny squints at me for a long moment ere she snorts again. "Mayhap. But given by who? You?"

I match her cool tone. "Mayhap."

She's fighting a smile, and it makes me want to slap her senseless. "You. Right. We'll see."

And Gwinny's off through the crowd like a hearthcat on the hunt, past shoulders and bundles toward Pluver, who is upending the poor ragpicker's cart. She glances over her shoulder and smirks as if she's caught me playing with dolls. Then she puts herself before Pluver and asks loudly if he's yet amerced a one-eyed brewster whose ale is watered and not up to scratch, and worse, has no license from the borough.

And it hits me—Gwinny is distracting him. She's daring me to teach him a lesson, as I said I would.

My father does not want to see the inside of Justice Court again.

But there's no filthy swine who deserves justice more than Pluver, and Gwinny will have to swallow that smirk.

I know just how to do it.

I circle wide, darting through the crowd and craning my neck, pretending to hunt for someone. Gwinny slants only one glance at me, then fixes her eyes on Pluver and raises her voice. Soon I'm behind Pluver, and his yellow-turd hat slides back on his greasy head as he aims gestures at Gwinny.

It won't really be stealing. He'll get his foolish hat back. Eventually.

In one motion, I rise on tiptoe, wick the hat from the filthy swine's fat head, and whirl it beneath my cloak as if I'm adjusting the drape. Then I move away as though I'm still hunting for someone, craning my neck and seeming peeved.

It's a few moments ere Pluver realizes he's bareheaded in a crowd of fairgoers, but by that time I'm watching from a good stone's throw.

Gwinny flings her hands up as if she's lost patience with Pluver, then stomps into the crowd. Pluver is patting his head and glancing around like a chicken with too much seed. He kicks at the mud and peers behind baskets and carts, all the while touching his head as if the hat will reappear through sorcery.

The ragman grins like a schoolboy as he rights his cart and scoops up sopping rags.

When Gwinny appears at my elbow, I move my cloak just enough that she can see the hat's fat yellow crown. She barely looks at it, though. She's staring at the ground, brow in knots, jaw working.

"You did it," she finally murmurs, as if I gave her a month off with double wages. "One of your own. And you did it."

"Not one of *mine*." I nod us toward the city gates, away

from the scene Pluver's making. "Justice for those who deserve it."

When we pass a massive dull-eyed hog tethered to a cart, I jam the levelooker's hat over the hog's ears and keep walking.

"Right enough," Gwinny mutters, "but how will anyone know the difference?"

I laugh outright. "Not by the smell!"

We move through every single handswidth of the fair. Gwinny isn't afraid to walk past the shady stalls that abut the city wall, the ones with goods of dubious provenance and therefore the best prices. She isn't even shocked that I suggest it. She doesn't protest that it isn't safe.

I suspect she wouldn't be afraid of climbing the city walls, either.

The sun is burnished and falling ere Gwinny and I return to the townhouse. Our shadows run out before us, tall and wispy like the banners of an invading army. Two faceless girl-shapes, heads lumpy from piled plaits, gowns fluttering about their feet like massive butterflies. They are so alike that betimes I must glance to be sure it's still Gwinny at my elbow, and not Alice or Agnes or Emmaline de Coucy.

Even though it's frigid in the workroom, I'm spinning before the window and ignoring my father. He's being completely unreasonable, denying me permission to go nutting. He says it's too wet and I might fall ill, but he says it while glancing at the blackthorn cudgel that's still propped in a corner.

Honestly, you'd think he's forgotten that the sheriff gave the ringleaders of that scene in county court a se'ennight on the gatehouse floor to study their lessons.

"*Tiiiiiit's of a fair young maaaaaaaiden who's walking in the wood*," I sing, badly, at the top of my voice so it will echo into the hall where my father is. "*Her voice was so mel-o-di-ous, it charmed him where he—*Oh, hey, Papa."

"Hay is for horses," he growls, gripping the doorframe. "What are you doing?"

"Singing." I smile and let my whorl spin. "Like Paul and Silas did while they were in gaol."

"They also prayed," my father replies through his teeth. "Try that. And you're not in gaol."

"Am I not? Can I go nutting, then?"

My father is growing steadily redder. "You're leagues too old to be fooling with such childish things."

"Fine." I tease out more woolen fibers. In a fortnight he will tell me I'm not old enough to go Catherning with the women, even though Mistress Glover already said over the fence and ten thousand bobbing blond heads that I could join her and Mistress Sandys and Mistress Pole.

My father's bootsteps clump down the corridor. I give him time to pour some ale and settle before the fire and let Salvo curl against his feet.

Then I warble, *"For if you stay too laaaaaaate to hear the plowboy siiiiiiiing, you may have a young faaaaaaarmer to nurse up in the—"*

The front door slams hard enough to shake the shutters. My father storms past, and by the look of him he's heading to the Boar's Head.

"Spring," I finish softly, and I let the whorl twist back and forth like a hanged man.

I enter the lady de Coucy's solar and drop my backside on the uncushioned bench reserved for me, but the lady drags me up by the wrist. She cannot believe I just shuffled into her presence like a plow horse after everything she's been trying to teach me.

"On my first day, you said my walk was wrong," I protest, and immediately wish I could have it back because it's not well-mannered in the slightest and the last thing I need is my father wroth with me when I'm trying to get him to buy me a new gown and all he can speak of is how we're going to eat this winter.

The lady puts one hand to her temple as if pained. At length she snaps her eyes up and demands, "What would you do if John de Havering walked through that door right now?"

She's regarding me so intently that I know she means to trap me. Should you behave toward a Crown official as if he's a borough official, God help you. Should you address someone as "my lord" instead of "your Grace," you may as well dump a privy bucket over his head.

Behind her mother's back, Emmaline catches my eye, then inclines her head and makes a tiny curtsey.

"Er . . . curtsey?"

The lady de Coucy's brows come down. "Do you even know who John de Havering is?"

I parse and parse. Surely my father has talked about him, mayhap even invited him to our house. Is he the sheriff? One of the other officers of charge? Surely not the constable of the castle—

"Oh, saints!" The lady groans and flings her arms wide. "He's only the justiciar of the Principality of North Wales, you ignorant girl! By the Virgin, I know not how you'll ever manage this if you're such a lackwit that you cannot even re-member the simplest things."

"Mother, please!" Emmaline tugs on the lady's sleeve. "She's really trying! Mayhap all she needs is a little more help. I can go to her house and—"

"No!" The lady de Coucy rounds on her like a mastiff. "No, you'll not be seen . . . Sit down, sweeting. And *you.*" She turns to me with knuckles upraised, but at length she lowers her arm and regards me as if I'm a sodden kitten that's just been sick in her lap. "No. It's not your fault. Poor motherless thing. It's not your fault you were raised in a byre by a ham-handed oaf."

If John de Havering walked through that door right

now, I'd spit on him just to see the look on this shrill harridan's face.

She's naming borough and Crown officials, and she gives me such an eyestab that I echo them after her in as frosty a tone as I dare. Because my father may be a hamhanded oaf, but I'll not have it said that he raised a lackwit who is not clever and brave enough to hoodwink a shrew with vaporheaded compliance.

Sacks appear one by one in our shed. They're full of milled barley and wheat and oats. I ask my father about them. He says the millers give him grain as part of his office of charge.

The millers must like him mightily if they gave up a share of the thumb's depth they've wrung from everyone else.

IT darkens earlier now that the season has changed. Mayhap the millers will be more accommodating, now that it's harder to be seen.

Knuckles against the door. And wait.

The Porth Mawr miller peers out. "You again."

Hold up the sack without a word.

He puts out his hand for the penny, for my se'ennight's worth of sweat.

Jab the coin into his hand.

The miller leaves the door ajar while he clunks about within. Then he thrusts out the sack, and it sways in his meaty grip like a wrung-neck chicken.

The sack is light. As if it's empty. Peek in. There's barely a dusting.

"Th-this isn't half what my penny brings." My voice is low and raw.

The miller spits. "It's what your penny brings now, after that worthless harvest. What will you do, call the Watch?" He laughs, ugly. "Off with you."

Raise my voice. "Give me my due."

"God rot your filthy soul, you ungrateful—"

Something hits my back hard and I'm pushed into the mill and harsh commands echo and feet scuffle in straw and my sack gets ripped from my hand and I'm face-first against the wall, gasping for breath.

A forearm across my shoulders and a hand at my lower back hold me pinned. Limewashed wattles gouge my cheek.

"Right, then, miller. Is this girl a burgess, pray tell, or are you trading on an unlawful day? And after sundown?" A cough of laughter. "Even better."

The arm at my shoulders pivots and a hand reaches beneath my underarm and cups my tit. Hot breath dampens my ear. Nipple gets pinched. Rubbed.

"What else can I amerce you for?" Heavy bootsteps clump across the room. "Will I find sawdust in these sacks?"

Something smashes. The miller cries out in dismay. Then there's a heavy sound, like a quartermeasure sack hitting the floor, and laughter. Several men, including the one pinning me.

The miller will get a fine. English will give me irons and time on the gatehouse floor. Or worse.

"I've done naught wrong," the miller says, but his voice quavers beneath a try at strength.

More laughter. Whoever's holding me rubs his groin against my backside, slow and deliberate. My hipbones grind into the wattle. He grunts softly.

"I believe I'll let the constable decide what you've done. He'll taste this flour and—"

"Saints, this sack of flour has opened, my lord." The

miller's voice is shaky. "I have no use for it. Why do you not, er, dispose of it for me? I would be in your debt."

Grip stray strands of wattle. Press my forehead against the wall. His grunting grows louder and the hand on my tit squeezes and rubs.

"Come. This mill is in order. Except for that open sack. Leverdon, take it to my shed."

Wince at one last grind of hips as he rocks away. Footsteps echo, and there's a whuffle of door.

"Whore, this is your fault! Show your face here again and I'll make you sorry!"

The miller seizes my collar and arm, gripping so tightly I cry out. Stumble out the door as he throws me.

Land, hard, on rocky ground. Lie crumpled there a long moment. Then struggle up and limp home.

Full dark now. Empty belly. Empty hands.

Gruffydd pushes roughly through the steading's doorway. "Dafydd's with me. Don't even start, hear?"

Bristle at my little brother ere I get a look at Dafydd. His face is raw and bruised, and he limps inside while Gruffydd hovers at the curtain, peering out.

Blink and blink and finally find my voice. "Wh-what happened?"

"I was well met last night," Dafydd growls. "Hauled out of bed and cudgeled something fierce. My door kicked in. My whole place sacked. Thatch everywhere."

"Jesu, why?"

Dafydd smirks. "My prospective neighbors within the walls wish to inform me that continuing to petition the English king for a burgage in Caernarvon is an endeavor to be conducted at my peril."

Fight to stay calm. Know not what else he expected. Especially after what happened at county court.

"You cannot stay." Say it kindly, but brooking no refusal. "They watch this place. Because of Da. They'd love an excuse."

"I'll certes put that in my next petition to the king. 'Your Grace, mayhap it would interest you to know that the officials who govern in your name visit the sins of the father upon his innocent children.' It'll go right after 'It troubles me to report that Caernarvon's gatehouse is enchanted. Upon leaving, men are rendered invisible for a fortnight, then turn up fatally beaten. At least, that's what your bailiffs would have you believe.'"

"Please." Regret my soft words already. Giving Dafydd anything is like oil on fire, and nay is easier said in blade-edged tones. "If they find you here, we'll all *wish* for time on the gatehouse floor."

Dafydd moves to rise, but Gruffydd at the doorway gestures him down.

"Nothing yet," Gruffydd reports. "Mayhap we lost them. That's enough, Gwen. Now's not the time."

Fold my arms. "Oh, come now, it's not the first time the

burgesses thrashed him, is it? Nor will it be the last. And I've no liking for this trick—"

"Gwenhwyfar." Gruffydd's voice is low and fierce. He's angled in the doorway like a beast in the furze. "Enough."

They're both muddy to the knees and covered in brush. Tense like foxes at the horn. Neither of them is smug.

This is not a trick.

Let out a long breath and summon brook-naught words, but one sidelong look at Dafydd and my voice betrays me with its catch. "The English will not tolerate your antics forever."

Dafydd straightens. "So be it. It's unlawful, what they're doing, and someone has to stand against them or the king will never know."

It makes no sense to stand when it will change nothing.

Gruffydd leans inside, eyes wild. "Go. Now. They're coming up the hill."

Dafydd runs a hand down my cheek ere I can pull away. His touch is warm and gentle, curse him.

By the time English cudgel into my house, Dafydd is gone into the greenwood while Gruffydd and I stand elbow to elbow, bracing to be questioned.

My FATHER is having winter firewood loaded into our rearyard. Cartload after cartload, and all I can hear is clumping hooves and blasphemy and the clatter of wood on wood.

I have never made a more crooked seam, not even ere the age of reason.

They must be quieter.

I stomp through the hall and into the rearyard to make them. The back door rattles on its leather hinges when I kick it open.

It's *him*. Of course it is. The one who *looks*. The one I made study his lessons, right in the middle of High Street.

He's chopping a massive heap of wood. With one smooth swing of his ax, he splits a piece, then reaches for another chunk while rolling the ax behind his shoulder. By the time his ax is upraised, the next piece of wood is on the block and ready for splitting. Again and again, fluid as a carole dance.

The last time we met, he was not sorry. He stood there in the High Street not being sorry for my gown or my convenience or his own brazen behavior in defiance of the king, who asked us to come here to teach them to behave.

Today he will be sorry.

I hook my hands behind my back and saunter toward him, swaying my hips and pushing my chest out. I stand just out of the way and watch him swing the ax up and bring it down.

He glances my way, startles like a cat, then whips his eyes back to his task.

He does not *look*. He *dares* not look.

And there is naught he can do for it.

"G'morn," I say sweetly.

"Better to you, demoiselle." He does not break rhythm or turn in my direction.

"What are you called?"

The ax comes down crossways, glancing off the chopping block. As he recovers and hoists the blade onto his shoulder, he mutters, "Gruffydd ap Peredur, demoiselle."

"Griff-ith," I repeat in my flattest English way.

He grimaces, shakes his head the smallest bit, then brings the ax whistling down.

I peer at him as if he's a hairy insect in my porridge. Let's see how he finds being looked at.

Under my scrutiny, his cuts become steadily less even and betimes he must chop the same piece twice. Betimes the ax must rest on his shoulder while he fumbles for another piece of wood.

"Begging your pardon, demoiselle," Griffith says to his chopping block, "but is there something you've come for?"

"Not particularly." I idle around to his other elbow, all hips and teases of ankle. "I've a right to be in my own yard, do I not?"

He scrubs a wrist over his eyes while the ax weighs down his shoulder. "Right aye, demoiselle."

I let him chop several more pieces, reveling in every wavering upswing and crooked cleave. One piece he must cut thrice, and he nearly crops a finger doing so.

"One reason we're here is to teach your lot to behave," I muse. "The king would have it so. And you're always looking at me. It's really quite rude. As if you really haven't studied your lessons at all."

The ax comes down hard, the blade half-buried in the chopping block. It takes Griffith nearly an Ave to work it free. Once he does, he looses a long breath and begins his rhythm anew.

"There must be some mistake," he finally mutters. "I've no idea what you're speaking of."

"Oh, I think you do. You're always looking at me. Now, let's see here. What could the reason *possibly* be?"

Griffith's expression darkens. He grips and regrips the ax, but when he speaks, his voice is quiet and level. "I must get on with my task, demoiselle. By your leave."

"Mayhap you look at me because you think I'm comely." I twitch the hem of my gown as if I'm going to lift it.

A look of panic crosses his face and he swipes a chunk

of wood, heaves the ax onto his shoulder, brings it down fiercely. Another piece, then another, as though all the demons in Hell are driving him like a mule.

"Do you?" I brush his shoulder with my handkerchief and he leaps as if stung. "You'd best answer."

"I . . . cannot . . ."

"So you think I'm plain." I make my voice all warpy like I've been weeping and throw in a stifled little sob for good measure. "I think I'll run into the house crying. My father will doubtless wish to know what's amiss. And he'll look into the yard to see what could possibly—"

"Oh, Christ, no!" Griffith sinks the ax into the chopping block and drops to his knees at my feet. "Demoiselle, please! I beg your pardon! Forgive me!"

I look down on him, right in the eye. And I smile. "Again."

Griffith closes his eyes, there in the mud on his knees.

Where he belongs.

"I beg your pardon." His voice is raspy, uneven. "Forgive me."

"Much better." It occurs to me to pat his head as though he's Salvo, but instead I angle my hand down in the *free dog* command. "Right, then, on with your task."

It takes Griffith most of the day to cut the wood. He cannot regain his rhythm. He's too busy glancing at the back door as if it's the gallows.

* * *

Ned comes to supper. My father is warming to him, for he tells highly amusing stories and always brings a pottle of very good hippocras.

Tonight Ned has a good tale of a Welshman who thought to avoid paying market penny by means of trickery. The Welshman wanted to sell goats outside the borough market, so he had a handful of reeds that he sold for the price of a goat, and if you bought his reed you'd get the goat for nothing.

As the bailiffs fell upon the Welshman, he protested that it was quite legal to sell reeds without license. It did not avail him, though. The Welshman's goats were distrained and he sits in the gatehouse awaiting gaol delivery, accused of defrauding the borough.

Tonight, along with his customary wine, Ned brings us a goat. She's in the rearyard tethered to the pig byre. Soon we'll have cheese every day, and mayhap some extra to sell at the market.

I sit at Ned's right. Beneath the trestle he leans his leg against mine.

I am warm to my core.

Then Gwinny tips a platter of custard in Ned's lap. He leaps to his feet and curses like a wharfside ganger. My father nearly bursts his belt laughing.

"Gwinny!" I gasp for words. "What—how could—?"

I'm still stammering like an addlebrain when Gwinny

serenely topples a mug of wine into Ned's boots and flicks gravy onto his surcote as she wipes up the spill.

Ned makes curt apologies to my father and leaves in a huff. He doesn't even glance at me on his way out.

If I wasn't unmarriageable ere this, I certes am now. And it's all Gwinny's fault, the clumsy lackwit.

She will pay for this.

Despite Mistress Tipley's feeble protests, I set Gwinny to shoveling the privy, scrubbing pots with lye, scraping hair from skins. While she's at her labor, I follow her from chamber to kitchen to hall, shouting how she ruined me and how she'll never get a moment's peace in my house and how fortunate she is that I cannot give her any worse than she's already getting. Gwinny leaves every day pale and wrung out, limping, hands bleeding.

It's naught she doesn't deserve. And she'd best get used to it, for I'll be cold in my grave ere I forgive her this.

Aline and Evilbeth are leaving Caernarvon. Emmaline begs me to come over and see them off with her.

"I'm going to weep and weep," she explains in a quavery voice. She clutches a handkerchief with stitches so uneven I can see them a league away.

I can think of no sight more welcome than that of those two vexing shrews growing smaller on the horizon, so I agree.

There's a knot of riders before the Coucy townhouse, but Aline and Evilbeth have not yet mounted. They stand with Emmaline shoulder to shoulder, their foreheads pressed together, clutching one another's forearms.

Promising, like as not, to be friends forever, no matter how far away they are.

Finally, reluctantly, they pull apart.

"Godspeed," I say civilly, nodding to Aline and Evilbeth. It's surprisingly easy to be pleasant now that they're leaving.

"I'm going to miss you both so much," Emmaline chokes out.

"You'll see us this time next year," Evilbeth replies. "Remember? For my wedding?"

Emmaline sniffles. "I suppose. In the meantime, Cecily will keep me from missing you."

Evilbeth cackles. "You certes won't have to worry about her getting married out from under you."

I glare at her ere I can stop myself, but Evilbeth only barks out a harsh laugh. She must have heard about Ned.

Rot that Gwinny, anyway.

Evilbeth and Aline mount their horses and ride with William and his companions out of Caernarvon. Tears stream down Emmaline's face and she dabs at them with her dreadfully stitched handkerchief. Even though I've never been happier to see anyone leaving, Emmaline's tears are making my own eyes sting.

So I say, "Would you come to my house, Emmaline? I must comb fleeces, but you could help."

Emmaline brightens, but the lady de Coucy pulls her toward the gilded Coucy townhouse and says stiffly, "Emmaline is occupied. You mustn't presume on people like that. Go on, now."

I'm burning to ask the lady de Coucy if a good woman of Caernarvon refuses comfort to a friend who's obviously in need of it.

But that wouldn't be well-mannered or attentive, so I stomp all the way to the townhouse, thanking God Almighty and all the saints that these customs will be easy to forget once I'm back home at Edgeley Hall.

On Saturday, while I'm supervising Mistress Tipley's marketing, I catch sight of Ned's russet cloak whipping into an alleyway. Mayhap I can salvage his attention. Mayhap all is not lost. I duck in behind him to beg his pardon for Gwinny's unforgivable behavior.

And I freeze.

Ned has a girl pinned to the wall and she's weeping something in Welsh while he scrabbles with the folds of her gown.

He looks fierce and terrible. Not at all fair to look upon.

I back out of the alley and walk home so fast my legs tangle in my skirts and I stumble unattractively. The hall is empty save for Salvo curled on his pallet near the hearth. I sink next to him and run my fingers through his warm gray hair, and he whuffles in his sleep.

Salvo came to Edgeley with my mother when she wed my father, and the hound did not like her out of his sight. My father says Salvo had to be tied in the hall for the first month of their marriage, so sure the poor beast was that his mistress was in mortal danger behind the bedcurtains.

My father is better than he could be, but my mother could not have known that when she stood with him at the church door.

But now I know something about Edward Mercer. And I'm too clever and brave to let it stand.

The linen my father gave me lies folded over my embroidery frame. Betimes I take it out and pin it, but then I only stare at the smooth, creamy expanse.

I keep waiting for my father to ask when I'm going to embroider something on it, but he seems to have forgotten he ever gave it to me.

Mistress Tipley comes into the hall. "Edward Mercer is here to see Cecily. He'd take her riding."

My father looks up over the knife he's sharpening. He's smiling, wary but interested.

There's naught like justice well served.

I make a greensick shudder. "Tell him to be gone. After what he did, I'll have no part of him ever again."

My father lowers his knife. His whole face goes granite. "What did he do?"

Mistress Tipley's eyes are wide. "Naught, my lord, I swear it. I've been with them every moment."

"Please don't make me speak of it." I cast my eyes down, pitch my voice calm with just a hint of disgust. "The mere thought of him turns my stomach."

I watch my father carefully over my mending. Sure enough, his face is darkening to that dangerous shade of plum and his fists are flexing like a plowboy's. He rises, rams the knife into its scabbard, and storms from the hall. I jumble my linen into a wad and hurry to the workroom window to get a good view.

By the time I crack open the shutter, Ned is already in the middle of Shire Hall Street, flat on his back in a shin-deep patch of mud. My father advances, wroth as a sunburned hog, with fists at his sides while Ned scrabbles back on his elbows.

I wonder if Ned will still like clever girls in an Ave.

My father hauls him up by the collar and bawls, "You worthless cur, don't you ever get within a stone's throw of my daughter again unless you want more of the same!"

"Wait—I know not—"

"If you value your manhood, stay off my doorstep! Now be gone!"

The front door clatters. I slam the shutter home and dash headlong for the hall. By the time my father huffs back to the hearth, I'm on the bench with my mending, all big eyes and curious frowns.

"Whatever happened, Papa?"

"Naught, sweeting," he gruffs. "He'll not bother you any longer. Should have known better. But it's done now."

I narrow my eyes and smile to myself.

Gwinny slides into the hall and begins to sweep. She is smiling narrow-eyed like me.

I think of the girl in the alley, tear-streaked, mud-hemmed, sobbing in Welsh.

Mayhap Gwinny is just as happy as I am to see Ned get his justice right in the middle of Shire Hall Street.

Mayhap what she did at supper was not an accident.

Later, when she's clearing up the bread and cheese, I seize her sleeve. "You knew about Edward Mercer, didn't you?"

She swipes some crumbs into her palm. "How could you not? He's infamous."

My stomach rolls.

"I'm glad you spilled all those things on him," I say firmly. "And I . . . regret that you were punished for it."

Gwinny stacks trenchers without looking at me. "Well worth it. Justice for those who deserve it."

Like Levelooker Pluver.

And there is naught like justice well served.

"I'd take back your punishment if I could," I tell her, and I mean every word.

She flings crumbs into the fire, stoops to give a stray crust to Salvo.

"Gwinny?" I take a breath. "Thank you."

Gwinny swivels, regards me as if I just offered her an ell of brocade. At length she nods, reluctant, as if she's heard something she never wanted to hear.

GRUFFYDD brings some bread. Gnarly. Half moldy. He won't say where it came from. Have learned not to ask.

Most of the wretched bread soaks in hot water for Mam. Cold saps the life from her. It takes more to keep her going in winter. More food. More fire. More cheer and old tales from nursery. More lies.

What's left we eat, Gruffydd and I. We crouch near the fire across from Mam. We do not speak. We say it's because we might disturb her. It's really because we don't want to speak of what's left to speak of.

Crown measures.

Men like Tudur Sais.

Pencoed's English lord.

When Gruffydd lifts his bread to take a bite, I mark the red crescents around his fingernails.

His fingers are bleeding. They have not bled in years. Not since his first few se'ennights of hard labor when we all wept in our sleep.

Seize his hand, hold it firm when he struggles to withdraw. Peer close. The skin around his fingernails is torn bloody. He's biting every finger till it bleeds.

This is not from labor.

He pulls his hand back. "Let it lie. I'll not speak of it."

"It's the wharves, isn't it?"

Gruffydd bites a finger.

Mutter a swear. "Walk past those Chester merchants twice and they think they own you. They might as well, since the Crown turns a blind eye to—"

"I *should* have paid the boon and worked the wharves! Then I wouldn't . . ." Gruffydd scrubs a hand over his face. "I have work. For now, anyway." He laughs mirthlessly.

Eye him. "Beg pardon?"

"It should have been simple work. And it was, until the daughter of the house decided on some sport." He swallows hard. "I did naught wrong. But it won't matter, will it?"

Christ help us.

"Thank your saint, she tells me. My father has all kinds of work that needs doing, and you're just the man for the job." Gruffydd laughs again, hollow. "It's only a matter of time ere someone comes into the rearyard. All he'll see is a burgess's daughter alone with a Welshman, and she knows it well."

Fist up both hands. "Quit. Don't go back."

Gruffydd doesn't reply. We both know why.

"There's other work. There *has* to be."

"Not if I say one of them nay. Especially not if I say *her* nay."

Sink back on my heels.

Mam's low, throaty breathing seems very loud.

Slide next to Gruffydd and put an arm about his shoulder. My little brother buries his head in my neck and his whole body shudders with a muffled sob.

He wept when they came for Pencoed. He wept when Mam stopped knowing who we are. He wept every night of that first month when he stood without the walls in the shadow of Da's swaying corpse, waiting for work.

I squint into the rafters until a telltale wink of steel looks back.

A FORTNIGHT ere Christmas, Nicholas comes roaring up before the house. He's brought a packet of royal missives for the mayor of Caernarvon, and he's permitted to remain until Epiphany.

There's a young man with him, and it's several moments ere I recognize my younger cousin. Henry actually looks like a man, furry across the cheeks and broad through the shoulders. Not the hare-toothed oaf with tousled hair and dirt beneath his nails who told one too many landlord's-daughter jokes.

I embrace them both twice and bring each a mug of hot cider while my father bids them come near the fire to tell the news.

"Mother's piles are acting up again," says Nicholas, as if my aunt Eleanor would like this information made public. "The miller's wife bore twins and had to swear her fidelity on the gospels. Agnes got married. I reckon there's some hope yet for you to unload this minx of yours, Uncle Robert. Someone saw the Adversary in the wheat field. Oh, and Father's brand-new bay mare went lame. I warned him not to buy from that . . ."

Agnes got married.

I slip out of the hall and drift into my workroom even

though it's withering cold, and I sink down before my empty embroidery frame.

They're both wives now. When they'd merely been far away, they seemed within reach. Now that they're married, they're gone for good, no matter what we promised.

Bootsteps behind me. Nicholas clumps into the work-room and shudders dramatically. "Brrr! Why do you not come by the fire, Cesspool?"

"That's all right. I like it here."

Nicholas kneels at my elbow and studies my empty frame. "She's happy, you know. Agnes. Alice, too. They live just around the corner from each other. In and out of each other's kitchens all day."

Just like a man to say the wrong thing and not know it's the wrong thing.

But Nicholas seems to realize something is amiss. "May-hap this will cheer you."

He offers a small parcel of grubby linen. Within are skeins of embroidery thread. A whole fistful, every color I could want. Even gold and silver. Good thread, too, not that coarseweave that bloodies your fingers. I squeal and clap and throw my arms about him.

"I know you were deprived of an altar cloth," Nicholas says with a smile. "Nothing could replace that, of course. But this will help you with another one."

Nicholas pulls plaits and laughs too loud and blames farts on Salvo, but he'll be here to hang the holly and ivy and light candles and offer me his elbow when we walk to Christ's Mass.

Henry has come to see Caernarvon. Nicholas has told him of the liberties and privileges given to burgesses, and Henry is weary of waiting for the chance to become a master gold-smith in the Coventry guild.

My father decides to show Henry the sights. After a little pleading on my part, my father relents and permits me to join them. We pass the Justice Court, the Boar's Head, and the murage trestle, my father rattling on about no tolls and cheap labor, until at last we find ourselves without the walls at the endowed cropland.

Henry stands openmouthed at the neat furrows of icy clods. "All this is yours?"

"Twelvepence a year," my father says. "No service owed. Held by simple burghal tenure."

Henry whistles low, shakes his head.

From somewhere nearby I hear a small noise I cannot place, so I move into the furrows and seek it. It sounds like a lost puppy, mournful and urgent. Mayhap my father would allow me to keep it. Salvo might enjoy a little company.

I top a small rise and stop short. Lying in the dirt, bound wrist and ankle, is the boy whose task it is to ward away crows. There's a filthy gag in his mouth and he struggles against his bonds. His hair has been so harshly shorn that his scalp is half torn away. Even his eyebrows are gone.

"Hey, Papa." I force my voice even. "Papa, Henry, I think you should see this."

My father and Henry cut the ropes in a trice and help the poor lad to his feet. He scowls at them and shakes off their hands, muttering in Welsh.

"Who did this to you?" my father demands.

The boy stares mutely, defiantly.

"It was those whoresons with blackened faces, wasn't it?" My father mutters another foul swear that unfortunately I don't quite catch. "Bastards think they can wreak violence on the few of you with half a measure of loyalty, do they? I shall see them punished, mark me."

"He will," I assure the boy. "He helped put all three of those women in the stocks last month, the ones who tried to sneak into the market without paying the toll. And those lads that sank that barge at the Grandison wharf. The bailiffs are still tracking down whoever carved those, er, offensive pictures into the city gates, but my father thinks the Porth Mawr miller knows who did it, so he's being questioned even now. Whoever it was, though, God help him. I doubt there'll be much left of him to hang."

The boy squints at my father and mutters something that sounds like *tooth-dee-din,* which I take to mean thank you.

"Back to your labor, then," my father says in a gentler tone. "Not your fault, lad. Mind yourself, though. Watchers are hard to come by."

The boy stumbles away through the furrows. Just looking at his clotted scalp makes my head throb, but soon the poor lad will have justice. My father will see to it.

My father needs some sacks of grain moved into the shed. I know just the man for the job.

I send one of the Glover boys for Griffith, and as always, he comes trudging up Shire Hall as if being led to the gallows. As he passes the house, Griffith looks up at it as if it will eat him bone and toenail, and when he sees me at my father's window he quickly drops his gaze.

I flutter my fingers and stare him into the rearyard. He does not look up anymore.

Gwinny is sweeping my chamber. I can hear the scratch of broomstraws on the floor as I sail down the stairs, tying my cloak and pulling on gloves.

The cold is searing outside the hall. I bounce on my heels in the storage chamber and rub my hands while my father gives Griffith his instructions. He speaks loud and slow and repeats himself thrice.

Then my father clumps back inside. He doesn't see me in the shadows, and I give him plenty of time to settle himself before the hearth with a mug ere I hitch my gown up just enough and stride into the rearyard.

"G'morn, Griffith," I say sweetly, even though the cold is crippling and it's hard not to curl into myself and shudder.

He freezes, his back to me and a sack on his shoulder. It's

heavy. I can tell by how he's listing. His whole body slumps like one great sob.

I smile. "I wonder how your lessons are coming today."

Griffith's gloves have no fingers and he has no cloak, merely a tunic that's seen more than one winter. His cheeks are already burned red and his ears are twice wrapped in wool, but still his hair tangles out like ribbons.

"Demoiselle," he finally says, "would you not rather be in by the fire? This weather is not fit for dogs."

It's rising Tierce. It's cold enough to freeze the beard off an icon. Yet he stands with a hundredstone weight on his shoulder while his rag-wrapped feet sink ever deeper into mud clods because he dares not answer and dares not ignore.

"Doubtless no," I purr. "I have *all* morning."

Griffith grimaces as he shifts beneath the weight. "By your leave, then? Should I get this finished, I can—"

"Are you *looking* at me again?"

He opens his mouth. Closes it. Shakes his head once, curtly.

I perch on the kitchen stump and get on with my teaching.

IT'S better when she's gone. Can pretend this house is Pencoed and it's my floor to sweep. My linen to hem. My hearth to stoke.

Pencoed was taken, though. Bastards took everything.

Wouldn't have it different. Having now means kneeling then. Kneeling before them, taking their king's peace.

Da would not. So English took everything. Even his life.

Cold. Bone-biting cold. Must sweep for warmth. All the dim corners and forgotten places.

Must close those rotten shutters.

Lean out to seize the straps. And see them. Gruffydd and the brat.

It grieves me to say it, she says with a smile of pure venom, but you're just not learning anything at all. What *would* the king say, could he see us now? Mayhap you'll never learn, no matter how much you study your lessons. Mayhap you're just not capable of it. I wonder what we'd have to do with you then.

Gruffydd is red and sick and scuffing the icy ground and not looking at her and it's *her,* it's the brat, she's the one plaguing Gruffydd and it's worse again than he ever let on and God help me I'll kill her dead and go to the gallows and not a vile

English soul in this Godforsaken town will hire Gruffydd's labor again and Mam will starve and freeze and die.

Lean against the wall. Gasping.

He was ready to kill them all with his toy spear when they came to seize Pencoed and Mam threw a blanket over us and told us to make no noise, not a sound, and I held my hand over his mouth and gripped him still while he fought to get free and things crashed beyond the wool and Mam wept and men shouted and I whispered over and over for him not to be afraid, that all would end up well.

Liar.

Rock away from the wall. Storm to the garment rod. Gowns hang there. Shifts. Hose and slippers and ribbons and surcotes.

Rose gown is on top. The one I put a thousand-thousand stitches into till my eyes hurt, and with no thanks. No notice of my bleeding fingers.

Seize that rag by the collar and rip. It tears in two with a satisfying groan and I laugh and sob and kill it some more, till it's dead in pieces on the floor. Sleeves like slain birds. Wrought hem like a gallows noose.

Throw its corpse down. Pick up the yellow gown and tear.

The lot of them should burn.

SOMETHING'S HAPPENING in the house. There's clunking and banging and the strangest other sound. Groaning?

Mayhap Ned has returned to try his luck against my father's rage.

Griffith is all but in tears. I've only permitted him to move three sacks. And I could easily stretch this work out all day. Whether I will or not I haven't decided. I sweetly promise to return as soon as I'm able and I swish all hips into the house.

The hall is quiet. My father is nowhere in sight, but Nicholas dozes before the fire in the big master's chair he's dragged from the trestle. Salvo sleeps on his feet.

The strange noise is clearer in the hall. It's not a groaning sound at all. It's a ripping sound.

Something is being torn abovestairs.

I take the stairs two at a time. At the curtain, I stop cold.

I cannot be seeing true.

There is clothing everywhere.

No. No, there are *pieces* of clothing everywhere. My garment rod is empty and there are skirts across the bed and sleeves on the floor and a leg of hose dangling from the shutter and scattered about are scraps that might have once been ties or hems or girdle lacings.

Gwinny stands in the middle of the wreckage, panting as if winded from a sprint. Her fists are stiff at her sides and both clutch handfuls of wool scraps. She looks poised to attack, like a mad dog or a boar.

Christ and all the saints but she will pay! And not just at Court Baron.

I seize her wrist and haul her from the room as hard as I can. She bangs an elbow on the doorframe and cries out.

"After all I've done for you, too!" I leap the last two stairs and heave her toward the hall. "My father will be furious and you will be *cartwhipped*."

Nicholas blearily rocks into a sitting position and Salvo creaks aloft his gray head.

I throw Gwinny before Nicholas and howl, "I've had all I can bear from this servant my father won't let me get rid of. I'd have her punished for ruining my garments!"

Nicholas blinks and rubs his eyes. "I'm sure there's naught wrong with your foolish gowns."

"She tore them all!" I lash a finger at Gwinny as if dealing the mark of Cain. "Every last thing I own is in ribbons!"

Gwinny says naught. Her eyes are red, as if it is she who's been wronged and betrayed.

Nicholas frowns and stretches. "This is something your father should—"

"My father isn't here!" I glare at him with all my hating. "Are you not a man? Punish her!"

"Wait here," Nicholas says grimly, and he goes above-stairs. When he returns, his face is terrible. He towers over Gwinny and demands, "What would make you do such a thing?"

Gwinny looks at me long and level, then turns her eyes to the floor.

"*Cart. Whipped.*" I snap each word as I cannot Gwinny's neck. "She has devils in her."

Nicholas's face is black as sin. He takes Gwinny by the elbow and roughly tows her out the rearyard door.

KNOW what's coming. Not afraid. Keep my eyes down, though. No need to make it worse.

The cold is blistering. Fingers stiffen in instants. Wind makes a mask of my face.

Oh, Christ. Gruffydd is by the shed, something on his shoulder. Catch his eye and shake my head. He must not step into this. The brat cannot know this matters to him.

Put both hands on the kitchen wall. Not afraid.

Brace.

A stripe of fire across my back. Curl my fingers against the wattles. Dig nails in.

A second blow over the first and I cry out. A third. Salted daggers carve from shoulder to backside, curling beneath my arms, nipping ribs. Christ help me, I'm dying on my knees in the snow while leather sings and my back opens and my throat goes raw and little ones look after littler ones no matter what the cost.

IT'S OVER ere I know it. Gwinny is sobbing in a heap in the snow. Mistress Tipley flies out of the kitchen, her sleeves still rolled to the elbow, and she falls to her knees at Gwinny's side.

"Happy?" Nicholas asks me curtly. He turns on his heel and strides into the house.

Griffith stands in the shed's doorway, gripping the frame as if it's the neck of something deadly. He starts toward Gwinny, then hesitates, cuts his eyes to me.

I will not be trifled with. That's the lesson he must study over all the rest.

I follow Nicholas into the house, but I don't stop in the hall. I don't even acknowledge his shaky voice offering me a drink of undiluted wine. I stomp abovestairs, grinding my toes against every step.

There are rags all over my chamber. Rags, where once I had gowns.

I kneel, collect a few scraps of rose wool. These stitches were strong, too. Tiny and doubled-up. Some of my best work, and like as not Gwinny's too. Now the edges are frayed and tangled. They'll not even be stitched back together in this state.

I close my eyes.

Later today I will show this mess to my father and he will shrug unhelpfully and give me the usual nonsense about how every penny he has will go to keeping us in bread this winter and there's no coin to spare for frivolities—that's how he'll put it, *frivolities,* as if my whole *life* isn't in tatters—and what's wrong with the gown I'm wearing, anyway?

Later today I'll have to go to the Coucy house. The lady de Coucy will eye my ragged cuffs and explain to me for the better part of an afternoon why ragged cuffs will mark me a *novi* and no good lady of Caernarvon should be seen outside wearing clothing in ill repair and I'd know that if I paid half a mind to her but apparently I'm too ignorant to even listen properly.

I gave Gwinny a gown. We saw justice done to a filthy swine of a levelooker who abused his position of power in the borough. She even helped me fend off the unwanted advances of a known scoundrel who sought to take advantage of my youth and gentle nature.

And this—this!—is how I'm repaid.

Gwinny will curse the hour she wronged Cecily d'Edgeley.

I don't give Mistress Tipley the chance to give her a soft task, tucked away in some warm corner of the kitchen. I call Gwinny abovestairs to clean this mess.

It seems forever ere there's a dragging on the stairs, then Gwinny appears at the curtain. She's the color of new cheese and she moves like a stiff puppet on strings.

"Pick it up." I kick a crumpled sleeve at her. "Pick it all up, damn you. Every last scrap."

Gwinny does not bend over to retrieve the wool. Instead she crouches and feels about till she gets it in hand. Then she rises like a water bird, her teeth gritted and her breath in gasps.

"All I had." I swallow and swallow but my voice is still warpy. "All I had that was mine. And only mine. And now I have naught. Because of you."

Gwinny leans heavily against the wall and falters, then she makes a garbled sound and collapses to the floor.

I jab her shoulder with my toe. "Get up, you lazy thing, else I'll give you such a cartwhipping that your grand-children will feel it. You're fooling no one with this dis-play of—"

"Merciful God Almighty!" Mistress Tipley crosses the room in three big strides and shoves me away from Gwinny.

I hit the wall hard, then rock away sputtering, "How dare you?"

The old cow glares up at me like a serpent from Gwinny's side. "How dare *you*, you wicked girl? Now help me get her on the bed."

"*My* bed? I don't think so."

"Fine, is it?" Mistress Tipley mutters to Gwinny as she tugs and wriggles Gwinny's gown over her head. "You most certainly are *not*."

Gwinny makes no sound as Mistress Tipley pulls off her

garments. She lies on her side facing the wall. Her hair spills like a matted hide around bony gray shoulders.

"Come here, girl," Mistress Tipley snarls at me, "and see what you wrought."

I don't have to come. I can see from here.

Gwinny's back is covered with a grid of cuts. Most are a fingernail's depth with edges that curl apart like long, gaping mouths. Where the worst cuts cross, the skin is peeling away in a limp triangle. Her whole back is a deep, angry red, smeary with blood and striped across with angry purple jags.

"No," I finally whisper. "I—I didn't do this."

"You most certainly did. Now help me get her into bed."

I hesitate. And hesitate. Then I pick up Gwinny's feet. They're freezing cold and rough like stones. Mistress Tipley gingerly hoists Gwinny beneath the armpits and we shudder her onto my bed, where she lies like a wet sack.

On my clean linen.

Gwinny moans something in Welsh. Mistress Tipley pets her ragged hair and dabs a rag wetted in my washwater against the cuts on her back. Blood fills the cleaves and stripes down her back, staining the linen.

I did not do this.

Gwinny would be fine had she not wantonly destroyed my property.

I stomp belowstairs and into the hall, and my father bids me a spry good morrow when I take my place at table before a trencher of maslin. Henry grunts a greeting through a mouthful of food, but Nicholas is nowhere in sight.

My father prattles about his foolish office between bites, how the millers are desperate cheats who'll do anything to avoid borough court and how Welshmen do any number of clever things to hide their handmills when they hear he's nearby, which just shows how well he's extending borough justice to the Welshry.

My father must not know yet.

I eat quickly, then excuse myself. He'll find out soon enough, and my father in a temper is pure wrothfulness, not justice.

I go to the workroom and sit before my embroidery frame. I pin and repin the length of linen my father gave me, then I unwrap my skeins of Christmas floss and try to imagine where to begin, what image to make.

It's no use. I give up on the linen and retrieve my spindle from beneath a wadded cloak in need of mending.

I tease out some wool, let the whorl drop. The fibers twist on themselves, and in a while I have a strand of yarn the length of my hand.

In the time it took me to make this strand, Gwinny tore apart every gown I owned.

I throw the wool and spindle across the room with a howl and hate Gwinny and her whole family and weep and hurl the half-mended cloak at the wall for good measure.

Someone will hear me and come. My father, or mayhap one of my lackwit cousins. They'll come to the workroom door with brows furrowed and ask what the matter is, and I'll weep and mourn my loss and they'll see justice done.

The moments stretch like year-old honey. Laughter from the hall, the clatter of crockery. No one comes.

My father does not throw Gwinny into the gutter when he learns what she has wrought. He does not even devolve into ranting. Because while I'm sulking in the workroom, Mistress Tipley plies him with claret and spins a fairy story about spats between girls, how easy it would be to overreact to something this silly, how things like gowns can be repaired, how he has a reputation in the borough to consider.

So he merely whistles low when I shake handfuls of rags in his face, and he jokes that he ought to hire Gwinny as one of his mill enforcers. He laughs aloud when I demand that he take Gwinny to Court Baron for recompense for my wardrobe, and he chides Nicholas for whipping a maidservant so hard. When I'm ready to boil over, my father gives that rotten Gwinny a clean-struck penny for her troubles. The hospitality of his hearth, he says, is hers till she recovers fully.

In the same breath, my father tells me I'm stuck with my one remaining gown unless I grow two handswidths during the winter, and even then he might just bid Mistress Tipley give me something of hers. Then he tells me to stop my caterwauling and mend my underclothes because no one has any business putting eyes on them anyway.

I'm in my workroom now. I cannot wait till tomorrow, when Griffith will be here to mend the byre fence and study his lessons.

1293–1294

CHRISTMAS

TO

ASSUMPTION EVE

IT'S CHRISTMAS. The holly and ivy are up. There's strong cider waiting when we get back from Mass and the Yule log stretches all the way across the hall, so we must step over it. I can close my eyes and everything is as it should be, all the mingled smells of roast goose and woodsmoke and bitter evergreen, the wind twittering, the crunch of feet in snow, the crackle of fire.

Then I open my eyes.

Nothing is right.

The goose is roasting, but it is Mistress Tipley's hand on the spit. Not my mother's.

Nicholas and Henry are cheerfully drunk on Rhenish and aqua vitae. They are planning to go out mumming later, which will inevitably devolve into misrule. They might even remember to wave to me through the window when they go, and they will come back pink and laughing and full of furtive looks and guffaws and secret jokes that they will tell me are not fit for my ears.

The holly and ivy are up, as crooked as only drink-addled male hands can make them. My mother would have straightened the greens, primped them, and tied tiny ribbons to the ends.

My father hasn't spent a Christmas sober since she died,

but this year he is staggering about town visiting houses, bringing a year's worth of good fortune with his dark hair. He says it's a civic duty. It's really just a way for him to get into the homes of the *honesti* even for a moment.

The same wind clattering about the eaves blows over her grave far away at Edgeley, and my wretched uncle and his mewling girl-wife will not place a bough of yew on the grassy patch that had all but sunk to ground level when we left for Coventry.

I am playing draughts with myself on the board my mother gave me the year my first milk-tooth fell out. I make a move, then turn the board and make a countermove.

There will be frumenty, figs, and all the plum pudding I can eat, but nothing is really quite right.

My mother was born on this day. She would go about with red ribbons in her hair. We'd play draughts and drink cider and sing ballads while the snow battered against Edgeley's tight walls and mourned about its door.

Not a day goes by when I don't think of her, but on Christmas I wear red ribbons in my hair and commend her soul to God.

I mend before the fire. Stitch by stitch, trying to put my wardrobe back together.

Gwinny lies up in my chamber behind shuttered windows and beneath piled bedclothes. Not only is her back in tatters, she's become feverish.

Just like my mother.

It's no use. Gwinny did her work too well. I can sew most of the cloth back together, but all the seams will show.

I hold up a bodice. It looks like Gwinny's back, all cross-hatched and frayed.

All of Edgeley prayed for my mother. *Pater noster qui in caelis es.* My father on his knees before the high altar for days at a time, unshaven, hollow-cheeked, gray from hunger. *Ave Maria gratia plena.* Saint Alrida's bell ringing to beg the saints to intervene on her behalf, day and night, day and night. *Miserere mi Deus.* Me in the corner with my hair in plaits, curling into a smaller ball and clutching my wooden paternoster while the household tiptoed past.

I go abovestairs and peek into my chamber. Gwinny lies motionless on my bed. Her back is covered with a fragrant poultice.

She must have known what I would do. She must have known the punishment would be severe. Nicholas even gave her a chance to explain.

Justice for those who deserve it.

Pater noster qui in caelis es.

Toward the end, they brought me to see her. My mother sweated and twitched beneath a mountain of bedcovers, too weak to do more than let her gaze fall upon me. The room was hot and close and damp. My father knelt at my mother's side, hands clasped and pressed against his forehead. His lips were moving and his cheeks glistened. My aunt Eleanor wept openly at the foot of the bed. The priest thumbed his beads in the shadows, the hall servants wrung their hands in the corridor, and all of Edgeley prayed.

Gwinny is alone here. No one to sit vigil by the bed. Mayhap even now someone worries over her, watches the door for her to burst in all surly frowns and blank bird-stares. That poor soul has no notion what became of her, where she might be.

Mayhap it's a child.

I bow my head and pray for Gwinny, as Edgeley prayed for my mother.

Mistress Tipley insists I help tend Gwinny. She says she has enough to do running the household that she cannot spare much bedside time.

"I can run the household," I tell the crone primly, but she just guffaws in that rude way of hers and hands me a rag and bowl.

I gather the shredded linen that no one has any business putting eyes on and stomp up to my chamber. As I drag the stool next to the bed, Gwinny glances over her bare shoulder with a look that's almost pleasant, but when she sees it's me and not Mistress Tipley, a hard look falls over her face like a curtain.

"I see you've come to reckon if I'm still alive," Gwinny says. "Sorry to ruin your game."

I gape. "What? No! I didn't wish you dead!"

"Deny it, then."

"I swear it on the Mass. I never wished you dead. Not once. Not *ever*."

Gwinny eyes me as if I'm on a spicemonger's scales. At length, she replies, "Right, then. You've done your good deed. Now you can go."

"I cannot. Mistress Tipley says I must tend you."

"I've no need for it. Go play lady of the house somewhere else."

"I'm trying to show you kindness," I say in little, bitten-off words, "and you are repaying it with scorn."

Gwinny laughs aloud. "God save me from any more English kindness!"

"I gave you a gown! We shared marchpane and wine at Michaelmas!"

She regards me levelly. "I spared you from standing at the church door with Edward Mercer."

"Exactly! I thought we'd reached . . . well, an understanding."

Gwinny snorts. "Oh, I understand. I understand quite well."

I frown. "So . . . you're sorry for what you did?"

"I asked the master's pardon. He has given it. He considers the matter closed."

"What about my pardon?" I brandish the tattery lengths of linen at her. "How could you do this to me? What have I ever done to you?"

Gwinny stiffens. "Don't you mock me."

"Or what?" I swallow and swallow to drown the warp in my voice. "What else do I have that you can destroy? Sorry to ruin *your* game, Gwinny."

In slow degrees, she pushes herself onto her elbows, wincing with each small movement. "In truth? You'd know what you've done to me?"

"In truth," I repeat firmly. "Because I want to hear you admit it before Almighty God. That I did naught. That it was spite and envy that made you do such a terrible thing."

Gwinny's jaw is working and she mutters something in Welsh. At length she sighs. Long, as if she's picking up something heavy. "If you say it's so, it must be so."

I lean back on the stool. "Good. Then do we have an understanding?"

She nods. She doesn't look at me.

"Here. You stitch these." I push a handful of linen scraps at her. "Something to pass the time."

When she shifts to take the linen, the poultice slides off her shoulder, revealing a long cut the color of day-old meat.

I did not do that.

Gwinny's stitches are tight and careful. Even flat on her belly, she matches me stitch for stitch, and ere it's time for dinner, we've put together most of a shift.

Mayhap I will forgive her. It's what my mother would have wanted.

* * *

My father takes Henry to meet formally with the mayor and the foremost *honesti*. They are very interested in having a goldsmith in Caernarvon, and there is a newly built townhouse in Palace Street they would have him view. If they find Henry agreeable, he could be living here by this time next year.

Mayhap I will speak to Emmaline about him.

Nicholas departs for the Boar's Head, so once again I'm alone, forced to spend another tedious day tending Gwinny. I have an armload of undergarments still in need of repair, but when I get abovestairs I find her asleep. The poultice is gone, and her cuts stand out against her flesh like claw marks from some unholy beast. The whole room still smells of pine and juniper. I stand shivering for many long moments to be sure Gwinny isn't playacting, but at length I sigh, toss my torn-up shifts on the coffer, and slip through the curtain.

The house is deadly still. No one will be home till supper.

I pace the landing like a tethered hound. My footsteps creak and echo. At length, I go into my father's chamber. There's his curtained bed and a stool with a tunic thrown haphazardly atop. Beneath the window lies the locked coffer containing my mother's gown and Heaven only knows what else that once was hers. I kneel before it for a long moment, my fingers tracing the lock.

Belowstairs, the workroom is cold and empty. My embroidery frame stands like a naked skeleton by shuttered windows that leak slats of thin gray daylight.

The hall is dim at the corners. The fire crackles and the trestle gleams with each flicker of orange light. Salvo on his pallet snores like a bellows.

Out in the rearyard, the kitchen windows glow. Mistress Tipley is holed up there, drinking small beer with her feet on the grate and dozing like an aging cat.

I go back to the workroom and throw the shutters open. A wall of crippling cold air drafts in, but so does a block of daylight, pale but steady. I pin my father's length of linen to my frame, take out my charcoal stick, and begin to sketch.

"Get down here!" My father, bawling like a boar. It's most unflattering. "That was Sext just then! You should be at the Coucys!"

I fold a half-stitched shift. Then I unfold it, smooth out wrinkles that aren't there, and fold it again. "Coming!"

"You'll regret it should you make me come up there!"

To my undergarments I mutter, "As if you'll get off your arse before that fire." Then, louder, "I said I was coming!"

I stand on tiptoe to drape the shift across the garment rod. "You deaf old badger."

Gwinny props herself on her elbows and watches me fidget and fuss with the shift. Mistress Tipley says it'll only be another few days ere she's well enough to get out of my bed and resume her duties.

"Do I look ill to you?" I ask Gwinny. "I could pinch my cheeks to redden them. And I can hoarse up my voice."

Gwinny shakes her head.

"Ahhh, you're right. He'd make me go even if it meant dragging myself from my deathbed. Anything to nuzzle up to those rotten *honesti*."

"You—don't want to go?" Gwinny sounds surprised.

"By all the saints, no!" I step into my felt slippers because I'll get an earful should I arrive barefoot. "I'd rather muck every pig-keep in Caernarvon."

Gwinny regards me with a mule-skinner's measuring gaze. "She'll make you one of them. Townhouse lady, servants all around."

"It's what my father wants." I scuff my heel. "He'd see me one of them."

Gwinny draws back, frowning.

"Cecily! *Now!*"

I tuck stray threads under my cuffs. I may not know my lord from your Grace, but I was raised with enough courtesy not to mention someone's ragged cuffs or call her father a hamhanded oaf.

Bootsteps creak on stairs.

I grab my cloak and fly for the door. My father glares me a warning as I hurry past.

On my way down Shire Hall Street, I drag my feet. I count chuckholes. I watch shiny green flies buzz over horse apples. For one sweet stone's throw, fifty-four steps if I make them small and Lady de Coucy–sanctioned, I can do what I will.

AFTER she's gone, shift—ow—margin—ow—by margin—ow—till I'm facing her coffer, her garment pole, the tiny shuttered window.

The brat will be gone till Nones, and she'll return in the foulest humor. The master will lecture her on how her ill temper is imprudent since it may offend her benefactor. He would have his privileges go straight to the bone, not merely lie skin-deep. He is *novi,* but men like him rarely stay *novi* for long.

Were it anyone but the brat, I might pity her.

Till Nones, then, peace.

Awakened by a shuff-shuff far away. The chamber is bitterly cold, even with the hall brazier brought up by Margaret. The sun's slant is narrower now, like a child's slice of pie. Not much peace left. Close my eyes. Flatten my hands beneath my chest for warmth.

Shuff-shuff. Shuff-shuff.

That had best not be what I think it is.

Grit to my feet. Handswidth by handswidth. Glide to the window as if my spine is kindling.

Gruffydd is threshing barley in the shed. Shuff-shuff as the flail comes down, sings across the floorboards, snaps up.

And she'll be home any moment now.

Too risky to shout. Cannot whistle. Work my fingers around the edge of the shutter and bang it against the house until Gruffydd pauses, glances around, then looks up. He grins like a sunrise, waves the flail.

Belowstairs, the front door slams and the brat's shrill voice rings out for the master.

Cringe my arm up in tiny jagged bursts, jab a thumb at the rearyard door.

Gruffydd frowns, makes a bewildered gesture.

Belowstairs, the master calls the brat into the hall. He bids her look in on me ere she starts her spinning or sewing or what-have-you, and listen for the laborer in the rearyard to be finished so the master can pay him.

Fling one last helpless finger at the rearyard door as Gruffydd steps out of the shed and shrugs expansively.

The stairs begin to creak, footfall by footfall.

Turn from the window. Lurch toward the bed. Must get clear ere she makes it up here, catches me looking.

Because then she will puzzle it out.

And Gruffydd will get worse again by tenscore at her hands.

Shuff-shuff. He's back to flailing. Shuff-shuff. The master has all kinds of work. Shuff-shuff. Say them nay and reap the whirlwind.

By the time the stairs fall silent, I'm on the bed facing the wall. Feigning sleep despite the agony spreading through my back. And praying to any saint who's listening.

Shuff-shuff. Go pick up your spinning. Your sewing. Shuff-shuff. For Christ's sake, leave him be.

The stairs begin to creak again, growing softer as she descends. She tells the master she's going to check on the laborer's progress.

Oh, little one. I tried.

Shuff—

How dare you look at me like that? Her voice is a whip-crack, like leather against tender skin. You'll study your lessons or you'll be very sorry.

Grip the brat's bed linens. Bury my face in them, so I cannot hear her bait my brother. Press tighter, so no one can hear me weep.

MY FATHER storms into the house bareheaded and reeking of smoke. His tunic is singed and his face is blackened with what seems to be soot. As he grumbles through the hall, what he mutters is not fit for my ears, so I try to catch every black word of it.

"Water," he growls over his shoulder as he clumps abovestairs. "Hot."

Charming. I get Mistress Tipley to haul up a basin of steaming water.

At suppertime, my father huffs into the hall wearing a clean tunic and surcote. His face and hands are pink-scrubbed, but he still smells faintly of smoke.

I don't tell him this. Instead I pour him some ale and ask, "Do you think it might rain?"

"Hope not. There's to be a hanging."

Just my fortune. Finally something interesting happens, and I haven't a thing to wear.

My father has a faint ring of purple shadowing his right eye. He obviously did not scrub his face as thoroughly as he thought.

The gallows stands on the market common, and it'll be nearly impossible to get a good view. All of Caernarvon has turned out to see two poor devils hang.

On the mill bridge, there's a man in a trencher-shaped helm wearing a white tunic crossed in red. He rests one hand on the pommel of the sword displayed plainly at his hip. At the end of the bridge, I can see two more men in white tunics, and another few near the gallows. It's easy to spot them because people skirt them like they've got the pox.

Even the castle garrison have come to watch the hanging. I'm pleased the king saw fit to grant them leave.

In Coventry they hanged a thief once, and the crowd bawled loud enough to deafen a post. But this hanging is curiously silent. There's no baying and howling, despite the size of the crowd. Every soul in the Welshry must be on the market common.

I draw closer to my father.

When we reach the end of the mill bridge, two men-at-arms fall into step on either side of us. My father opens his mouth, but one of them shakes his head curtly.

"Save your breath. Captain's orders."

My father cuts his eyes over the crowd. "Surely they wouldn't dare. Not in the very shadow of the walls."

The man-at-arms shrugs. "Best not to tempt them. Besides, it's not just you, is it?" And he tips his chin toward me.

My father grunts something like agreement, and now the crowds part for us as the men-at-arms lead us to the foot of the gallows, to the place usually reserved for victims of the condemned.

I brought some rotten cabbage from the shed wrapped in old sackcloth, but now I'm not sure I want to throw it. Not up here. Not in front of every soul in the Welshry. Not even with men-at-arms at my elbows.

There's a crunch of wheels on dirt as the condemned are rolled toward the green on a cart. I hop and weave, but it's no use. All I can see are two dirty hoods.

I let the cabbage roll off my fingertips and stomp it into the mud.

"What did they do, Papa?" I ask, wiping my hands on the sackcloth.

My father does not answer, but one of the men-at-arms mutters, "Crimes against the borough, demoiselle. Don't worry, though. You're perfectly safe."

He says this as he grips and regrips his sword-hilt and runs his eyes over the crowd.

The cart heaves to a halt before the gallows. The condemned stumble out and drag themselves up the steps, closely flanked by more men-at-arms. Both prisoners' faces are streaked with soot, as if they escaped a house fire on the breath of God.

Two nooses stand out against the crisp sky. The condemned stand beneath the dangling ropes.

The crowd is buzzing now. Not hollering. Not baying for blood. Muttering. Fidgeting. And though those gathered keep a healthy distance from the men-at-arms, I can feel thousands of eyes on us up here, in the very shadow of the gallows.

Two men-at-arms no longer seems like a lot, even though they're built like mastiffs and armed with daggers and broadswords.

The hangman cinches a noose tight over the neck of the first man, then the second. The first one says something in Welsh, something calm and bold, something that redoubles the crowd's murmur and turns more eyes to us than ever.

I grip my father's elbow.

The hangman puts a hood over each man's head, then steps back to the tether. There's a drawn-out swiff of rope and both men sail into the air, wriggling like worms on a fishhook.

The crowd falls utterly still, as if they're deep in prayer.

My father insists we stay till the bodies cease swaying. When we finally leave, much of the crowd remains. Some are kneeling as if it's a vigil.

The men-at-arms escort us to our dooryard. One offers to stand post outside for a few days, but my father thanks him and says him nay.

"This," my father says, gesturing to the house, "I know they wouldn't dare."

The man-at-arms shifts beneath his leather armor. "I've been here long enough to know better than to guess at what the Welsh will and will not dare."

My father laughs and sends him and his fellows on their way. I watch the men-at-arms disappear around the top of Shire Hall Street, then I go into the rearyard and put both hands on the walls that keep things like sooty felons and the need for armed guards safely without.

When I arrive at the Coucy house for my se'ennight's bad-mouthing, I find the lady de Coucy arranging strips of linen and foul-smelling pottles in a basket.

"Oh, you're leaving." I clasp my hands and study the floor so she cannot see my good cheer. "Beg your pardon. I'll just be off."

She pulls a bright cloth over the basket and reaches for her cloak. "You'll be coming with me. Emmaline, too. It's nearing Mistress Glover's time."

"Time for what?"

"For her child to be born, silly girl."

I step back. "I—I'll just be in the way."

"Nonsense, Cecily. Helping at a birth is one of the most important things a good woman of Caernarvon does."

It's Mistress Glover's hundredth child. Like as not she just has to sneeze for the baby to come out.

Emmaline takes my elbow. "Mayhap we'll be allowed to hold the baby!"

Mayhap I'll be allowed to hide in the garden shed.

Mistress Sandys is already at the Glover house when we

arrive, as is Mistress Pole. They're fluttering up and down the stairs bearing lengths of linen and basins of water. Someone has brought a relic to aid in the birth—a girdle that Emmaline swears belonged to Saint Margaret—and draped it reverently over the mantel.

The moment the lady de Coucy walks into the Glover house, she takes charge of everything. She sends Emmaline abovestairs with some rosewater for Mistress Glover's brow, and she gives me the task of opening and untying. Leaving even a single knot tied might tangle up the baby or wrap the cord about its neck, and a closed door or shutter could stop up the birth canal. It would be all my fault. So I throw open every shutter and untie every knot in the house, down to the laces in Saint Margaret's girdle on the mantel.

After I finish, I edge into the shadows of the hearth corner. Borough ladies wick by me, eyes to their footing or their burdens. Betimes they mutter in hushed voices that put me too much in mind of a sickroom for my liking.

I haven't a paternoster, but I whisper a prayer for Mistress Glover.

Then there's a thin, spindly cry from abovestairs. A baby's cry.

Emmaline appears at the bottom of the stairs. Her hands are clasped and she's bouncing like a wagon on the low road. "Oh, come and see, Cecily. He's just the sweetest baby in all of Christendom!"

Babies ruin your garden, even when they aren't yours. They get lost and worry you ill, even when they aren't yours.

But I follow Emmaline abovestairs and into the bedchamber, where Mistress Sandys has just lifted the tiny baby dripping from a basin. She dries him off and wraps him tightly in crisp white linen, then tucks him into his mother's elbow.

The baby is a deep glowing pink. He isn't stinky or screamy. He looks weary but content.

Emmaline shyly asks if she can hold the baby. Mistress Glover hands him up and Emmaline settles him in the crook of her arm as if he's wine from water.

"Would you like to hold him next, Cecily?" Mistress Glover asks.

I shake my head violently and the women laugh, but not in a mocking way. Then Mistress Pole says she'd never even held a baby until the moment her eldest was placed in her arms, and Mistress Pannel cackles when she says she tiptoed around her eldest's cradle for a whole fortnight after he was born, afraid to wake him. She'd have to pick him up then, she explains, and she was sure she'd drop him and break every bone in his body.

The good borough ladies laugh and brag and best one another with outlandish stories, and it isn't long ere we've all drawn stools around Mistress Glover's bed. Someone produces a flask of claret and starts it around. Mistress Glover smiles and closes her eyes while Emmaline hums a lullaby and sways the baby like a dancing partner.

Mistress Pole places the flask in my hand without thinking twice. She does not seem to notice that I'm a *novi* who will never be one of them. The wine is strong and sweet. Not bitter at all.

I've saved what I can of my tattered wardrobe. I manage to piece together two shifts, two pairs of hose, and my bedrobe. What's left is a mass of fibers that cannot even be unraveled, tied together, rerolled into a skein, and rewoven. They are finely spun, expensive rags.

So I do what you do with rags. I bundle them up for the ragman.

I find him at the market one Saturday, the same wizened ruffian whom Gwinny and I avenged when Levelooker Pluver was plying his odious trade. We surely got the best of Pluver that day. I laughed like a madman when Pluver finally found his hat crushed beneath that hog's filthy trotters.

Neither Alice nor Agnes would ever have done anything so clever and brave. They would have pressed hands to mouths and fretted about being caught.

The ragman offers me a penny for my bundle. I tell him I cannot take less than five, and show him the quality of the rags.

He chitters like a jay, rubs them, then asks toothlessly, "What possessed you to stove up such fineries?"

I pet the rose wool. I could be *wearing* this gown, and thinking about it still makes me want to kick something.

But I toe a line in the dirt and quietly reply, "I know not what I was thinking."

Gwinny is finally well enough to leave. Mistress Tipley tries to persuade her that it's too late for her to walk home, that the men with blackened faces do terrible things to collaborators, but Gwinny shakes her head firmly.

She totters into the hall, stiff like a lance. I'm grinding bits of beechnut hull for dyestuff. She nods to me as she fumbles with her cloakstrings.

"Gwinny."

She's halfway out the door, hands already balled in her cloak against the cold, and she winces as she sidles back into the hall.

I put aside the beechnuts and approach her. She lifts her chin. She does not cringe, but she seems to be bracing for a blow.

I untangle her hand from her cloak and lay her wages in her palm. Three pennies that catch firelight.

Gwinny gapes at the coins. The bird-look falters and she begins blinking rapidly.

Then she inclines her head, fists a hand about the pennies, and disappears into the deepening winter twilight.

MAKE no haste. Couldn't if I wanted to, but I don't. What awaits me at the steading will be the same regardless of haste.

It'll be bad. Scavengers will have been at the corpse.

She'll have died alone, weeping for her babies.

That is what the brat will pay for. Whatever the cost.

Uphill takes months and years. Must move in tiny margins. Mustn't bend. Scabs are still raw enough to tear.

Cannot smell the corpse yet. Mayhap the cold holds it down.

Limp inside and blink. There's fire.

Go cold all over because fire means Gruffydd has foregone labor to tend Mam and it'll be se'ennights ere he sees even half a chance at a penny again.

But it's not Gruffydd who rises from the shadows. It's Fanwra from down the vale, and she gestures shyly to Mam.

"She's a tough old girl," Fanwra says in her wispy little voice that makes me think of baby birds and dry grass.

"You're kind to come."

Fanwra worries her ratty sleeves. "Gruffydd asked me to stay with her. There's not much I'd deny him."

Her words hang there, waiting for me to dignify them,

to bless her devotion. Not in this lifetime, though, nor in any spare moment of the hereafter.

"You're kind to come."

Fanwra finally flutters toward the door, muttering well-wishes and prayers for Mam. The moment she's gone, I sink in fits and measures to my knees while keeping my mincemeat back in a rigid column.

Mam whimpers for water. The leather bucket is empty. Look at it and look at it, as if one wrung-out plea will make it fill itself. Then rise, every margin a blade of fire, and edge downhill toward the creek with the bucket swaying from my hand like a hanged man.

They come at night. Gruffydd goes with them. He darkens his face with ashes and pulls Da's spear from the rafters without flinch or hesitation, as if he'd known where it was all along. His eyes scream like jewels from the soot.

The others say little. They stand without the door, flat against the steading. A mass of shadows, men and weapons, curves and angles and blades.

Don't see them. Don't know them. Cannot betray them.

Da went out. Da never came back. They left his body on the walls till naught but scraps were left.

Gruffydd wears no cloak. Cloaks catch and snag on brush. He shivers already.

My little brother. The boy who once wept for injured

hares and maidens ill-served in nursery tales. Now there's down on his cheeks. Scars across both hands.

Da went out, called up by his prince. Da stood with the prince when he fell at Cefn-y-bedd, and all Wales with them. He stood after, while men submitted in droves to save themselves, their lands. He stood against their king till English hanged him from the walls of Caernarvon.

They come at night and Gruffydd follows, disappears into darkness.

A SE'ENNIGHT after Candlemas, we always feed the poor in honor of my mother.

At Edgeley, tenants filled the great trestle tables in the hall and spilled out into the yard. Every man, woman, and child in the village left full to bursting. Meat and ale, bread and cheese. Wine for the reeve. Cakes for the children. Whatever was left we sent home with each family, wrapped up in linsey.

When we return from Candlemas Mass, I ask my father how we'll feed the poor this year when our house is so small.

"Oh, sweeting, it'll be hard enough to keep our bodies and souls together till spring." He runs a hand through his hair. "And it isn't as if this is Edgeley, where the tenants would be at the door with pitchforks should I think to go against custom."

I frown. "You mean we aren't going to feed the poor this year?"

"I'll pray for them, sweeting. These people aren't my tenants. There's no custom binding me to them."

The custom doesn't bind us to the tenants. It binds us to her.

But he's got that don't-make-me-cuff-you look about him, so I duck my head like a good girl and say naught. Instead I wait for him to put on his boots and pick up his questioning cudgel and go out to officer the mills. I hide behind the garden shed until Mistress Tipley lumbers into the yard privy, then I dart into the kitchen and liberate three big loaves from the trestle. I put on my cloak and find Gwinny plaiting hemp in the hearth corner.

"Can you walk? I'm going without the walls and I'd have you with me."

"What for?"

"I'm feeding the poor."

Gwinny's eyes jerk up as though I've crowned myself dunghill princess. "You are not."

My mother had hair the color of a new-brushed roan. She was always moving, never still, and she walked chin up with a jingle of keys, with Salvo ever her shadow.

I hold up the bread.

Gwinny lays aside her task and rises in stiff margins. "If you say it's so, it must be so."

"Does that mean you're coming?"

Gwinny smiles in a way I'm not sure I like. "Wouldn't miss it."

It's rising Tierce. Midmorning is achingly cold and the color of wallstone. The bread in the satchel against my back is no longer warm and grows heavier by the moment. The serjeant at the trestle marks Gwinny at my elbow, but I meet his eyes steadily until he steps aside and lets us through.

Outside the gate, I drift a few paces, then stop ere I even

get across the quay bridge. I didn't think this through very well. I haven't the first idea where to even look for the poor.

"You still want to feed the poor?" Gwinny stares into the distance, her hair snarling into her eyes. I nod and she says, "Come."

She leads me toward the market common. Along the trodden toll path, huddled like piles of wet laundry awaiting the clothesline, are whole families with cheeks like slack sails, and graybeards with fingers all knuckle. Dozens of men, women, and children, and I have but three loaves.

"The poor," Gwinny says expansively, gesturing. She's appraising me sidelong, not quite smiling.

She's waiting for me to run away screaming.

The poor are ashen and malodorous. They're not like the poor of Edgeley. Those were people I knew. Every one of them. Down to their livestock. They were a part of Edgeley and therefore mine. But these poor wretches are living skeletons, something straight out of a sermon on sin. If I stay too long in their company, I'll end up one of them.

But I'll not give Gwinny the satisfaction of leaving. Besides, I'm not here for her.

I slide my satchel off my shoulder and fumble with the bread. Nearby is a gaunt mother of two tiny redheads who are covered in rashy scabs. I tear off a chunk of bread and hand it to her.

She gapes and stammers something to me in a voice that sways like a bird on the wing, then breaks the bread in two and hands one piece to each child. She closes her eyes as they gulp it down.

Some of the poor, the stronger ones, rise and lurch toward us, and Gwinny says something to them in Welsh in a sharp, no-nonsense voice. They stop and retrace their steps, some mutinous, some hopeful.

"I told them to make a queue," Gwinny says to me, "and that you'd go along and give everyone something."

So I do. I break off pieces as equally as I can, placing bread in every palm that's put toward me. They eat as if they've never seen bread ere this. As if they'll never see it again.

When the bread is gone and my satchel twice tipped for every last crumb, I smile and shrug and look to Gwinny to say something to them. She does, and when she's finished, I gesture to the city gate and she falls into step at my elbow.

I cannot recall ever running out of food when we fed the poor at Edgeley.

"This isn't even the worst of it," Gwinny says quietly. "These are the ones with strength enough to crawl to the common to beg."

My mother was always moving, never idle, and had she been starving on the roadside with me beneath her arm, she would have gone without so I could feel full just for a moment. She would have wept to see me hungry, to have no way to feed me.

"Why?" Gwinny asks, so quiet the wind nearly takes it away.

"Why feed the poor?" I ask, and she nods. "Er, because they're hungry?"

Gwinny frowns as though she's heard me wrong. "Because they're hungry."

I nod firmly, because I don't trust my voice to speak of my mother. Especially not today.

Back at the townhouse, my father is roaring at Mistress Tipley for taking the bread that was to last us the better part of a fortnight, and Mistress Tipley is cowering before the hearth and blubbering that she didn't take the bread and cannot imagine where it has gone.

As usual, it's up to me to make things right.

When my father pauses to take a breath, I clear my throat. "Papa, I know what became of the bread."

All three turn toward me—my father in rage, Mistress Tipley in mute hope, and Gwinny in disbelief. But I'm no fool. I'll feed the poor, but I'll not take a thrashing for them.

I blame the one creature in the house guaranteed never to feel my father's temper.

"Please don't be wroth with him, Papa," I say, "but I saw him coming out of the kitchen with the bread in his mouth, and when he saw me, he just gobbled it down ere I could get it away from him. I tied him up after that, but he must have eaten the other loaves ere I caught him. He's just so hungry, poor beast. Like the rest of us."

My father's color is still high, but his fists are sliding to his sides and relaxing. He looses a long breath and mutters something to Mistress Tipley that might be an apology or permission to depart. Either way, she bobs her head and all but flies out of the hall.

I go to the rear storage chamber to fetch my father a mug of ale, but when I see the level in the barrel, bring him half a mug instead. My father sulks on one of the trestle benches and glares at Salvo, who lies against the warm hearthstones in dreamless sleep.

We eat naught for dinner, and for supper there is only watered maslin and some old squishy turnips that smell like unwashed hose.

I bite my tongue, though. If I'm hungry, someone else isn't, and I'm that much closer to her.

Rain and cold have killed the winter crop. Not just here, but on Anglesey, too. The barges have stopped poling in after Nones.

The prices at the market jump to twice and thrice the summer rates. On one Saturday alone, there are three knife-point robberies and a whole rash of petty thefts.

Even though no victims were English and none of the assaults were carried out on market grounds, my father assigns one of his mill enforcers to escort Mistress Tipley and me when we market. He is called Geraint, and he has curls that beg to have hands run through them. He is the tallest of the mill enforcers by a head and muscled like a bulldog.

I must admit I like having Geraint along. Not only is he fair to look upon, the toll-table queue falls away like meat from a bone when we approach. So do the poor who still crowd the market path. The ones strong enough to crawl there.

I pray for them, then I thank God Almighty and my father and the millers of Caernarvon for the modest surplus in our rearyard shed.

Not long after Prime, Gwinny comes into the workroom, where I'm mending a massive tear in one of my father's tunics. "The lady de Coucy sent for you."

I groan. "But it isn't Monday! Why in thimbles does she want to see me *now?*"

Gwinny shrugs, but I don't expect an answer from her. And the good Lord knows my father will raise Cain should I ignore a summons from the oh-so-important Coucys, so I put on my cloak and head up the road.

A mousy servant answers my knock and shows me to the solar. The lady de Coucy is spinning, so I discreetly clear my throat. She looks up and startles.

"Saints! Child, what are you doing here?"

I bite down on the smart-mouthed retort that will make its way back to my father and end in trouble I don't want. "You sent for me."

The lady de Coucy slowly shakes her head as if I'm a babbling halfwit or speaking Welsh or both. "Why under Heaven would I send for you? Now be gone. I'm busy."

"But . . . you . . ." I stifle a grin and nod politely and hustle out of the room ere she changes her mind. I'm so delighted that I've been spared an afternoon of harangue that I'm halfway up High Street ere I reckon why Gwinny would tell me the lady de Coucy wanted to see me when she obviously didn't.

When I get to the townhouse, Gwinny is shivering in the gutter out front. I approach her, but ere I can speak she says, "You're wanted at the Glover house. Mistress Glover hopes you'll mind the baby while she sleeps."

"Mayhap in a moment," I tell her, "because first I'll know why you . . . told me . . . What is that sound?"

Shuff-shuff. Shuff-shuff.

I crane my neck to peer down the greenway at the garden shed, but Gwinny puts herself firmly in my path.

"I must have been mistaken. Mistress Glover said to hurry."

It's a flail against the shed floor. And that can mean only one thing.

"How do I know you're not, er, *mistaken* again?" I ask in a voice of honey. "Mayhap you should run over there and be sure."

Gwinny shakes her head. "I'm not. Just go."

She's standing like a mastiff between me and the greenway. I move to pass her and she puts herself in my path. I slide to one side and she matches me, smooth and even, as if we're dancing.

And it dawns on me.

"You don't want me in the rearyard, do you?" I fold my

arms and smile. "That's why you sent me to the Coucy house. And that's why you'd trap me under the Glover baby."

Gwinny lifts her chin. She makes no reply, but she's girding herself as if she'll tackle me if need be.

I smile again, slyly. "You're sweet on him, aren't you?"

"No! I—I—"

Gwinny is usually so calm and deliberate. It's amusing to watch her redden and stammer in a mix of Welsh and English.

At length she closes her mouth, draws a few long breaths. "To think you almost had me hoodwinked. With your pitiful nod to justice and your feeding the poor. More fool I, thinking you were any different from the rest. Especially the likes of that shrew in the gilded townhouse you cannot complain of enough."

I stiffen. "I am nothing like her!"

"You will be." Gwinny narrows her eyes. "You're already well on your way."

"Name one thing she does that I do!"

"Murder!"

"I—*What?* Are you *mad?*"

Gwinny's words are clipped and haggard. "Your hands won't be on the rope, but mark me, his blood will be on your hands. A fine little game. You just love your little game. To *Hell* with you *and* your Goddamn game!"

The blasphemy is shocking enough that I step away, into the gutter. Gwinny looks a heartbeat away from weeping or throwing a fist, but one wrong word and she'll do much worse.

"Whose blood?" I gesture toward the rearyard. "His?"

She doesn't answer, but she doesn't have to.

"What is he to you?" I ask quietly, because she's crying now, but by no means is she getting out of my way.

"My brother," she chokes, "and he's all I've got, rot you! He's all I've got and he's going to end up dead because of you!"

We're in the churchyard, my father and I, and before us is her grave, freshly mounded with dark damp earth. My little white hand is tight in his big brown one, and he's holding it hard enough to crunch my bones to powder. He whispers, mayhap to me and mayhap to himself, "Just you and me now, sweeting. You're all I've got."

I draw back, pull my cloak about my shoulders. Gwinny's stance relaxes but she never takes her eyes off me. "What did my brother ever do to you, to deserve death?"

"But he *doesn't* deserve death!"

"*Then why are you doing this to him?*"

I toe the mud that's caked on my shoe. "Er . . . he needed to . . . I . . . well . . ."

Gwinny presses a hand to her forehead. "So it's true. You'd call down the wrath of Caernarvon on an innocent man just for the sport of it. Jesus wept. You should be grateful all I could do was rip up your worthless clothes."

For an instant I see scraps all over my chamber. Scraps, when once I had gowns.

Gwinny took the whipping of her life—for vengeance.

"I—I never would have let it go that far!" I protest. "You must believe that! I would have put a stop to it ere they *killed* him!"

Gwinny swipes at her streaming eyes and cries, "How?"

"Well, I'd just—just—"

And I shut my mouth. Because I am too old for nutting. Not old enough for Catherning. Girls do not go mumming. Walk this way your Grace my lord—

I turn on my heel and hurry into the townhouse, down the corridor and abovestairs and onto my bed and under the bedclothes. The window is shuttered, but I can still hear the muffled shuff-shuff of the flail hitting the shed floor.

1294

ASSUMPTIONTIDE

TO

SAINT JOHN'S EVE

ONE of the tenscore Glover lads appears in my garden unannounced at dawn and spades the whole thing up. He is sullen and grumbly, but he makes a good shift of it. It's early for planting, but I take a chance and sow the fresh cold earth with seeds and cuttings. Ere midmorning, there are neat rows marked with stakes and tiny linen flags.

It's hard to make things grow here, harder than Coventry and twice as hard as Edgeley, where everything green sprang up even where it wasn't wanted. But there's something about coaxing life from ground that shrugs at you, that makes you tend it with fish guts and holy water, coddling it as if it's an old sick hound. It matters more. You harvest every blade and seed and grain. You cherish what the earth bestows.

Soon I will have tansy, rue, and coltsfoot.

This year, I will put up a baby fence.

It's Easter. I've been a whole year in the king's borough of Caernarvon.

My wretched uncle Roger is still hale and still lord of Edgeley. The Crusader sun has not yet finished him off. There's still hope, though, for there's been no smug announcement of a birth or even a quickening. My new aunt is not much older than I, but may she remain childless till she's gray as a mule's back-end.

My father offers frankpledge for our street every month and never misses Court Baron. He says he finds borough service most rewarding. He swaggers down Shire Hall like lord of the manor. It's as if he's forgotten Edgeley even exists.

That cur Edward Mercer has kept his distance, but he hasn't taken an interest in another girl. Mayhap he is pining for me. None of the *honesti* girls looks twice at him, and their fathers are never far away when he's about.

Edward Mercer is still shivery-fair to look upon, especially when he flashes that carefree smile, but the shivery only lasts a moment and does not blur my vision.

Mistress Tipley still holds the keys and directs the kitchen. I've not given up, though.

We walk the liberty stones, every burgess and his family. The mayor leads the procession bearing his big mace, the priest at his elbow flicks holy water, and we all tromp dutifully after, trying to keep the mud from our finest clothes.

Up rise the city walls, steep and solid and grand like holy Jerusalem. The view from down here is so different from that atop the walls. Down here there are no glowing rooftops, no endless fields. Down here there is only mud and stone. Up there is utterly out of reach.

Not till I pass through the gates do I feel like myself again.

Just after Compline, my father calls, "Come here, sweeting. Come look at this."

My chamber is dark and I'm just about to undress for bed. I put my obviously restitched bedrobe over my shift and slip through the curtain to my father's chamber.

He's at the window. The shutters are flung wide and the sky beyond is a rich, deep blue, nearly fallen to black. The land is black, though, and across it lie hundreds of flickering sparks. The tiny dots of orange cover the ridge and spread like pinpricks into the dark distant hills.

I lean against my father's shoulder. He's warm and solid and smells faintly of horse. "It's pretty. What is it?"

"The Welsh herdsmen are burning carcasses," my father replies. "Every beast that has murrain must be killed and its body burned."

"So much fire for one little animal."

"We would not see one beast burning, sweeting. Those are bonfires. Dozens of animals must be destroyed. Hundreds."

My father puts his arm about me and I lay my cheek against his shoulder while the hills glitter and twinkle as if all the stars have fallen.

When time comes to hire a man to clean out the shed, I send one of the Glover lads for Griffith. The poor wretch comes up Shire Hall Street like a soul into Purgatory.

He knows what happens to him here. And yet he comes anyway. He dares not cross me. The cost is too high.

The cost of many things in Caernarvon is too high. That's a lesson both of us have studied.

I bid Mistress Tipley give Griffith his instructions, then I spy on him from my chamber window as he carries crates and sacks from the shed.

At first Griffith cringes with every snap and rustle. He even drops a crate when Salvo lurches outside to drink from the rain barrel. But after a time his whole body loosens. He ceases looking over his shoulder and lingering within the shelter of the shed. He shoulders his burdens with an easy grace that's lovely to watch. He even whistles. When he sweeps the shed floor, he twirls the broom like a dancing partner and flourishes his ratty cloak.

I withdraw two pennies from my father's strongbox and bid Mistress Tipley give them to Griffith for his labor.

Her eyes get big. "Twopence? For merely cleaning the shed?"

"And whatever bread that's idle in the kitchen," I tell her firmly.

"There isn't—"

"Give him mine. I'll go without."

When the old cow trundles outside, I hurry abovestairs and watch from the window. Mistress Tipley hands the coin to Griffith along with a linen-wrapped parcel. Griffith glances about furtively as if something's going to pounce, then takes a whiff of the parcel. He says something disbelieving to Mistress Tipley and she shrugs.

Then Griffith inclines his head and departs through the greenway, carefully stepping over my garden.

I'm curiously warm. As if there's something sweet and delicious baking deep in my vitals.

As if I'm holding the reins of the whole world.

It's raining. Again. Little wonder naught grows here. We ought to sow the fields with fish.

I'm finally ready to stitch. It took innumerable sharpenings of my charcoal stick and three washings, but the design is right at last.

It's the Holy Family. They're on their way to Nazareth. Saint Joseph is holding the Christ Child while the Virgin prays at the roadside. The road winds through a stand of thick woods, and beyond the woods is the sea. High in one corner is Caernarvon, castle and town.

It took us a whole winter, but we turned out an altar cloth that all but marched off the linen. Three of us, shoulder to shoulder before a single frame, giggling, pushing, drinking cider till we lined up for the privy. All three of us together for the last time, not knowing to cherish it, thinking we'd be together forever.

But they're lost to me, and Emmaline de Coucy cannot

sew a straight seam to keep her soul from Purgatory. A pity I cannot ask Gwinny. My undergarments are stitched as tight as wine casks.

So this piece will be my own. It will take me longer, but every stem stitch and knot, every curl and vine and wallstone, will be mine alone.

I sort through the thread Nicholas gave me and choose a deep brown for Saint Joseph's robe.

THE brat is in an ill temper. She's had me sweeping and tidying the hall since sunup, cleaning out corners I've cleaned thrice.

There's a knock at midmorning, and in come the Shrewcys. Mother and daughter, and both have baskets over their arms.

The brat smiles and bids them enter, but she's stiff as a days-old corpse and her smile is too cheerful.

Stand in the corner as she bade me.

Mother Shrewcy wrinkles her nose and asks has the brat never heard of garlands? The brat's smile goes frozen. She opens her mouth in a way that makes me brace for the scolding. But the brat ducks her head and says she merely forgot and begs Mother Shrewcy's pardon.

Saints, that I was fool enough to agree to your education, grumbles Mother. At least your boorish father knew enough to beg the right woman. You'd best not shame me, girl. I mean it.

As Daughter Shrewcy entreats the brat to try harder, the brat's ancient dog limps into the hall and noses Daughter's hand. Daughter shrieks and whips her hand away, pulls out a handkerchief, wipes her fingers.

Send that mongrel out of doors, Mother snaps.

The brat pets the dog's gray head and says, The poor creature is as old as the hills. The damp's not good for his bones.

Put him out, says Mother firmly, and the brat squares up like a toll-table serjeant.

We are nowhere near your grubby little manor, Mother goes on in a blade-cold voice. Those who think to become *honesti* will do well to remember where they are and whose favor they need.

The brat blinks hard, kneels, puts her arms around the dog's neck. Forgive me, she whispers to the beast, then walks it at its shambling pace into the rearyard.

She's gone for many long moments. Slip into the rear chamber, peek into the yard. The brat idles near the kitchen, knotting, reknotting, and unknotting a length of rope around the dog's neck.

Mother and Daughter in the hall discuss whether the brat's table linen ought to be replaced or mended.

The brat brings a pan of water to the dog, pets its head, picks at tangles in its hair.

Daughter Shrewcy comes to the rear door and tells the brat that Mother Shrewcy is waiting and it's time to show the master her walking.

The brat heaves herself up and scowls murder at the kitchen. Then she fixes that false, pained smile and trudges inside.

Have seen that look ere this. Know it, down to my white-hot core.

She walks the way they tell her. She holds her feet, her shoulders, her hands just as they do. The master looks on as if she's made of gold. The brat's smile does not change, unless it grows sharper. As if anyone within an armslength would end up bloodied should that look leave her face and flow through her fists.

She could be one of them. Townhouse lady, servants all around.

It's what everyone wants but her.

BECAUSE THERE is the off chance I might enjoy myself, my father has forbidden me from Midsummer porch vigil at Saint Mary's.

"Midnight is too late for you to be out alone," my father says. "If I didn't have Watch and Ward, I'd be happy to escort you."

"You're *always* on Watch and Ward," I sulk.

"They've stepped up the guard. The whole castlery is a tinderbox since the murrain, to say naught of the Welshry. And then there's the October collection of the tax of the fifteenth drawing nearer. I'm sorry about porch vigil, sweeting. Mayhap next year."

"But Emmaline de Coucy is going to porch vigil!" This is a lie, but it's a lie square in the pride.

My father straightens his cloak. "I believe I said you nay. Don't make me repeat myself."

I put on my best air of offended but obedient dignity, for I have every intention of sneaking out after Vespers and sitting on the church porch until the souls pass by. I want to know right away if my uncle Roger will die in the coming year.

I can barely believe my fortune when my cousin Henry rides up in a splatter of mud a whole month early. I sail out to greet my dearest cousin, call for a Glover lad to take his horse to the common stable and for Gwinny to bring him the coldest buttermilk in the house. When Henry is resting in the big chair with his feet up and his throat wet, I ask him pretty as you please if he plans to attend the Midsummer festivities in our fair town.

"Would that I could, Cesspool," Henry replies, "but the foremost *honesti* will be here tonight to discuss my prospects for taking the privileges."

Thimbles and pins! Not even Fortune will take my side.

My father leaves explicit instructions to me in Henry's presence that under no circumstances am I to leave the house for porch vigil and that it'll be Henry's hide as well as mine if he is disobeyed.

Henry warns me with a single look, then bids Mistress Tipley fetch our second-to-last cask of ale from the cellar.

I defy my father by sitting in the rearyard and throwing hempseed into the mud. It's supposed to grow and my future husband is supposed to come rake it behind me. All it's doing is giving the pigling something to root for.

At dusk, Henry calls me inside and banishes me to my chamber with an awkward but genuine apology and the assurance that the hall will be no place for me tonight. And judging by the houndlike singing and hallooing and laughing that fills the house as the pillars of Caernarvon arrive to discuss Henry's prospects, he may be right.

Exiled, I throw my shutters open and lean out my window as far as I dare. I can see only a shade of the rear wall of Saint Mary's, but mayhap I'll catch sight of the souls on their way to the porch. Mayhap my uncle's soul will be among them. Then my father will be back in possession of Edgeley. By Christmas I could be walking the same floorplanks my mother once trod, and Salvo could be buried at her feet when his time comes.

In an Ave, I'm bored.

So I sit at the top of the stairs and listen to the goings-on in the hall, trying to piece together how Henry is doing, how the burgesses are taking to him.

How good a chance there is that he will become our neighbor.

Apparently they took quite well to him. The *honesti* have extended an official invitation to my cousin Henry to consider the privileges of Caernarvon. He has accepted. He will take the oath at Christmas and move into the townhouse on Palace Street.

Henry goes on at length about how envious Nicholas is and how Nicholas swears as soon as he gets his spurs he'll come to Wales and take so much of that twopenny land that he won't be able to ride its boundaries in a day. Baby Henry has finally beaten Nicholas to something, but I'm still trying to catch them both.

Now that Henry will be our neighbor come Christmas, I cannot wait to show him the market and the Water Gate,

Saint Mary's and the wellheads and the place where the Seiont pools cold and quiet, where small fish come to nibble your toes.

The evening ere he leaves for Coventry, Henry clears his throat and casts about and does worse than ruin my life.

He ends it.

Henry ends my life with the black news that Thomas d'Edgeley was born to my wretched uncle Roger and his worthless slip of a wife on May Eve.

My father cheerfully throws on his cloak, seizes Henry by the elbow, and calls over his shoulder that they're off to the Boar's Head to drink to the babe's good health.

I sit at the empty table and stare into the dying hearthfire.

It's gone.

The snug little hall with its brand-new chimney, the glowing garden, the dovecote, the turn of stream where quiet fish would gather in a silvery cloud. The pasturage where goats would crowd their necks through the fence for a handful of clover. The churchyard with its ancient yews and graves. The swing, swaying from an oak limb, that my father made from a length of hemp and an old cart-slat.

Edgeley was to be mine. My mother promised all of it to me on my saint day when I turned seven and she let me carry the keys on a piece of twine tied about my waist from Prime till Compline. I could open every chest and door and lock. I spent every moment of that day at her side, hurrying to match her calm, swishing stride, and Salvo followed us both.

At Vespers I was hiding from her in the dovecote, clutching the keys together to keep them from clanking. She had the grooms combing the yard for me, as it was long past my bedtime. The poor lads called and called, but they were grown and had forgotten the best places to hide. I could have stayed where I was till the Last Trumpet, and I planned to. I could not bear for the day to end.

My father came out as far as the trough and promised me the whipping of my life should I not immediately present myself before him, but I held the keys tighter and moved not a margin.

My mother finally came into the yard herself, holding up the horn-paned lantern. "Cecily, sweeting, one day it will all be yours. Every post and barrel, and there won't be a day that goes by that those keys aren't at your belt. You must be patient."

One day felt like the morrow when she said it. I came out and put the big ring of keys in her keeping. And I did get the whipping of my life.

And ere the season turned, we buried her.

Edgeley is his now. The rotten usurper mewling at his girl-mother's breast. It's all his, every post and barrel.

Now we're stuck in Caernarvon. We're stuck here for good, and my father doesn't even seem to care.

Hywel shuffles to the steading door. For a moment I'm wroth, Dafydd sending his cousin to ply me with more fruitless talk of marriage. But Hywel looks hagridden, his eyes red and his face blotchy. He's been weeping.

"All of them," he whispers.

He loves them like children. He names them and weaves crowns of flowers for their horns.

Step away from the fire. "You had them up high. How could they have caught it?"

Hywel shrugs, scrubs a wrist over his eyes. "I know not. They're all dead. Sweating and staggering. Yours. Mine. Every beast in the vale."

They're all dead. Cattle. Goats. Sheep. The murrain leaves nothing on the hoof untouched. No meat. No milk. No butter. No cheese.

No food left but what's doled out in Crown measures for ten times its worth.

"Forgive me," Hywel whispers, as if it's his fault. Tears slide down his cheeks, winding through bristly beard-fuzz. "They all had to burn."

Beckon him in. Give him some mead. He refuses half an oatcake. Cannot eat, he mutters.

Best eat now. Soon enough we'll all be too hungry to care about the morrow.

A thrash. The stumble of feet. Something being dragged.

Awake. Instantly. The door-curtain wicks back to reveal a square of deep night-blue and a harsh silver wash of moonlight.

They've come. As they did for Dafydd. Cudgels and thatch everywhere.

On my feet, grappling for something heavy.

"Gwen, it's me!" Gruffydd's voice is strained, as if he's winded or bearing something heavy. "Help me. Right now."

Cannot move. Can barely breathe. The cooking pot slides out of my hand.

From the dark comes gasping. Harsh bursts of sound a man would make were he drowning.

Or hanging from an English rope.

"Gwenhwyfar!"

Kneel to stir up the coals. By the raft of sickly orange light, I can make out Gruffydd on his knees. Covered in blood.

Sweet. Merciful. Christ.

"Hssst! No fire! They'll be looking for light!"

Swipe up Mam's water and douse the struggling coals. A great billow of smoke rises with a hiss of steam and the stench of burn.

"No." Whisper is choked. "Oh, Christ, no."

"It's not my blood, Gwen. Please. He's dying. Help me."

For a long moment, all I can do is tremble.

Not his blood.

Then I feel my way across the steading, moving toward Gruffydd's voice. The disembodied gasps dry up as I near.

"What happened?" Even as the words come out, I bite my lip. The less I know, the better for all. "To him, I mean."

"Cut," Gruffydd replies tersely. "And never mind. He's gone. God rest his soul."

Bump into Gruffydd and kneel at his side. Press my shoulder against his.

"They got Cadwgan and Rhodri ap Tudur. Naught we could do. Bastards will hang them on the morrow. God *damn* those English sons of whores!"

Stickiness spreading over my shoulder, soaking in. Not Gruffydd's blood.

Reckoning the fire now. Lackwitted of me to cast water on the coals. Somehow I'll have to get the fire started again ere I leave for the brat's.

"Someone will have to tell their wives. And their mother."

This is why. Because I cannot bear to lose them both.

Gruffydd beside me still draws his breath unsteadily.

One day, a shadow will come to my door. He will push his hood back and scuff the dirt with one heel, and he will tell me to go to the market common should I want to say farewell ere the hangman does his work. Or that my brother died well in some anonymous way, calling down the only kind of justice the likes of us have recourse to.

Then I will have naught left to lose.

1294

SAINT JOHN'S DAY

TO

MICHAELMAS EVE

MMALINE'S father is accused of murder.

I'm not supposed to know a word of it, of course, but it's impossible to get a moment of marketing done without absorbing who's with child by whom or who's fighting with her mother-in-law or whose baby has rump rash bad enough to blister.

As near as I can figure out, Sir John de Coucy was out on his endowed cropland and caught a Welshman foraging in the stubble. Apparently there was a struggle and Sir John slew the Welshman with his falchion.

My father keeps combing a hand through his hair and muttering that it could have been him, it could have been him.

Murder is the Crown's jurisdiction, not the borough's, and the royal justice itinerant will be coming from Conwy to hear the case.

The Coucys' mousy servant appears on our doorstep with the message that the lady de Coucy will not expect me this Monday, nor on any Monday until further notice. My father says that no man can blame her, even though the look about him suggests that he's a man who could. I merely glance up from my embroidery frame with my good-girl smile *that says whatever the lady de Coucy thinks is best* and all that rot.

And I spend Monday peaceably for a change, outlining the city walls of Caernarvon with a strand of purple-gray thread that seems made for the purpose.

It's high summer, and that means there isn't much hired work to do around the townhouse. I explain to my father that Gwinny is worried about her brother, who's finding it hard to get a job of work, and I ask if there's something that needs doing at one of the mills.

My father has some sort of merry wine-tinted exchange at the Boar's Head with the provisioner of the castle garrison and learns that one of the timber gangs is a man short. If Griffith wants the work, he's to report to a man with the rather unsavory name of Snagnose John at the Newdale site on the morrow at dawn.

One of the Glover lads is dispatched to inform Griffith of the offer, and I dance toward the kitchen to tell Gwinny what I've done, but I pull up short the instant I step into the rearyard.

She'll think it's a trick. And she'll tell him not to go.

I hesitate in the doorway for a long moment.

Then I take myself to my workroom and plant my backside before my frame.

I know he takes the work, though. I know because

Gwinny comes in one day smiling in a way that makes her every step light as she sweeps and tidies.

Gwinny is rather pretty when she smiles. I wonder why I never noticed ere this.

Emmaline de Coucy turns up on my doorstep unbidden and unannounced. She's robed in servants' linsey and her eyes are red.

"Mother doesn't know I'm here," she whispers. "Won't you please let me in ere someone sees me?"

I bite back the choice words I have for the lady de Coucy and show Emmaline into the hall. I pour her a mug of new cider and steer her to the hearthbench, away from Salvo's pallet.

"Forgive me breaking your peace." Emmaline's voice quavers. "I couldn't bear to be alone. I'm so worried about my father. What if the royal justice finds against him? They hang felons! Just like those two poor Welshmen, God rest them!"

I pour myself some cider and take a long drink. It could very well have been my father who drew steel on a trespasser, and me weeping secretly at Emmaline's hearth.

If the lady de Coucy allowed it.

"Do you think the king would truly hang your father?" I make my tone reasonable. "Sir John de Coucy? Burgess and *honesti* of Caernarvon?"

"Yes! His Grace the king is adamant that this province

be governed by statute and his law applied evenhandedly regardless of blood." Emmaline wipes her eyes. "If the mayor himself were found guilty, he would be hanged."

"His Grace the king is rather generous," I reply. "Mayhap he has never been here and met the Welsh."

Emmaline chokes on a giggle. "The king knows the Welsh very well. He would have them as subjects, so he must trust his officials here to govern as he bids. And he must trust us to treat the Welsh as neighbors."

"Neighbors," I echo. Neighbors who pay all the taxes. Neighbors who rob one another at the market out of hunger. Neighbors who cannot get a decent job of work without the intervention of a burgess.

"Oh, Cecily, my father had no murder in his heart!" Emmaline toys with a loosening stitch of her handkerchief. "It was all misadventure, but out there in county court there will be Welshmen on the jury. They'll want vengeance, not justice."

Out there. Without the walls. I pat her shoulder as she sniffles into her handkerchief. "All will be well. Truly. His Grace the king would not suffer a man to be punished wrongfully. Especially a man like your father. There will be justice. You must believe that."

Emmaline worries the stitching on her handkerchief. She doesn't believe it. The king might want Caernarvon ruled by statute, but it's hard to insist on it when he's so far away.

* * *

It's not even Tierce and it's sweltering. The market is dusty and the basket is heavy and I'm thirstier than a year's worth of Augusts. Mistress Tipley bustles ahead. I sway behind her, heaving the basket because this task is rightfully mine.

At the bakery, Mistress Tipley hands over the five wads of bread dough. The baker pulls out five loaves and pushes them across the counter.

"Are you not supposed to keep one?" I ask him. "To feed the castle garrison?"

The baker shakes his head. "Don't need it now. The garrison is being thinned since the order to muster came down."

"What order?"

"Every man of military age in the Principality is summoned to fight for his Grace the king in Gascony and— Demoiselle, what ails you?"

No.

Not him, too.

I tear out of the bakery, leaving Mistress Tipley and the market basket behind. Past shoulders and around carts and over puddles and he's a trial and a goose but the king cannot make him go to Gascony, he just cannot!

I burst in, slam the door, stumble down the corridor. My father is in the hall buckling on his wrist braces. I fling myself at him and hold on hard.

"Don't go! You cannot go!"

My father peels me off gently and steers me toward a bench. "What's all this, sweeting? Where can I not go?" He sits on the other bench, forearms on knees, all wrinkled brow and downturned mustache and gray at his temples.

"Gascony! The baker said that all the men here must fight for the king in Gascony!"

"Sweeting, that summons isn't for the burgesses. His Grace is summoning the Welshmen of the Principality to his standard. They're the ones who must fight abroad."

I lift my head, scrub my eyes. "The Welshmen? Not you?"

"No, sweeting. I owe for my burgage twelvepence a year. I owe no military service abroad. I owe no service in England, either. All I must do is defend the king's interests in the Principality. Remember?"

My father is not going to Gascony.

I let out a long, shuddering breath.

"Now, your uncle Roger," my father says with a smile, "is responsible for equipping two and a third serjeants for service in Gascony, if he does not go himself."

I giggle. Two and a third serjeants. I wonder what good a third of a serjeant would be to the king.

My uncle Roger owes service for Edgeley. He must pay taxes like lastage and passage and a fifteenth of his movable goods when the king requests it. He must trade on market day.

We don't have any such restrictions. Here in Caernarvon, we're friends of the king.

"That's my girl." My father embraces me and rises. "I'm

off. The mayor is expecting a report on the state of the mills. Have you seen my counter-roll of fines?"

"In the coffer. Where it always is."

"Good girl."

And he's out the door with a tromp of boots and a whuffle of wood.

Thank Christ. Thank Christ and all the saints for our friendship with the king.

Gwinny stands before the hearth, clinging to the broom. She looks like a corpse, bloodless and stiff.

"Oh, Gwinny, your brother!" I press a hand to my mouth. "Your brother will have to go."

She sinks to the floor and runs both hands over her hair. The broom clatters behind her. She looks greensick.

"He's all I've got," she whispers.

Gwinny looks so small crumpled like a dishrag in the hearth corner that I sift for something to say that will make her feel better.

Someone else might try, "Mayhap it'll be a good thing. His Grace the king pays wages, you know." Or, "Griffith will be fine. He'll come back with a purse full of silver and tales of heroics in Gascony. And September is a long time from now."

But I keep my mouth shut.

Because if anyone had said those things to me an Ave ago, I might have clawed her eyes out.

TAKING. They're always taking. Da. Pencoed. Coin. Beasts.

Now they want my brother.

Hands out, rattle parchment, cry it down in grating, rusty English.

Those who do not give freely lose all.

Know not where I first hear the name. It rises from the dusty ground, from the powdered ash of charcoal bones that once were live and lowing and keeping us from hunger.

Madog.

It's breathed like prayer from the very soul of the Welshry, wreathed round the horns of distrained cattle peaceably browsing Watched burgess land. It's in the Crown measures, the market pennies, the chalk.

Madog ap Llywelyn ap Maredydd ap Llywelyn ap Maredydd ap Cynan ab Owain Gwynedd. Disinherited son of a slighted line, trembling with quiet rage in some forgotten corner of this land.

Know not if he's even real, and if he is, know not what to make of the mutters men pair with his name.

They are the mutters of sharpened staves. Of spears hidden in the rafters. Murdered fathers and seized estates. *Con-*

tra pacem, they said. Da had taken up arms against the king, *their* king, a man he never swore for, so they took all.

Madog. Breathe it like prayer. Madog ap Llywelyn ap Maredydd ap Llywelyn ap Maredydd ap Cynan ab Owain Gwynedd.

Please God let him be real. We are all becoming men with blackened faces, even with the gallows in plain view.

POTTAGE AGAIN. Miserable, misbegotten refuse better suited for filling gaps in the wall slats.

I cheerily serve a plate of it to my father. "Look at the delicious pottage, Papa. How much I love eating it day after day. So delightful that we may eat it for breakfast and dinner, too. And such flavor! Not at all like the mud pasties that the Glover children serve one another."

"Sit down and eat it," my father growls. "Not even the mayor has a haunch of meat."

I do, but now I'm thinking of wall plaster and every bite goes down that much harder for it.

Thank all the saints that my father thought to stockpile the oats and barley given him by the millers of Caernarvon as part of his office. Even if he does stand over Mistress Tipley like a mastiff and see that she measures out shares for all four of us for breakfast and supper. If he hadn't thought to keep that grain back, we'd be down at the market paying the price of ten horses for half a quartermeasure of crawling rye.

Or going without.

I'm terribly glad that I can use the workroom again. In winter, we were packed into the hall because every other room was so cold that our breath came out in puffs. There are precious few times I can bear my father's feeble attempts at humor and smile politely at his tales of millers attempting to get out of castellaria or Welshmen who hid their handmills to avoid the fine.

"The sacks were in the byre, if you'll believe it! A little, er, *persuading* and he came out with them." Or, "Thought he could hide the handmill in the dunghill, but that fool surely didn't think I'd throw him in to find it!" And so on. It's tiresome.

But now it's summer and he's hardly ever here. If he's not officering the mills, he's in and out of *honesti* houses or meeting with castle men or putting himself forward for extra turns at Watch and Ward.

Gwinny enters the workroom and stands quietly till I look up from my embroidery frame.

"Mistress Tipley says to come to supper."

"Very well." I flex my fingers. They ache like penance, but Saint Joseph is finished and the Holy Child outlined. I stow my needle and stretch.

Gwinny regards me as if I'm on sale at the market but she's not sure of my teeth. Then she brings something out from behind her back and holds it toward me.

It's pink. A most familiar rose pink.

I let the small folded packet fall open. Sure enough, it's the rose wool from my Michaelmas gown, but it's been carefully trimmed into a square and stitched around the edges with tiny, precise stitches to stop the fraying.

A handkerchief. From one of the scraps.

Gwinny lifts her chin. "Taking all of it makes me no better than you."

I hold the handkerchief close to my chest. At length I whisper, "I'm sorry, too," but Gwinny has already gone.

Saints keep me, the constable of Caernarvon and the justiciar of North Wales are coming to our little house! They will be here for supper and the kitchen is in an absolute uproar, eel sizzling and pots bubbling and fingers flying and Mistress Tipley shrilling.

My father pulls me aside. "Now, sweeting, I need not tell you how important these men are. I'd send a child to her chamber to keep her out of the way, but you are old enough to serve us at table. I know you'll make me proud."

Not only will I make him proud, I'll prove that I've learned *honesti*craft like the paternoster and therefore never need suffer the goodwill of the lady de Coucy again.

"And it'll give you a chance to be seen." My father winks. "Both of these men have sons who need wives."

High-ranking borough officials will expect naught less of a man with ambitions toward *honesti*hood, and my father would have himself seen by these men just as much as he would me.

When the guests arrive at Vespers, the hearth is blazing with fragrant pine. The constable of the castle is called Adam de Whetenhale, and he has the reddest hair of anyone I've ever seen. I already know the justiciar's name, and, very well, I'm glad I know to curtsey.

They sit on either side of my father at the trestle, and he has both men laughing within moments.

I walk like a fine borough lady. I pour wine from the right and cast my gaze down and smile when one of them makes a jest, but not too much because of my crooked teeth. Emmaline could not have done it better.

But they're not even looking at me. They're talking about Sir John de Coucy's *problem*, as they call it.

"We cannot ignore it," my father warns. "Not with the king's Gascony edict atop the famine and *taxatores* on their way. The Welshry is demanding justice. And the whor—men with blackened faces will see that they get it one way or another."

The justiciar grins. "They'll get the justice that's coming to them. But Coucy will be tried by a jury of his peers. And that's why we're here."

Mistress Tipley appears in the rear storage chamber with a tray of fried eel that demolished our savings. I glide over to take it from her, but it's hard to remember to keep my eyes down and not trip over my hem and keep the tray level all at once.

"We need you for Coucy's jury," the justiciar says to my father. "A fortnight's time. The bailiff's clerk will come for you."

My father frowns. "I owe no suit at county court."

"County court, mayhap," the constable replies, "but not a county jury. God forbid."

I slide the tray onto the trestle where all three can reach, then step back, hands clasped and head bowed. Surely one of them will tell my father what a charming and lovely daughter he has. They will say what a fine borough lady she is, and how any man would be fortunate to have her to wife.

But they don't. Three daggers spear slices of eel and the men tear in like beasts, swigging wine and spitting out stray bones.

They don't even notice me.

"Coucy is a burgess of Caernarvon, and he'll be tried by his *peers*." The justiciar smiles like a sated cat. "He could cut down half the Welshry and that right would still be his. Matters little *where* Coucy sits for judgment, for I have every confidence that you lads will hear the oathgivers and come to the right conclusion."

My father squints thoughtfully for a moment, then grins big as market day. He clasps wrists with both visitors and agrees to serve as a juror. Then the three of them attack their meal once again with relish.

I stand in the hearth corner trembling with rage. I did everything I was taught. Everything, just as an *honesti* lady might. And it gained me naught.

HE was tried by his peers. Fellow burgesses. English-men all.

This is justice, they tell us. English justice.

Out in county court, away from stone and mortar, he should be judged by a jury of Welshmen.

But the Crown looks away.

English returns to Caernarvon in smug horseback tri-umph. He killed a man in cold blood and the verdict is Not Proven. Twelve of his peers see to it.

1294

MICHAELMAS

TO ⊙

CHRISTMAS EVE

MICHAELMAS dawns clear and blue, the kind of fierce autumn sky that promises endless summer. I lean on my window frame, shutters thrown wide, and breathe the thick, briny wind.

Today is the fair. Today is jugglers and trained marmosets and pasties hot from carts and ribbons and carole-dancing in the street. It's Michaelmas!

As I reach for the shutters, I smell something strange. A dark haze is rising over Anglesey, smearing the blue.

It's almost like smoke.

First the crop failure, now a fire. Anglesey must have done something to anger the Almighty. God willing, next year will be better.

My father is much more sober this Michaelmas. He eats his porridge in measured mouthfuls while staring at the hearth. There are fresh scars on his forearms. He's still on his first mug of ale.

"Papa," I purr, sliding into my place at his right hand. "May I go to the fair?"

"If you stay within the walls, sweeting. Take Gwinny and be careful. The countryside is still hot."

"Could I have fivepence to spend?"

He makes a show of choking on his ale. "Fivepence? Surely. Let me just pull that out of my purple and ermine tunic!"

I fold my arms and huff big. Good old pinchpenny Papa. "How about three?"

"Two, you little spendthrift," he says, tugging my plait. "Honestly, you'll have to marry an earl. Only blooded men will be able to keep you."

"Give me his hand and point us toward the church door," I reply, and my father laughs aloud. He pulls out his purse and hands me the pennies. I kiss my father's bristly cheek, then Gwinny and I are out the door and into the whistling, singing, stomping, and shouting.

This fair seems smaller than last year's. Not nearly as many sheep on tethers, or skeins of wool. The prices are higher, too. A stall in front of the Glovers' wants a half a penny for a single honey cake!

Surely there are better prices. I have but twopence and I want to stretch them. With Gwinny in tow, I thread through Shire Hall Street and move down High.

Someone screams.

Man or woman, I cannot tell. It came from the gates, though, and I strain on tiptoe for a glimpse. Betimes the Watch will hack off a cutpurse's ear while the wronged man watches, or they'll thrash a minstrel for singing in the street.

No such fortune. All I can see are hooded heads, bobbing and plodding and swaying.

I tug Gwinny's sleeve. "Come, let's go see what the excitement is!"

Gwinny stands like a sighted hare.

"It'll be fun!" I hop and crane, but I can see naught. "We surely don't want to miss out."

"Madog," she whispers.

A boy flashes past me. At least I think it's a boy. He was running too fast to be certain. Then another boy, then a woman dragging a child by the wrist, then men.

There's a rumble like thunder far away, yet the sky is so blue it hurts the eye.

And there's screaming and shouting and the shing-shing of metal and the dull thud of blades in flesh, like a hallful of people eating meat with daggers in both hands.

I turn.

High Street is rushing toward me in a massive wave. Men, women, children, dogs, goats. They thrash and tumble and scrabble away from—

Welshmen. Welshmen who chase them like animals, cut them down with sword and spear and falchion and dagger, leap over the corpses and hack at whatever's moving.

They're running past me, men and women and boys and dogs bumping me shoulder and elbow, and I cannot move.

Gwinny will help me. She'll intercede with the butchers,

tell them I'm to be spared, that I gave her a gown and kept her fed and found her brother a job of work.

But Gwinny is not at my elbow. Or up the street. Or anywhere.

A Welshman shoulders in a door not an armslength from me. He plows inside with several fellows on his heels. Things crash and there's screaming. And then sobbing. And then silence.

I must get home. My father will protect me. He has a big sword and a falchion and he'll hold the door against them.

I fly up High Street, straight through the gutter. Already it's full of blood.

A Welshmen startles as I wick past and he stabs his spear at me. Two brutes peel off and pursue me at a dogtrot.

Christ, no.

I stumble over a limp arm and hit the gutter face first. I come up mired with mud and blood and it reeks and purple stars dazzle my eyes and my mouth waters and I vomit my porridge and cream.

Footfalls behind me. I heave myself up, retching, swiping at the mess gobbeting my gown. The arm I fell over hangs limply in the gutter.

It belongs to one of the Glover lads. His belly is cut open and his guts are sliding out.

And I'm off, away from feet crunching mud and rock, away from the Glover boy, and crossing myself with every other step, falling over my hem and gagging at the smell of myself and dodging bodies and getting home so my father can pet my hair and keep me safe.

The racket is hellish and everything smells like burning. I round the corner of Shire Hall. Smoke pours from the windows of the Tutburys' house on the corner. The screaming comes from everywhere at once like the sound of some unholy choir. Ahead I can see our house, and I pray to every saint who's listening that it's not afire.

It's not. God is merciful to sinners.

I try the door, weeping and weak in the legs, but it doesn't budge. Not a margin. And the two brutes are rounding the gate and four more are following, all of them ragged and raw-eyed and brandishing blood-smeared weapons and looking right at me.

"Papaaaaaaaa!"

I screech and pound and kick the oaken slab and they're going to cut me up for the pigs and it's forever ere the door opens a crack and a slice of my father's face floats beyond. His eyes are wild. I throw my shoulder into the crack, trying to cram inside, but a massive palm slams into the door a handswidth from my ear. The door flies open and my father staggers back from the force of the blow. Welshmen crowd through, one after another, pushing me ahead of them.

I hit the wall hard. Black pain over my eyes, then I'm blinking and the wall is holding me up.

My father is in the middle of a crowd of Welshmen, all elbows and fists and knees, flailing like a drowning man.

They're going to kill him. They're going to beat him to pulp right before my eyes.

Even in my own house, I can still hear the screaming.

"Papa!" They're killing my father. And I'm standing here.

"Get out!" His voice is raspy, as if he's swallowed ground glass.

I cannot move.

Gwinny appears from the rear chamber and points through the hall, jabbering in Welsh. Men troop past with grain sacks from our shed on their shoulders, and she directs them to the door with stabs of her finger.

The Welshmen are dragging my father toward the stairs, but he's fighting them knuckle and jab, tooth and backhand. He's bleeding from nose and mouth, and clumps of his hair are missing.

I stagger across the room and fall into Gwinny. "He's going to die! They're going to kill my father!"

She snorts. "Aye. They are."

"Stop them!"

Gwinny shrugs. "I couldn't even if I wanted to. He's been digging his own grave with every fistful of barley, every handmill fine, every door kicked in, every word in the bailiffs' ears."

They've got him halfway up the stairs. All I can see of my father are his boots, catching winks of hearthfire as he kicks and struggles. Another Welshman follows with a length of rope.

I'm weeping at Gwinny's feet and clutching her hem and I can still hear the screaming above my own shuddering breath.

"Help me, Gwinny," I sob, "please, for the love of God. They'll come for me next. Help me. Do something."

The hem jerks from my hands and swishes away. I look up at Gwinny, up and up and into her bird-black eyes.

"Justice," she hisses, "for those who deserve it."

Then Gwinny swings a quartermeasure sack over her shoulder and follows the men out the gaping front door.

There's no more scuffle abovestairs, no thumping or scraping or dragging. Only cheering and hooting.

Get out, he said. He cannot mean alone.

I stand up. My legs are watery. Heavy footfalls drum on the stairs. Toward me.

I stumble through the storage chamber and out the rear door. The rearyard is a shambles. The henhouse is tipped over and kicked in. The pig and goat are missing. The rain barrel has a foot-shaped hole in the side.

I totter through the wreckage and peek through the kitchen door. No sign of Mistress Tipley. Pots and kettles and spoons and paddles lie scattered like driftwood. The shelves are bare.

I slip through the greenway toward the street. This time I do not run. Running draws their attention. Welshmen heave past, toting lengths of wool and quartermeasure sacks.

They storm along Shire Hall bloody to the knees with blades drawn. The screaming is louder here. The whole town is screaming for mercy.

In front of my house, I search the street for someone to help me. Anyone. Master Glover. Sir John de Coucy. Even Edward Mercer. But there are only Welshmen, smoke, and blood.

Something creaks. Something behind me, in what's left of my house.

It's my father. Hanging from his chamber window. Stripped naked. A handmill dangling from his neck, strung on the cord of his bedrobe. Neck awry, eyes bulging, blank.

I'm running. The ground flashes past my feet in smears of brown and green. My stomach is hot and stabby and I land in dirt as I retch and retch but nothing comes up.

My garden. I'm in my garden. I'm crushing tansy and borage.

The shed door has been torn off. I grapple my way inside and sink into the corner nearest the door, pull knees to chin, and weep.

I'm little. Not more than three or four summers, because I'm small enough that my father can throw me high in the air in Edgeley's sunny yard. He catches me in strong, sure arms and I crow *again again again* because I know he will never let me fall. A wooden top with a red plaited pull-string skitters over Edgeley's trestle and clatters to a stop and I squeal and my father smiles and pets my hair and oh Christ he's gone he cannot be gone because I was going to buy him some gingerbread with one of the pennies because I did not think to tell him farewell.

Get out, he said. Ere a handful of whooping devils put a rope round his neck and pushed him out his chamber window.

I heave myself up. The screaming is muffled here, but somehow that's worse. If I go through the streets, they'll see me. I'll have to follow the walls through rearyards till I get to the gate.

I check my rearyard. Empty. So I make myself walk. Running draws their attention and they're in the houses, tipping coffers and seizing garments by the handful. They'll see me through shutterless windows and sweep down.

Near the fence, I step on something furry. It's Salvo, lying peacefully on his side as if he's asleep on his gorse bed. But he's not. His throat has been cut. A collar of shiny red from ear to ear. Bleeding a scarlet fan into the mud.

I cross myself and keep walking.

Next door's rearyard is torn up like a byre. My shoe sucks into the mud. Then the other. So I leave them. The mud squishes cold and gritty around my ankles.

At the corner, I peer down High Street. What's left of the Michaelmas fair is strewn and thrashed. Broken carts and dead sheep and ragged scraps of bunting still clinging to smoldering buildings. And Welshmen bearing plunder, sacks and crates and bundles. Welshmen with torches, setting town-houses afire. Welshmen everywhere, armed and wroth as de-mons loosed from Hell.

It's about a stone's throw across High Street to Church. And I must cross High in plain view of these butchers.

I'll never make it. They'll descend on me like a pack of dogs.

I take a deep breath and step into the road. Chin up, eyes forward. The walk that earned me penance from the lady de Coucy.

Over my shoulder is the castle's gray profile. The cross of Saint George does not fly above the Eagle Tower, nor the arms of the constable. There's another banner, one I don't recog-nize. A red and gold banner, quartered.

The Welsh have taken the castle.

All dead. The castle garrison. The porters at the city gate. No one's left. They'll spare none of us.

Cannot stop. Welshmen everywhere. One foot before the other, slipping in blood.

An apron drifts across the Sandyses' greenway. A shift, too. Three adjoining townhouses are ablaze, smoke pouring from the windows. A baby cries somewhere in a pathetic, straggling wail.

If I survive this I will confess my sins like an anchoress, for if Hell is anything like the fall of Caernarvon, I want to be perfectly certain of my soul.

* * *

Follow the wall. Drag my hand against it. Don't look too closely at limp shapes in corners or furtive movement behind sheds. Stand still as a hare when Welshmen pour out of townhouses, smearing sooty handprints on doorframes. Count towers till I reach the Penny Tower, then the city gate.

At the gate, Welshmen stream in and out weighed down with plunder, making a great din with their shouting, singing, roaring. Somehow I must get through that gate. It's the only way out of Caernarvon.

I lean against a shed. Suck in trembling breaths. My feet are raw. My legs are like cooked parsnips and I cannot go on. Not another step. Not through that gate.

Get out, he said to his only living child, the light of his otherwise meaningless life.

Grip my muddy gown. Let out a shuddery breath. Then I plunge around the shed corner and plow through the alley toward the city gates.

One gate has been torn from the hinges and trampled to splinters. I fix my eyes on the bridge that spans the river beyond the dark arch. Welshmen stagger and storm through the gate-hole. I look through them as I pass. They do not exist.

There are scrape marks on the ground where the toll trestle stood. Not even a splinter remains.

Outside the gate, I choke on acrid smoke. The wharves are burning. Every last boat sends diagonal flames to the heavens and the canals are crammed with charred flotsam.

Chin up, stride even. Running draws their attention. I

pray to every saint who's listening to surround me with angels bearing swords.

Something snares my plait.

The saints are elsewhere today.

I reel backward and twist, but whatever has me jerks my hair downward and slings me hard against the bridgehouse. The whole world is naught but purple stars and agony from scalp to backside.

Then a Welshman appears before me and pins me by the neck to the bridgehouse with one big hand. His other hand pushes my gown up in scrabbly grips and grabs. He's grinning. He's missing teeth.

The sky behind him is glowing blue while all the world burns.

No one is coming to help me. They're all dead.

The Welshman gets my gown over my knee and I kick. I kick as hard as I can between his legs and he roars as if I've killed him. I hope I have. He falls away bellowing like a poorly stuck pig and that's all I see because I run for the bridge, attention be damned.

There's a clamor of harsh noise behind me but I don't look back. I fly across the bridge through a crowd of Welshmen fighting over plunder and getting drunk off tuns of wine that must have come from those burning ships.

Mayhap they chase me. Mayhap they don't. They don't catch me. I stop running only when I'm deep in the greenwood gasping for breath and there's not a soul around save birds and insects and quiet, ancient trees.

No more screaming. No more smoke. Only riversong and the chirring of birds, the wet, woody smell of earth.

My legs give way. I collapse in the brush. Take breath after breath. My skin burns. My neck. My legs, where his damp eager hands dragged upward.

Caernarvon stands on its plain while a curtain of black smoke rises as if the Adversary himself has come to claim it.

I'm out.

I'm alone.

It'll be dark soon. Were there any bells left, they'd be ringing Nones.

My gown crackles, a stiff sheet of blood and muck and vomit. It reeks like a midden in August. My feet are laced with cuts and blistered from sun-baked ground, stinging as if full of pins.

Water murmurs somewhere nearby. As on the outing with Emmaline and her kin all those months ago. When angry Welshmen pelted William with rubbish because he was a *taxator*.

And I was wroth because of my ruined gown.

We'd regret it, the poor wretch swore, sweltering at borough court as serjeants hauled him away. Every last act of it.

I crawl beneath a tree. Curl up. And tremble.

They murdered my father. They hold Caernarvon, seat of his Grace the king's government in the Principality of North Wales. My house will soon be char and timber if it isn't already. I am without the walls with naught in the world but the clothes on my back.

And it'll be dark soon.

Someone's coming. There's no time to hide, so I huddle as small as I can, a cat in January. No tromp of boots, so it's a Welshman.

Go past. You don't see me.

But he does. And his face darkens.

It's Griffith.

He's smudgy with soot and his tunic is torn. He squares up like a boar and looks me up and down, as if I'm something to scrape off a shoe.

Tremble and whimper and my breath comes in tiny gasps as if I'm pulling air through a reed.

Griffith snorts, shakes his head, and starts toward the ford, disappearing in margins over the hill.

Swipe at my wet cheeks again and again.

Then he stops. For a long moment he does naught, and I will him on his way with every bit of will I have.

But Griffith comes back up the rise, piece by piece, face, shoulders, torn tunic, till he's standing over me like an idol.

Get out, he said, ere they killed him in cold blood. He did not mean like this.

"No. It won't do." Griffith sounds weary, as if he is a thousand years old. "The worst is coming. Here."

He holds out a hand.

If whatever's coming is worse than the sack of Caernarvon, Hell must be opening its great maw.

"Go away." I try to stand. If he knows I cannot fight back, I'm done for. But I cannot even climb to my knees.

Without fanfare, Griffith hauls me up like a wet pallet, looses me roughly, and leaves me swaying like a sapling on legs that won't make it ten steps.

"Wh-where are we going?" I whisper.

He makes no reply, merely fixes me with a look that shuts my gob very quickly and jerks his chin at the greenwood. So I make myself stumble behind him on colt-legs and feet burning like sulfur.

Mayhap it'll be quick. Please, God, let it be quick.

We walk. The sun sinks. One foot before the other. Days and se'ennights and years we walk.

Just when I cannot go another step, we come to the bottom of a wooded hill.

And I collapse.

So Griffith drags me step after staggering step toward a sagging hovel decaying amid thick brush. He shoulders the curtain aside and lowers me before a ring of embers. Next to me is a pile of moth-eaten blankets outlined faintly in orange light. He hangs the quartermeasure sack from a hook in the rafters, then approaches me.

Flinch. And flinch. Dear God, this is it.

But Griffith only kneels to build up the struggling fire. He's close enough that I can smell him, smoke and sweat and soot, but he does not so much as look at me. The coals glow like stars. At length, flame licks up the tinder and begins to crackle.

I can see better now. There are wattled walls, patched and repatched. Dirt floor, damp at the edges. The whole place smells of mold and rot with the faint whiff of goat.

When the fire is busy, Griffith goes to the sack hanging from the rafters. He withdraws a hand-sized wedge of cheese and a loaf of bread. The bread is bloody on one heel, but he cuts a slab from the other end and sets it in a shallow vessel.

He has not cut my throat, raised a hand, pushed me down. He does not seem to even want to.

Behind me, someone screams as if cornered by a haunt.

Gwinny's in the doorway. She's wearing three cloaks dangling with silver cloak-pins and brooches and armor-buckles. About her waist is a man's belt stuffed with two daggers and a length of silk, and she clutches quartermeasure sacks in her fist like a wilting bouquet.

And she looks like the Adversary's Hellspawn daughter as she storms across the room, raving in Welsh.

THE brat is in my house. *The brat is in my house!*

I storm across the room to serve her with the back of my hand what I served the other English of Caernarvon, but Gruffydd catches me in a tight embrace. "Gwenhwyfar, thank Christ! You weren't . . . I didn't . . ."

My little brother is hugging me as he hasn't since we were small. I hold him close for more long moments than I can count, and I'm the one who pulls away first.

"Jesu, lass, you look . . ." By the look of him, Gruffydd is casting about for the word *vengeful,* but seems unwilling to say it aloud. "Were you trapped there? Did any man hurt you?"

I take off the cloaks one at a time and they jingle to the floor. Then I toss down my quartermeasure sacks and slide out of the belt. I take off the too-big felt shoes and dump coin from both. I look at him in triumph.

"I'll be damned," he murmurs, and he cannot keep the admiration from his voice.

"I'm perfectly sound. I was not trapped anywhere. Not today." I prime a mighty slap and turn toward the brat, but Gruffydd catches my hand and holds it fast.

"Leave her be."

"I'll not suffer her in my house." With my free hand, I fling a shoe at the brat. It bounces off her back and she squawks like a wrung-neck chicken. "English at their best are still bloody well English. But now I'm rid of them all. I'm free."

Gruffydd tightens his grip. "We're not rid of them, and we're certes not free."

I hiss and wrench toward the brat, ready to pummel, but my little brother pulls me up cold.

"I said leave her be."

I snort. "If you're not man enough to give her the justice she deserves, be assured that I will."

"Vengeance," Gruffydd says in a low, dangerous voice, "is not justice."

The brat looks up. She knows we're speaking of her, though she cannot understand a word of Welsh. It is Justice Court, then, and I am justiciar, bailiff, and hangman. I am handing down a sentence in a foreign tongue and carrying it out with the rope.

I narrow my eyes. "You of all men can say such a thing?"

"No. Yes." Gruffydd runs a hand through his hair. "I cannot, but I must. She . . . tried to make it right."

"By taking the boot off your neck? How charitable."

"How do you think the likes of me got on that timber gang?" Gruffydd jabs a finger at the brat.

I flinch. "It was never! You're mad!"

"Her father has the ear of the *honesti* now. She leaned on

him, and the castle provisioner passed over all the lackeys who bribed him for months and what do you know? Gruffydd ap Peredur with his tainted malcontent blood has a place on the most sought-after work gang in the Principality."

I press my lips together. Study the brat crumpled before the fire, tattery and pale and small.

"I know not why she did it," Gruffydd says. "I only know that she did it knowingly, with intent."

"You're as much a fool as Dafydd." I fold my arms. "We must get rid of them. Every man, woman, and child. Every brat and dog."

I say it in English so she'll tremble and cower.

"Is that what you think this rising is about?" Gruffydd shakes his head as if I'm a child. "Destroying the English? Pushing them out of Gwynedd?"

"We took the seat of royal government. I watched Madog ap Llywelyn wipe his arse with the town charter while the whole Exchequer burned."

Gruffydd smiles faintly. "Gwen, the English king will come with a massive army and put the rebels down. But then he will want to know why he had to. Have you any idea how much it cost to raise that monstrosity in stone and mortar? Do you really think he'll just let Caernarvon go?"

I toe my pile of goods. There's blood beneath my fingernails.

"When the rising is all over," Gruffydd says, "the rebels crushed and Madog ap Llywelyn hanged from Caernarvon's walls, the burgesses will come back. They'll rebuild Caernarvon, but they'll remember what happened here. As will the English king. The burgesses have learned what happens when Welshmen are pushed to the wall, and they will not push so hard again."

Da went out, but Caernarvon happened anyway. Ten years he's been dust, and English have learned naught.

Gruffydd nods at the brat. "This girl has learned it better than most. And now she's the sole holder of her father's burgage. She'll bring her husband into the privileges of Caernarvon and tell him exactly what to think of us. That's who we'll live under. Those who remember the aftermath."

Not if she doesn't survive the aftermath. Not if I turn her out, let the men with blackened faces take care of her.

Sharp pain shoots up my arm and Gruffydd's breath rushes past my ear. "I see it in your face, Gwenhwyfar. And believe me, I'm sorely tempted to let you, but by God, we are not animals, no matter how many times they say as much."

I pull free, glare down at her.

"She stays," Gruffydd says in a ragged voice. "Come what may, we will not harm her or allow harm to come to her."

The brat is trembling now. Hard. Ripping at a loose thread on her cuff as if it's biting her.

Like as not she thinks she's escaped a terrible fate, but she'll come to envy those who fell in Caernarvon.

She is without the walls now.

* * *

For the first time in as long as I can remember, I don't get up at bare dawn. I lie abed till the whole sky is pink, stretch like a hearthcat, and smile up at the thatch.

Then I rise and spend a long, delicious moment deciding what I'm going to do next.

Sometime in the night, the brat moved. She's huddled near the door even though it's the coldest place in the house. She's staring hard at the floor, and there are stark lines down her cheeks where tears have carved runnels through the grime.

I ignore the brat, stir the fire to life, tend to Mam. Gruffydd comes in with a bucket of water and she flinches hard, even though he thumps right past her without a look.

Gruffydd and I are eating bread and cheese when we hear a shuffle, and there she is before us. She's trembling so badly she can barely keep her footing, but she stands chin up, shoulders back, as if she's priming for hemp about her neck.

The brat swallows several times, then chokes out, what will become of me?

Gruffydd glances my way, but I fold my arms and shrug. "She's here because of you," I tell him in Welsh. "You deal with her."

He glares at me, then fixes the brat with a cool stare. That depends, he says in English. Have you anyone that will come for you?

Yes! She jumps on it, clings to it. My cousin. Nicholas of Coventry. He's a squire for Sir Reginald de Tibetot. You'll find him at Wallingford. He'll come. I know he will.

Gruffydd nods and tells her, we'll ask the priest's boy to fetch him here. Should you value your life, you'll not stir from this house till your cousin arrives. Those men out there are not to be trifled with.

"And until then," I say in Welsh, "you work." I pick up the empty bucket and shove it into her arms. "Go fetch water."

What did you say, she asks, and I grab her wrist and rough her toward the door.

"Water! Go. Fetch. Water."

The brat frowns at me in utter bewilderment as she clutches the bucket. Her clawed-up fingers stand out white and stark.

"Best hope you're a fast learner." I smirk and narrow my eyes. "Some of us learned English beneath the rod."

She blinks rapidly, then squares up like a cornered beast.

You're savages, cries the brat, the lot of you are savages who killed my father!

"And many other swine besides," I reply. "The master was decent enough, but the Officer of the Town Mills deserved worse than the nice clean hanging he got."

Her grip tightens on the bucket rim. She isn't moving.

"Do what you're told or it'll go hard for you." I point to

the door and she follows my finger with the round eyes of prey. "I can make things go *very* hard for you."

The brat swallows. She gets ten steps into the yard ere she asks, where is the water?

I stare her down from my doorway. She is within *my* walls now. I will show her what it is to be mistress.

All at once she falls, shoulders and back, scowl and teeth, and she shrinks like a helpless child. Then she shuffles around, stumbles downhill, and disappears in the brush.

When I return to the fire, I take the bread Gruffydd offers and say firmly, "No harm."

Gruffydd smiles. "God's honest truth? I enjoyed every moment of that."

The brat does not return till well past midday. Brambles in her hair and gown soaking wet, a gash across her forearm and muddy to the knees. But the bucket is full and she drops it at the fireside, jaw clenched, gallows-defiant.

I wait till she collapses by the fire and pries a crust of burned oatbread from the bakestone. Then I pour the water into the cooking pot and hand the bucket back.

"Go fetch water," I tell her in Welsh.

The brat trembles to her feet. Staying upright is costing her, but every line of her is mutinous, furious.

She is coming undone slowly. First her arms, then her hands, then her eyes.

She would strike me.

Do it. I've been waiting for this moment longer than you know.

But she masters it. She closes her eyes and bites it back. Hard through the arms, stiff like a fence-rail. The brat throws the crust down, takes the bucket, and sweeps out the door.

This will not last. She will break. And I will laugh till I weep while the brat nurses bruises and a split lip with naught to look forward to but more of the same. Day in and day out. Because the vale will give her ten times worse just for being English.

Because I'm her only hope.

And she knows it.

The brat sleeps heavy, like sodden wool. Day after day, I kick her awake and work her. From bleak not-dawn till long past sunset, she fetches and carries. Cuts firewood. Bears water. Tends Mam. Dirties her hands with pitch and shit and ash and mud. Day after day.

There's no spinning. No embroidery or hemming.

The brat does not break.

She looks bad, though. Her skin is gray. Even her lips. She keeps wrapping her hair behind her ears as if her fingers need busying.

One day I catch her idle in the clearing, the bucket at her side, staring at the soot-smudged walls and crumbling towers of what was once the king's borough of Caernarvon. There's no fear about her, though. No anger. It's more as

though she would reach down and embrace it, gather it together and rebuild it as a child might a castle of stones.

Her father still hangs from the window. Like Da once,
from the walls.

The next day, I find the priest's boy and send him for the
brat's kin.

SHE CALLS me lazy. At least I think she does. What she doesn't know is that I cannot sleep with my cheek against dirt and I cannot close my eyes without fire and blood and smoke and the red-raw terror of his last moments of life.

Nicholas is coming.

I don't sleep, exactly. Betimes I close my eyes, then blink awake to Gwinny shoving the leather bucket into my hands and barking something in Welsh. The hempen handle digs into my palms so hard that I don't think about how the rope must have roughed up his neck as they shoved him toward the window. I close my eyes and picture the market on a bright blue day. I'm meeting Mistress Sandys at the well, letting her lanky half-grown son draw my water. Trading Mistress Glover a handful of thyme for a length of thread.

I'll startle awake when Gwinny piles my hands with slimy privy rags and growls more commands I cannot understand. When I'm wringing the rags out in water so cold it reddens my knuckles, I don't think about crisp autumn air against his bare flesh, the terrible weightless instant ere the drop. I'm walking home from Mass in my best kirtle, holding one of Nessy Glover's hands while Emmaline holds the other, and betimes we swing her, squealing, high in the air.

Nicholas will come. I know he will.

Gwinny piles on task after task, then watches me like she might a limping horse. Or mayhap a colt in the breaking pasture, mouthing the bit.

But every bucket of water I haul is one less whiff of soot, one less flash of steel to wake me gasping. Every armload of wood I gather is one less reason for Gwinny to put me out of her house and leave me at the mercy of men who will not be trifled with.

That's a lesson I've no need to study.

Get out, he said.

This is the only way out.

I'M in the yard picking tiny rocks out of a bucket of barley when there's a crunch of brush and Dafydd angles out of the greenwood. Gruffydd slings the leather tunic he's working over his shoulder and nods a greeting.

"Give me another day or two," Gruffydd says, holding up a corner of the garment. "They're heading east, so they should be easy to find."

Dafydd shakes his head. "I came to tell you to go ahead of me. I've some things I must do ere I join Madog's lads."

My mouth falls open. "You? Joining the revolt?"

"If this is the only way to get the king's attention, so be it." Dafydd must mark my disbelief, for he smiles and adds, "I'm not afraid to fight, Gwenhwyfar. It just has to be the right fight."

There's a tiny flicker of motion just inside the doorway. The brat, disappearing into the shadows. She's still convinced I'm going to beat her senseless or Gruffydd's going to have his way with her. She regards us as if we're capable of anything.

"Who's that?" Dafydd asks.

"She's the heiress to your townhouse." I smile, blade-sharp. "It would be a shame should anything befall her. Shall I turn my back?"

Dafydd shrugs. "Should anything befall her, they'll just give the house to another Englishman. This doesn't work if we profit at their expense. It only works if we're granted what they already have—and the Crown enforces it."

Gruffydd busies himself with his tunic, the coward, so I face Dafydd steady on and reply, "I want no part of what they have."

"I do," he says. "I would be a subject. Not one of a subject people."

This is why, Dafydd. Because you're so damn sure it's even possible.

"And you believe that rising in revolt against their king is the way to gain that?"

"The king will be wroth, true enough," Dafydd replies, "but not just at us. He'll demand a reckoning from Havering and Whetenhale and it'll all come out. How they weren't governing according to the king's laws, but for their own profit. How their abuses were what turned us to such extremes. Once the king learns all this, he'll be forced to act."

I swallow. "And how do you know that the result won't be ten times worse than it was ere this?"

Dafydd smiles sadly. "I don't. One way or another, though, Caernarvon will never be the same."

"And given all this, you'd still see us married?"

"Tomorrow. If not sooner."

"Why?" I fling a hand. "It would change nothing!"

Dafydd meets my eyes and whispers, "It would change *everything.*"

I don't reply. And don't reply. And don't dare look at him again.

Know not when Dafydd leaves. Too blurry. Only know when I look beyond the bucket and his feet are no longer there.

A FAINT LIGHT filters through the doorway. It's not yet dawn but the curtain is pulled back. Gwinny and Griffith stand in the doorway, murmuring intensely in Welsh. Griffith wears one of Gwinny's plundered cloaks and shoulders a weathered spear.

He's leaving. I catch enough words in Welsh to realize Griffith is going somewhere. Somewhere dangerous.

I catch words in Welsh.

They embrace, fiercely. Then Griffith pulls away and disappears. Gwinny snaps the curtain shut and slumps against the wall. In the stillness, her tiny sobs fill every corner.

It's blood and fire and they're all dead and I cannot keep the tears down.

Gwinny turns on me like a Fury and snaps in English, "Shut up! Don't you dare weep or by God I'll put you out of my house this moment!"

I picture Anglesey out my window, the silky band of green held at arm's length by the shimmering strait busy with boats. I'm in my chamber and the gulls are crying and daylight is just beginning to seep in and it's going to be a lovely brisk day.

At length I master myself, steady my breathing. Gwinny's

shoulders relax bit by bit, but she still glares damnation at me. "You will not weep for my brother. I will not have it."

I don't tell her I wasn't weeping for him. There's no way those words will come out properly.

"You've no right to even *think* his name. Should you be so bold as to utter it, I'll douse you in blood ere I turn you out."

I don't remind her that Griffith told me that I could stay, that I shouldn't try to leave if I valued my life. He's not here to say her nay. He's not here to seize her hand.

He's gone somewhere dangerous, and he's all she's got.

I lick my lips and say, "I know that . . ."

Gwinny fixes me with a venomous look.

"I thought to . . ." That's when I hold my tongue, for Gwinny's jaw is grinding like a millwheel and what I thought to do cannot erase what I did.

"Is it true?" Her voice is gravelly. "About the timber gang?"

Mayhap she's trying to trap me, but I haven't the strength to lie. "Yes. It's true."

Gwinny grunts. "Had I known, I would have told you where you could shove your pity."

"Not pity. Justice."

Gwinny draws back as if I've struck her. She repeats the word in English as though she's never heard it ere this. And she regards me so intently that I swipe up the water bucket and hurry toward the stream, trembling every step of the way.

THEY come at night. I tell them that Gruffydd has already gone, and I give them the knives I plundered from Caernarvon in memory of Peredur ap Goronwy, who once stood with men like them.

They don't loot the house. Out of respect, they say. I bid them Godspeed and they disappear into a vale that's bracing for the worst.

I return to the fire, sit with Mam. She does not move. Her flesh is still warm. Her chest still rises. But she takes only tiny mouthfuls of breath. She drinks less every day.

Once they've been gone for some time, the brat creeps out of the byre where she had the good sense to hide. She's panting like a lathered hound as she edges toward the fire.

I thought they were going to kill you, she says. Right in your own house.

"The rebels are only ravaging," I reply. "There's not much to take, so we'll be rid of them soon."

The brat blinks rapidly, whispers, r-rebels?

"The rebels, fool. The men of Gwynedd who follow Madog ap Llywelyn to finish what they started at Caernarvon." I even out my voice. "Men like my brother."

The brat gapes like a fish.

I say it in English so there'll be no mistake. Rebellion.

Welshmen have taken and trampled your worthless borough and even now reduce it to rubble. They'll take their spears and blades to the Perfeddwlad, where they'll run roughshod over your worthless king and with God's help send him to Hell where he belongs.

Whether any of it is true beyond the sack of Caernarvon I have no notion, but it puts such a panic on the brat that I press down.

More men gather every day. Ere long, all Wales will be in revolt and not a single English man, woman, or child will be safe. We'll be rid of you ere Christmas. Every last damn one of you. And then we'll take apart your castles and boroughs brick by cursed brick until the very land forgets you were ever here.

Rebellion, echoes the brat. But that means that Nicholas . . . mayhap he won't . . .

I smile all teeth. "Well then, best pray hard for my continuing good health."

He'll come, she whispers. I know he will.

The brat speaks clear and sure, a voice that does not match her slumped shoulders, her clenched jaw, her hard stare at the fire.

The same voice I use to say that Gruffydd will return alive. Clear and sure, the way Mam once spoke of Da.

Fanwra's baby is stillborn. I wrap half a plundered cheese and bid the brat ready herself. The brat watches the cheese disappear beneath cloth. Hunger is not a ghost she knew within the walls.

I ready Mam. Firewood, linen, a rag soaked in liquid porridge. Then I pet her hair and nod to the brat.

The brat gestures to Mam and asks, what of your mother? Who'll care for her?

"The saints. Come."

She follows me outside while saying, any manner of man or creature could come through that flimsy curtain. How can you leave her?

"Where shall I start? The part where your lot dictates what jobs of work lads like Gruffydd can do for how much coin, or the part where they tax us so heavily that girls like me have to take up work to keep breath in body?"

The brat rakes her hair behind her ears thrice, glances over her shoulder toward what's left of Caernarvon. At length she says, I'll stay with her.

"You'll not. You'll come see the piteous creature my neighbor bore."

The brat looks as if she'll protest, then wisely closes her mouth and nods. As we walk through the greenwood, she flakes the biggest chunks of filth from her ratty gown. The stains remain. They will never wash clean.

THERE'S A SWEET, burny smell. Just ahead is a wide patch of blackened earth scattered with what look like tangled branches till I get closer and realize they're bones. Scorched and melted and left to bleach.

Animal bones. Cows and sheep and goats. A twinkly star fallen to a black landscape. Ones and dozens and hundreds.

That's bad enough. Then I see the bodies.

Three of them, two men and a woman, hanging from a tree not far from the path Gwinny forges. Purple faces. Crooked necks. Pecked-out holes where eyes once were.

The woman is Mistress Sandys.

I'm on my knees in mud and gasping and choking and they're all dead and all I want is my father back even if he does his fool dancing before every window in Christendom.

A hand on my shoulder, and Gwinny is hauling me up by one arm. "Don't look. Take my hand. Face ahead."

I do as she tells me. My gown is heavy with clinging mud. We're a hundred breaths away when she says, "It'll get better. Not for a while, but it will."

I want to ask Gwinny why. Why the Welsh of the countryside attacked Caernarvon with such sudden violence. Why they hanged and cut down the innocent. Why they tore up the market and looted the wharves and reduced the toll trestle to a pile of splinters.

I don't, though. I think I already know.

FANWRA'S steading is damp and airless. There's no fire. The brat hovers in the doorway and I jerk her in, stumbling. She does not twitch or gag as I expected. She bears up straight, despite her bloodless face.

I kneel at Fanwra's head and smooth her sweaty hair. Then I tuck the cheese into her hands. I do not ask how she fares.

A bundle lies beside the door. The creature within is colorless and smooth, oddly calm. Like statuary, or a figure cast in wax.

I shove the bundle into the brat's arms. She shudders and scrambles to hand it back.

"You'll hold it," I tell her. "You did this. So have a good look at what you wrought."

Her eyes widen and she says, I did not do this.

I pinch the warm pink flesh of her upper arm. "This is hunger's work."

The brat rubs the reddening patch and says, your poor neighbor. Who will look after her? Where is her husband?

"Husband?" I snort. "She should be so lucky. I reckon you believe I gave Edward Mercer justice merely for your benefit."

The brat swallows hard. She looks greensick. She whispers words in English I do not recognize.

Fanwra eats the cheese as if it will disappear.

Ave Maria gratia plena, whispers the brat, and she holds the bundle close as if it's a live, breathing child.

The walk is the same as before, same tree-stump hillsides and stolen fields, but now I stride through those fields that by right should be Gruffydd's. The Watchers have been scattered, the cattle loosed, the struggling barley thrice trampled. I grind my heel into the parched, prickly roots. Give me salt enough and I would sow every handswidth.

The market trestle is splinters, scattered like kindling. Even the walls don't seem as high. The market common is torn up, littered with rubbish. No bodies, though. No bodies anywhere.

There are no more gates, only hinges clinging to the walls like broken spiders. I can look all the way up High Street to where it curves like a spine, obscuring the Water Gate and the strait beyond. Men on what's left of the towers watch me enter the gravetown, blades shouldered, careful.

They must be Madog's men, guarding their prize. As if there's an English soul within a day's ride who still breathed God's air.

Already they're taking Caernarvon down. Brick by brick, timber by timber, plank by miserable plank. By the time the English king arrives, this place will not be worth fighting for.

Farther up High, I pass men bearing long rolls of canvas slung between them. Little wonder there are no bodies. Madog's men are disposing of them.

They must plan to be here for a while.

The master still hangs from the window, sightless, gray, withered. I pass beneath him and into the house, into the brat's old demesne.

Not a stick of furniture remains. Not trestle nor coffer nor wall-cloth. There are only bare, battered floors and sooty walls. I put it to memory. I will tell her every spill and scorch, every last absence.

I will enjoy watching it hurt.

Something is wadded in the corner. It's head-sized, washwater-colored and lumpy like vomit. I toe it and it becomes linen. A ray of glowing blue turns over. I kneel, peel apart the folds.

The castle appears first. The castle and a walled town. It's unmistakably Caernarvon, notched and purple-banded in tiny tight stitches high in the corner. Then Saint Joseph, his cloak a field of backstitches and his curly hair spilling over his collar while the Holy Child sits serenely on his arm, haloed. The Virgin is unfinished, an outline cast in blue and scarlet.

The castle appears first. Even she has built it.

Caernarvon, in stitches and thread.

I jab the tip of my plundered knife beneath the stitches

and twist. Thread catches, strains, and I gouge hard. More thread falls, tiny worms of purple and gray. I rip and stab Caernarvon from the linen even as Madog's men pull down walls and townhouses.

Finally there's no more thread. I've cut myself twice and my blood stains the frayed edge.

But Caernarvon is not gone. There's a faint outline on the linen where the stitches were, tiny holes suggesting towers, walls, gates, rooftops. Ghosts of color where thread rubbed cloth. Caernarvon still presides over the Holy Family, present even without substance.

And I look out the half-shuttered window at the castle just clipping the sky, dark as rain. My throat tightens and I grip the brat's linen in both hands because Gruffydd is right, curse him, and it's all for naught.

The extents and rolls may be ash, the town charter may be naught but privy rag, but none of these acts can undo Caernarvon. Brick and plank have stood. Kings have blessed. Men have seen. Girls have stitched. We could pull it down again and again. They'll come back. They'll always come back.

Outside, I ask one of the labor gangs carrying corpses to cut down the master and bury him. I wait till the crow-pecked body is wrapped in canvas and laid in a grave ere I fold the brat's linen into a tight packet and head home, dirtying my feet through once-Watched fields.

EVERYTHING," Gwinny says, and she smiles as if the Adversary himself did the wrecking.

"Everything," I whisper.

"Every trunk and chest and wooden spoon," she prods, still smiling. "Not a splinter or scrap remains."

"Did you see Mistress Tipley or Mistress Pole?" I ask. "Emmaline de Coucy? I would give much to know they're sound."

Gwinny draws back and eyes me. "Naught remains in your house. Everything you have in the world has been kicked in or made off with. Your precious embroidery frame. Your colored threads. Your mother's gown."

I swallow. "What of the Glovers next door? There are so many little ones, and Mistress Glover bore her baby not long ago. Surely they wouldn't have slaughtered children. Would they?"

"Madog's men garrison the town," Gwinny says stonily. "Should any English remain, God help them."

"They must have fled." I nod, fierce and sure. "They must have."

Gwinny narrows her eyes. "Fled home, you mean. Back to England. Where they belong."

"Emmaline has no memory of England. All she knows is Caernarvon. That's her home."

"It's not her home. It's not *your* home."

I square up and look Gwinny in the eye. "I would that were true. But it's not. My home isn't mine any longer. He took it, and I must make shift with what's left me. Caernarvon is my home now."

Gwinny flinches, blinks, turns away.

HORSEBACK English, a decree from their king, and the new lord of Pencoed rode right up to the hall door and kicked it in and that's all I saw because Mam threw the blanket over Gruffydd and me and there was screaming and clatter and ere long we found ourselves in a ditch tangled in that blanket a stone's throw from the hall and Mam next to us was weeping quietly and there was nowhere to go but into the greenwood, away from that timbered hall that the prince himself granted Da, where I was just old enough to kneel before the prince during his final days on God's own earth.

IF I close my eyes I can see it still, the new chimney, the dovecote, the endless rolling yardlands of barley and oats and rye.

But it's his now. It'll never be mine, and even if I go back, I'll be at their mercy. My thieving uncle Roger and his wretchedly fertile girl-wife and their little pink baby. I'll have to pretend to like the howling brat who stole Edgeley from me and mayhap even play nursemaid to it.

Gwinny said everything I had in the world was kicked in or made off with, but that's not true. I have what's left of a townhouse on a plot of ground sixty feet by eighty on Shire Hall Street in the king's borough of Caernarvon. Out of one window you can see Anglesey, green atop green like layers of infidel silk. Out the other, houses and roads and the walls curving around it all like a great embrace. On one side the Glovers, on the other, the Poles. The church downstreet, the castle up, the middle alive with dogs and children and neighbors.

I'll find a way to have what's mine. What my father made mine because he'd have more for me than the lot of a steward's daughter on an estate, hers by right, that she could never have.

Get out, he said.

He did not mean forever.

I'M pounding barley between two stones when Dafydd appears in the doorway. He's dressed for weather even though the sky is holding blue well past the time it should have hunkered down for winter. He leans on the frame, flashes that damn carefree grin.

"I've come to ply you ere I go to war," he says cheerfully. "I've ten reasons why you should agree to be my wife, and I'll not leave till you hear every one."

There's a swish and a grunt, and the brat lurches past Dafydd into the steading, slanting beneath the water bucket. She greets us in English as she sways toward the hearth with a long and purposeful stride. She does not seem to notice that her hem is caked with mud or her hair is streaming from its plait like a halo of snakes.

She looks nothing like a borough lady.

Daughter Shrewcy would be in pieces by now, weeping for her veil and her blistered hands. But this girl looks as though she doesn't even care.

The brat would care.

"Reason number one is—"

"I will." My voice is low and steady. I thought I'd want my words back right away, but I don't.

Dafydd closes his mouth. "You . . . what?"

Now that I've said it, I cannot take my eyes off him. "If we both survive, that is."

"I'd hate to think you were mocking me," Dafydd says in slow, measured words. "I've never once played you false."

"I'm not. I mean it. I'll marry you should we both survive this."

"You'll pardon the question, but I'll not have you unconsidered." His voice wavers. "What's happened?"

The brat wipes muddy hands on her gown, steps around the leaky place in the thatch, heads for the door with the water bucket. Dafydd steps inside to let her pass, then watches her stumble down the hill.

"Ah," he says quietly. "The crack. Caernarvon just wants one."

Dafydd kneels before me till I look up from my grinding, then takes the stones out of my hands and lays them aside. He pulls me gently to my feet and draws me into an embrace so deep it feels as if he's been saving it up, as if he'd never let go should the choice be his.

I curl beneath his arm and let him hold me, my cheek against his shoulder, and all at once I'm back in his bed, snug beneath the woolens and listening to the muffled beating of his heart, ere he single-handedly took on the task of undoing the English stranglehold on Caernarvon's privileges with the simple act of requesting a burgage. All these months, and he's still warm and solid, like city walls. He's still flippant, maddening, and irresistible.

He'd still have me.

After this is over, everything will change. One way or another, Caernarvon will never be the same again.

Rain is pelting the steading as if we're under Heaven's eaves. The roof is leaking in no less than a dozen places, and the smell of moldy thatch is stronger than usual.

Gwinny is sharpening her meat-knife, sliding the whetstone down the blade in lengthy, irritable shings. She's in a foul mood because it took me too long to figure out she wanted me to patch the wall wattle, which I'm doing now, coated to the elbows in mud.

"When you're done," Gwinny says in Welsh, "something something roof and fix the something something."

I almost glare at her. She cannot be serious. Assuming I could get on the roof *and* had half a notion what to do, the rain would wash me away like all the sinners in the Flood.

"I hope your cousin never comes," she taunts in English. "I'm growing quite used to having a servant. How idle and dissolute I've become. Almost like a fine lady of the borough."

"He'll come." I slap some mud on the wall hard enough to spatter my face. "I know he will."

"You *hope* he will," she drawls. "Wallingford's a long way from here. Anything could happen to the priest's boy. Imagine a lad that young trying to cross a countryside in revolt, to say naught of him finding one knight among hundreds. It's already been what, a fortnight? A month?"

I want to tell her to shut her mouth, but instead I picture the sun streaming through my workroom windows and spread some mud on her wretched walls.

Nicholas is coming.

He has to be.

"And what if your king calls him and his lord to the royal standard?" Gwinny presses a hand to her cheek in mock-horror. "Surely he could not say your king nay. And you'd have to stay here. Unless I put you out. I could always do that. How far do you think you'd get? Do you even know which way to go?"

If she's going to put me out, I would she'd just get on with it. I cannot contain a glare, and she's on me like a ratter.

"Don't you look at me like that! You'll be in the ditch ere you turn around!"

Picture the market. Picture the hall, the table set with broadcloth and pewter.

But all I feel is cold on my skin, raw terror in every direction.

Gwinny is smiling.

"You'd best hope it's the wolves that find you," she purrs. "They'll merely kill you."

"Stop it!" I fist up both hands and brandish the mud spreader like a dagger. "Do you take pleasure in this? Why are you doing this to me?"

And I freeze. Lower the mud spreader.

Justice for those who deserve it.

Gwinny rises slow, draws shallow breaths as if she's run to London and back.

"I'm done," I whisper. "I'm done playing games."

And I turn back to my task because there is naught like justice well served. Mud up my arms, over my face. No one can even see my cuffs anymore.

I've studied my lessons, but now it's too late.

After a while, there's a shuffling behind me. Gwinny crosses the small room, takes up a second mud spreader, and wordlessly begins to patch the walls alongside me.

ENGLISH collapses into sleep within moments of gobbling her corner of bread. Without the walls, labor is a ghost she has come to know painfully well.

Those first few se'ennights are the hardest, English. Ere calluses roughen everything on you and in you. Barely a month bereft, you're still pink and raw.

You'll have to harden, though. Even if you weep as it happens.

At least it's just you. You've no one who wept for trapped hares and maidens in nursery tales, pushed beyond your protection then and now and forever.

The steading is still. I withdraw English's length of linen from my apron and unfold it.

The linen is cleaner from several washings, but the shadow of a ruined Caernarvon still towers over the Holy Family. Saint Joseph and the Christ Child, faded but finished, all but leap off the wrinkled gray cloth.

Da went out. Gruffydd went out. Should I ever bear a son, he will go out. He will meet the same fate. He will die for this realm already twice lost.

English whimpers in her sleep. Her cheeks are wet.

The burgesses will come back and she will be among

them. She will bring her husband into the privileges and tell him what to think of us.

I have not harmed her. I have not allowed harm to come to her. It's more than her lot has ever offered me, and English has seen what befalls them when they press the boot on our necks. She has survived the wages of justice through luck, mettle, and wit enough to open her eyes.

English finally sees.

If I'm to be ruled, may it be by those who see.

GWINNY AND I eat the last of the plundered bread. The loaf-end has deep finger-holes, one of which is bloody. I cannot look at the bread while I eat it, but nor will I stop eating.

The pile of blankets near the fire begins to quake and gasp like a rusty bellows. Gwinny drops her bread and flies to her mother's side.

The old woman's eyes roll back in her head and her tiny frame shudders as if throttled. Gwinny holds her mother down at the shoulders and kneels on the blankets to still her legs. The poor dame's face is bloodless and her blue lips stand out like leeches.

"Fetch the priest," Gwinny snaps as she wrestles a piece of wood between her mother's clattering teeth.

I can barely find the stream. I shrug helplessly.

Gwinny groans like a wounded beast. "Then you hold her!"

The old woman looks like a corpse, all waxen and pale, but I kneel and gingerly lean my hands on her shoulders as much as I dare. Her shoulderbones poke like peg hangers.

"Hold her steady," Gwinny says, and out the curtain she races.

Gwinny's mother jerks like a puppet on strings and there's a fresh privy stench. She must have loosed her bowels.

I gag and retch but I don't let go. She's gasping low and harsh at the back of her throat and I beg her not to die till Gwinny comes with the priest, till she can be shriven and have her own daughter holding her head as she goes.

Her struggles are fading. I'm losing her.

I pray. I pray, clinging to the old woman's shoulders as I might a paternoster. I pray with my every fiber that she not die, not yet, not like this.

Something tugs at my collar. It's Gwinny, with a cold-eyed priest hovering over her shoulder. I let go. I stumble away and they both kneel at the old woman's side, blocking her from view. I'm in the corner again, overlooked and passed by.

Rattly gasping drowns out Extreme Unction and the viaticum. Gwinny's profile stands out against the dark wall like a new-stamped coin. Tears slide down her cheeks and my face is wet and I'm in the corner praying and we're the same, Gwinny and I, we're the same.

I BURY my mother. All those who knew her gather at the grave and commend her to God.

English comes, too. She stands at my elbow and wipes away tears as four graybeards lower Mam's body into the frozen earth.

She's brave to show her face at this burial. My neighbors glare at her sidelong and mutter, but she does not look away from the grave. Her lips are moving. Her fingers, too, as if they're sliding over beads on a paternoster.

I should be weeping for my mother. I should be tearing my hair and smearing my face with soot. Or at least drying tears, as does English, who barely knew her.

Instead I feel light. As if I could float away on the wind, somewhere far from here.

Ashes to ashes. Mam is buried. My neighbors cluster, pushing English aside.

Your mother is with God now, they say. Her suffering is over. Beyond the cares of the world.

It's like saying the sky is blue or the Pope is Christian.

I lag behind till they strip away and head for their own hearths to what's left of their children and beasts. Soon it's just English and I, heaving uphill toward the steading that's mine now. Empty and mine.

And English says, even when you know it's coming, it still hurts. She squeezes my hand and whispers, I'm sorry . . . Gwennaver.

She's filthy and tattered and hungry, waiting on a cousin who may never arrive. Her hands are blistered raw and her cheeks windburned, but she looks me in the eye and she hasn't broken and she's sorry.

Now mayhap time can do its work.

NICHOLAS ARRIVES when the wind off the strait is flinging angry snow against the steading. He lurches up the hill on a half-dead horse and leaps from the saddle as if it's afire. His face is mottled red and his hands are like leather, but I throw my arms about him and hold on hard.

"Thank Christ," he whispers into my hair. "Oh, Cecily, I never thought I'd see you again in this world."

It's Nicholas. Lop-eared, gingerfool Nicholas. My eyes sting.

"I had a look at Caernarvon as I passed," he growls. "They will pay for what they've done, mark me. His Grace the king is even now massing forces at Chester."

"What they've done," I echo, in the shadow of hungry crofts and churchyard graves and toll-table splinters.

"Come, we ride for Chester," Nicholas says. "Father will meet you there and take you back to Coventry."

He's tugging me toward his horse, but I pull away. "First I must bid farewell."

"To whom?"

She puts the bucket down as I near the steading door. We regard each other for a long moment. She's a lot thinner than the girl who came with my house, but she stands just the same. Chin up, shoulders squared, steady as the Adversary's throwing arm.

But I understand why.

"*Pob llwyddiant,*" Gwennaver says. "*Hwyl.*"

"*Di-diolch yn . . . er, fawr,*" I stumble, and I mean every word. I need every bit of good fortune I can get, and although a simple thank-you seems inadequate, it's the best I can do with my new words.

I turn away, but Gwennaver catches my sleeve and presses a folded packet into my hands. Ere I can respond, Nicholas manhandles me atop the rickety horse and leads it away.

I look over my shoulder, but she has already disappeared.

"Barbarous," Nicholas mutters. "I cannot believe Henry thinks to return once these beasts are put down."

"What else is he to do?" I ask, and Nicholas grunts.

What else am I to do?

Swaying on Nicholas's horse, I unfold the packet Gwennaver gave me. Saint Joseph and the Christ Child wait while the Virgin, still merely an outline, prays at the roadside. Caernarvon has been torn away, but its outline remains. It will not be hard to restitch.

I fold the linen and stow it close to my heart.

I wish Gwennaver health and Griffith safety, for both will need it for what's coming. Then I pray for my father's soul.

From this far, Caernarvon looks just as it did upon our arrival. Gray and weathered and solid as Jerusalem, and it's only because I know to look that I see the makeshift gate and crumbled tower-tops.

The king will have it back. The burgesses will return. They will all remember what happened here, and why.

My cousin Henry will be among them. He will need a chatelaine to run his house and preside over his kitchen. Someone who knows the market and the countryside, someone who knows the Welsh and how to treat with them. Someone with a townhouse two streets over, held in trust till her marriage, when she will become its lady. Someone who'll not dishonor her father's memory and give up her new birthright as if it's worthless.

I know just the girl for the job. She will walk her cousin's townhouse amid a faint jingle of keys while a wolfhound puppy follows at her heels.

HISTORICAL NOTE

Caernarvon in 1294 was a great place to live—as long as you were English. A decade earlier, after two hundred years of near-constant conflict, the English brought about the final collapse of native government in Wales with the battlefield killing of Llywelyn ap Gruffydd and the execution of his brother Dafydd, the last Welsh Princes of Wales. Although the fall of Wales was not his precise intention, Edward I, king of England, quickly consolidated the old princely lands into what became known as the Principality of North Wales.

Once Edward held Wales, he wanted to ensure that it never troubled England again. To that end, he instigated an extensive— and expensive—castle-building, urban development, and settlement program to maintain control of the land and its inhabitants. A critical aspect of this project was a series of walled towns like Caernarvon, intended to attract English settlers to support the castle garrisons and help develop the local economy.

These towns were very much on the frontier, surrounded by a hostile, newly subjugated Welsh population—people like Gruffydd and Gwenhwyfar—who were still becoming accustomed to English government. Cecily's concern that she would be murdered was not entirely unfounded. Wales had a fierce reputation in the thirteenth century, so Edward had to offer settlers an array of privileges to entice them to take burgages, mostly in the form of tax breaks and subsidized farmland. One of the few requirements was residence, and one of the only burdens was a modest yearly rent. In the Middle Ages, this kind of offer was almost unheard of.

But Caernarvon was not the best place to be if you were Welsh. The same conditions that attracted English settlers to the Principality made life very difficult for the Welsh, who had until recently been governed by a familiar and long-standing set of laws and customs. Gwenhwyfar would have been raised on stories of Welsh princes who resisted encroaching English domination with diplomacy when they could and with the sword when they had to. It was not an easy transition for the Welsh, and Gwenhwyfar's resentment toward her new English masters had ten years to simmer.

On the surface, the introduction of English rule to Wales was surprisingly lenient. There were no wholesale executions of Welsh nobility, and only a few, like Gwenhwyfar's father, who died fighting the English, lost their lands. Edward made no attempt to ban the Welsh language or any other type of cultural expression. In many places, Welsh civil law remained in effect, and it was only for criminal cases that English law was imposed. Although he enacted a number of underhanded, semilegal measures to protect the castles and new walled towns, Edward went out of his way to ensure as peaceful a transfer of power as possible, mainly because he was more concerned with events on the Continent than with those in Wales.

Since Edward's attention was elsewhere, he placed a number

of officials in charge of Wales with express instructions to govern according to the Statute of Rhuddlan, a document issued by the king in 1284. But the burgesses in the walled towns had different ideas. They were nervous already, outnumbered fifty to one by a disgruntled populace, and they harbored a certain sense of entitlement due to their presence on the front lines of a hostile frontier. Some of them had lost loved ones in the two wars leading up to the fall of Welsh native government. All of them saw the opportunity to profit from a demoralized and marginalized population that was in no position, legal or otherwise, to fight back. It wasn't long before corruption set in, and Edward's officials either looked the other way or benefited right alongside the burgesses at the expense of the Welsh.

The first hint of trouble was a famine that swept through Wales and England in 1290. Famine was not uncommon in the Middle Ages, but in the subsequent year, 1291, Edward called for a tax that amounted to a fifteenth of the movable goods of all of his subjects—including, for the first time, his Welsh subjects. Welsh landholders didn't object on principle to being taxed, but medieval taxation was assessed and collected in such a way that the burden per capita fell more heavily on the Welsh because of their lower population, and also because the burgesses in the walled towns were not subject to this type of taxation.

By 1294, Wales had been suffering under four successive years of famine and three years of a tax many Welsh landholders saw as unreasonable and dangerous in its precedent. In the summer, when the king proclaimed that Welshmen of military age like Gruffydd and Dafydd would be compelled to serve overseas under the royal standard in Gascony, it became clear to the Welsh that things in the Principality had to change.

By all accounts, the English were taken completely by surprise by the events of Michaelmas 1294—not just the sack of Caernarvon, but the simultaneous attacks on castles across Wales, nearly all of which were successful. It was Christmas before Edward could divert enough troops from his campaign in Gascony to deal with the rebels. The rebellion was put down conclusively by the summer of 1295, but there were no mass executions or crippling legal retributions. The royal inquiry into mismanagement that Dafydd predicted did in fact come about, and the outcome told Edward all he needed to know about how to secure peace in the Principality. Wales was not taxed to any significant degree until well into the fourteenth century, and the next time he needed fighting men for his army, Edward did not attempt to conscript the Welsh. Instead, he invited them into the army at full pay, the same as English foot soldiers, and they volunteered by the thousands.

When the burgesses returned to Caernarvon after the revolt, they were forgiven the payment of their rents for ten years to help them recover. Although the rebellion stirred up a lot of English mistrust and hostility against the Welsh, it wasn't long before all the boroughs in North Wales recovered from the physical damage and experienced a social and demographic shift. By the middle of the fourteenth century, every walled town in the Principality had some Welsh burgesses, a few of whom had made their way into civil government. This social shift was a result of interactions very much like those among Cecily, Gwenhwyfar, and Gruffydd. Each community had to come to terms with this new world, and such exchanges set the precedent for cooperation, even if it was initially reluctant.

As the frontier became less volatile, and indeed stopped being a frontier at all, local government became more diverse and the culture of the walled towns began to better reflect the communities that shared the space. These changes took time, but the cracks that began in Caernarvon shaped Wales well into the future.

In chronological order, my sincere thanks go to . . .

My mother, for reading to me every night till I was nearly twelve. And for patiently fueling my teenage research interests with a never-ending stream of interlibrary loan materials.

My father, for buying the first book-length manuscript produced by thirteen-year-old me, thereby ensuring I kept writing through a very dark time. It's quite possibly the best ten dollars he ever spent.

Kelly Stromberg and Dean Rieken, two AP English teachers who tolerated my teenage hubris, doused my writing in red ink, and held up a mirror at all the right times.

The staff and librarians at too many research libraries to count, but particularly those at Bryn Mawr College, the University of Pennsylvania, and the University of Washington.

My husband and son, for their love, encouragement, and most of all, patience. Living with a writer is no easy thing.

Mary Pleiss and Sara Polsky, my beta readers. Without their time, insights, and raw honesty, this book would not exist. Thanks also to Mary Cummings for her valuable comments on an early draft.

My agent, Ammi-Joan Paquette, for her excellent advice and tireless work on my behalf. I'm very fortunate to have her in my corner.

Reka Simonsen, my editor, for her wisdom and enthusiasm. I couldn't ask for a better hand on the tiller.